SUSAN DAITCH'S
THE COLORIST

"Susan Daitch is a marvelous writer. An elegant stylist, she surveys narrative trajectories as if they were suspects of a crime. Her novel unfolds with the inevitability of dominoes, but dominoes that have been arranged in a beautiful and exotic calligraphy. I can't think of anyone else writing today who offers such proportionate measures of élan, erudition, and humor."
—Mark Leyner

"*The Colorist* forges relationships between art and so-called reality that probe at the heart of fiction. . . . Intelligent, inventive and surprising."
Lynne Tillman

"Susan Daitch is a young writer who is going to move up into the big leagues. . . . Her writing drifts with an exquisitely tight control."
—*San Francisco Chronicle*

"*The Colorist* is the work of a remarkable writer with much to say about the visual world and the way we live in it. The images are sharp and telling. This is a fine, unique novel."
—Joan Silber

THE
COLORIST

THE
COLORIST

SUSAN DAITCH

VINTAGE CONTEMPORARIES

VINTAGE BOOKS

A DIVISION OF RANDOM HOUSE, INC.

NEW YORK

A Vintage Contemporaries Original, January 1990

FIRST EDITION

Library of Congress Cataloging-in-Publication Data
Daitch, Susan.
The colorist / Susan Daitch.—1st ed.
p.   cm.—(A Vintage contemporaries original)
ISBN 0-679-72492-3
I. Title.
PS3554.A33C65 1990
813'.54—dc20   89-40109
                                                     CIP

Illustrations by George Krenik

Manufactured in the United States of America
10 9 8 7 6 5 4 3 2 1

TO JOHN

The author would like to thank
Charles Long for the use of the cinema hat.

THE
COLORIST

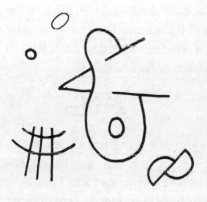

On the wall behind a table was a big mural labeled *Civilization Teeters*. Dogs chased half-naked women, columns tumbled. You didn't know what kind of teetering was being discussed on the part of civilization: falling or laughing. Sometimes when I walk into these places, I feel invisible. Sitting at tables, at the bar, even in this basement, everyone has conversations, arrangements to make. They look very intent, but it's a veiled kind of intention, at any moment intention could fly apart, go to the dogs. Urgent and under control, as if they're applying for government jobs. I imagine when you apply for such a position, you are subject to surveillance. When you think no one is checking your behavior, you're wrong. Behind closed circuits everyone is being watched, assessed by NASA, for example. All of them except me. I'm not in the running, not being watched. NASA isn't interested in Julie Greene. I'm invisible.

Walking home, past a woman in a blue dress, a row of sequins unraveling from along its hem, leaving a bright blue trail; another in a cracked plastic skirt, buyers and sellers mixed together, young men with no hair baiting everyone who walks by, shadow men painted on the sides of all kinds of buildings; someone painted a smiley face on one, the smiley face was between the legs of another. I watched a couple, arms linked, hair sticking to their backs in the heat. One put her hand under the neck of the other, lifting hair matted into dreadlocks. Even at night, every sensate thing must have felt as if it were melting into whatever was beside it.

A friend of mine made an object called a cinema hat. It's a box-shaped object you put on your head. The inside of the box looks like a small movie theater. Your eyes are where the projector is. In front of your face are small seats, and the place where the screen would be is open, so whatever you see in the room, in the street, that's the movie. Your life as it happens, that's the film. You are the leading actor and the audience at the same time. This method puts random events, especially unpleasant ones, in a dramatic context. You run into a skeleton from your closet at large (everyone has these; sometimes you get lucky and have two or three), you see a man dressed like Cardinal Richelieu, or another like a ragtag Sheriff of Nottingham throwing imaginary arrows at everyone on Seventh Street and it's all part of the script, the story.

Sometimes the super next door would leave his paintings out, hung from his ground-floor windowsill as he painted until early in the morning. Little slips of paper fluttered in bits of wind: $15.00 for a metallic green starling, $20.00 for an island with palm trees, self-portraits were usually around $10.00, a painting of his granddaughter's little dog was $5.00. The pictures were flat, wet, oil paintings. Three carved heads with large hats also sat on the sill. For months these were unpainted, dry wood, then he colored them in. A sign which read *!Libertad a Puerto Rico¡* was painted on a map, had no price tag, and he never took it in. He drew wide blue columns on the inside of one of his rooms, the one which faced the street. The columns were wavy, and each had a different capital, some overlapped onto the ceiling. He was not my super and rarely smiled or said hello, but he would tell me if someone had been looking for me or Eamonn. He painted late at night by whatever light came in from the street, drinking and singing and leaning out the window. His granddaughter lived with him and played with his paints on the sidewalk while he swept the stairs and corridors. She was a very thin child and never seemed to grow any taller.

○

When Eamonn told me not to take so seriously the hidden images of my bad dreams, he made a mistake, but I learned: never demand a leap of faith from a man who sees himself as a professional fly in the ointment. Dreams: a random helter-skelter tipping of the hat to the hieroglyphics of my childhood. In these nightly dramas Eamonn saw only signs of mental anarchy. He had his own insubstantial apartment performances. He wore a torn sweater as though it were a relic from the 1916 Easter Rising, and he'd just been dragged from the

Dublin post office, riddled by British bullets. I have a couple of torn shirts, but I can't pretend they're anything.

Suppose I saw a ghost in the apartment during the day when I was awake. If it disturbed no furniture, made no noise, and even made itself at home, I don't think Eamonn would notice the thing. Even if I could think of nothing else, he would say it was an afterimage and we would never speak of it. What kind of afterimages would I see? The sidewalk painters, turning blocks of concrete into temporary mosaics? The cinema hat worn out, its chairs in unhinged bits?

Eamonn Archer left Ireland when he was twelve or thirteen. He told the story several different ways. Exiles or expatriots—sometimes he called his family one, sometimes the other. There were no jobs, and his father had died. They weren't starving or fleeing Ulster constabulary, British soldiers had not yet arrived, but his mother had gotten work with Aer Lingus in Galway. The job finally brought them to New York. Eamonn's accent was fragile, there was barely a trace of it left. A casualty of fifteen years here, it resurfaced when he said certain words: London, Shankill, terror. In bodegas in the neighborhood, he spoke Spanish quickly, as if he'd lived in a country where Spanish was spoken, but no, he told me. His grandmother had never heard of Franco. She had lived in Derry all her life.

I moved in with Eamonn after I was attacked in the hall of my building on East Ninth Street. I remembered the boy was tall, had a filed-down screwdriver, took me up to the roof. All I had was ten dollars. He knocked me to the floor. It was then I understood the moments in *Frenzy*. "You're my kind of girl, Babs." He took off his tie, and the camera withdrew down the stairs, backed up and out of the building; the sound of traffic grew louder. Hitchcock said the audience would subconsciously think, Well, if the girl screams, no one is going to hear her. A murder is happening, a man buys a newspaper, life in London goes on, and in New York, too. Murder or potential murder goes unnoticed, like someone shouting in a language no one within earshot understands or has any inclination to pay attention to. In history books, medieval cities are often described as if all daily activities neatly dovetailed, a self-contained enterprise: markets, water systems, collection of tithes, one religion (nearly), the distribution of justice, and all the lunatics were placed in ships of fools and set adrift. In reading of early cities, so conceptually grid-like in places where the streets made no sense, I imagined them harmonious. People were diligent, delinquency was rare. History proceeded with a sense of progress. Citizens clumped together, formed cities, conducted business, grew more secular. Here it is the twentieth century, and cities, for a moment, appear just as self-contained, especially in a long shot during a movie. I was a woman on a roof looking at the pointed end of a screwdriver. He said he knew my address and he'd be back. I believed him. The murderer in the movie lived on Southampton Street, above a publisher called Duckworth and Company, Ltd.

Eamonn helped me pack. His offer seemed more convenient than potentially Faustian. It was as if an intangible abstraction (not my soul but something like it) were sold and tossed into the exchange. The habits given up when I no longer lived alone were part of the arrangement. Eamonn presented me with a logical choice, nothing more complicated than an apartment a few blocks away, with the same telephone exchange and low rent. Hidden clauses, overlooked riders that might turn up later in unpleasant ways, tipped no scales. I didn't change my mind because the screwdriver could turn into a knife or a Saturday-night special. Eamonn was sympathetic in the way a witness might be who was essentially untouched by the crime and had nothing to risk as far as being the object of a stranger's revenge. Concern had its charms and helped move boxes and a couple of suitcases, but I was resistant to showing the depth to which I'd been shocked by the incident on the roof. Betrayal on Eamonn's part didn't mean he might confess our arrangement had its conveniences or that he might fall in love any moment, and just by chance. Betrayal meant giving away confidences, meant ridicule. He would meet someone on a train, or at a newspaper office, and say, "There was no one on the roof really, she imagined there was someone in a shadow, behind a pigeon coop, but there wasn't anyone there. Heard a knife clatter to the sidewalk; it was just birds." To the listener, the third person, Eamonn would dismiss my fear that the man on the roof might return. Or, taking a contradictory position, he might enlarge the moment on the roof as if it meant I would become terror-stricken in an elevator, on the street, anywhere. There was betrayal in his confusion, even if the confusion was faintly altruistic. The responsibility involved in rescue can grow into assuming certain things are always true about the victim. I didn't want him to be the man I would remember as having known far too much. Conversations recollected with embarrassment first, mortification later on, these would be part of his arsenal, so I wouldn't give him too much to misinterpret.

Eamonn spent several days moving, arranging, and throwing out rolls of unused, out-of-date film, old Polycontrast F paper, empty yellow-orange film canisters, including the flattened one on which I'd once written my telephone number under the word Kodak, neck straps long ago removed from the cameras they came with, old bottles of bleach and chemicals, selenium toner and Edwal FG-7, cracked tongs for shuffling prints around in solutions, and old newspapers. He cleared enough space so if I wanted to do any drawing I could begin whenever I wanted to, but certain objects never moved. His dry-mount press, like a square-jawed alligator, abutted a roll of drawing paper. The surface bore dents every seven inches.

He didn't take my picture often. In a few months he might if he thought I was becoming a problem. Eamonn would start clicking away as soon as I got out of bed, not stopping until night, or until I moved out, whichever happened first.

He was the shutter savior, providing automatic rescue by virtue of the act of recording the scene of the (social) crime. The camera would prove things; could universalize and make Eamonn feel less marginal. He was there somehow, not in the literal picture, but he wasn't altogether invisible behind the lens. How is packing a box like taking a photograph? How is an embrace like a rubber raft? They're not alike at all. Acts of virtue, help, amelioration; generally I'll defend you but sometimes not. I had seen newspaper photographs taken just after the bombing of a department store in Paris. I asked Eamonn how the photographer got there so fast. The two women put their hands up before the camera as if it were a gun. The one whose face was visible bore an expression of anger and affront. They felt pursued by the camera. What mattered to Eamonn was that people didn't know what was ultimately going to be good for them. Eamonn knew about the private, personal shocks dotting the landscapes of public catastrophe, and he knew about fighting fire with fire, or so he was fond of implying. Just as members of certain clubs feel affinity and understanding with one another, Eamonn thought most of the people whose pictures he took would feel a partnership with him. He didn't quite understand how they might find his snapping and clicking invasive, and in his blindness I misread a kind of vulnerability. He constantly put himself in a position of being told off. If Eamonn thought he wore a sign which read I'm on your side, there were moments when it was hopelessly illegible. He was no longer an immigrant but not yet a citizen. Eamonn sometimes made a profession out of the role of a displaced person. When I complained about my job or the strips of negatives hanging in the bathroom, Eamonn would tell me there were genuine tragedies in the world and whatever I was talking about wasn't one of them.

In a few months he might inadvertently photograph my assailant. As unlikely as that was, it was an event I anticipated. I would barely recognize the blur, and I wouldn't say to Eamonn, "That's him. That's the one. Where did you take this picture?" The man was gone and had only been in front of Eamonn for a second, longer than shutter speed but no time at all really. He could be anywhere. The picture, if it was taken, would be an accident.

In the future we would both forget how Eamonn helped me pack, and how he spoke about the provisional government that took over after the 1848 revolution in France, recruited murderers and thieves to be part of the *garde mobile*, battalions of adversarial proletarians. They were still a mob, *les gens sans feu et sans aveu* (People without fire or faith, he would quote Marx in French). They were paid and given uniforms, but they were still useless. I hadn't wanted him to talk about the underclass at that moment, even if there was some historical fact in what he might say. Curtains, plates, boxes, Eamonn packed and stacked with a kind of enthusiasm I wasn't sure had anything to do with me. It was an opportunity to talk about *les gens sans*. I had known Eamonn for two weeks.

Madder lake, manganese blue, titanium white used to lighten them later on. I had a job coloring empty frames for a serial comic called *Electra*. Sometimes I needed to go on color searches. If I couldn't literally see or envision a color in the offices of Fantômes and Company, Ltd., I would go out to look for it. This was often a ruse, I admit, for leaving work, but I was rarely questioned if I came up with the perfect hue.

It was the middle of the summer, the middle of the day. Electra's spaceship had been taken over by hybrids which looked like lascivious New Guinea hibiscus with Venus flytrap offshoots. Their germination and subsequent growth went through complex stages from spore to adult plant. The black-and-white frames had sat mutely on my desk while I experimented with greens and yellows. None of them seemed right. *I need to look at flowers*, I said, *I'll be back tomorrow morning*. I took a train to Brooklyn, to the Botanical Gardens, to look at the tropical plants.

The subway was nearly empty. My hair grew less sticky as the car sped under the river, and blew in my eyes in the air-conditioned breeze. I hold it out of my face and I remember looking at the three other passengers when the car came to a stop and the lights went out. At first the car was quiet. Trains frequently stop in the middle of the tunnel, then they start up again, but too much time passed. A woman sitting across from me began to panic, talking out loud about trains which could instantly electrocute everyone in a blaze of sparks. A conductor stumbled into the car and said we would have to walk to the next station, a problem with the next train, an accident, an underground fire, or a passenger was ill. I don't remember the cause. I might not have been listening anyway. The subway doors were opened mechanically and I stepped onto the tracks. A man with a camera was ahead of me and the woman, who trembled uncontrollably, was behind me. I took her hand. A rat scurried by in the water near us. The man with the camera reached for my hand, causing me to drop my journal of color notes. The present tense had evaporated. I was thinking about how I would tell everyone at the office about panic and danger in the tunnel. Rats, smell of smoke, nearly pitch-black, nervous attack, the walk went on forever, like the Resistance tunneling under a German munitions pile. Everyone would laugh, and the stalled car would seem more like an adventure than a nuisance, but I wanted my notebook and there was no way to get it back. It had fallen near the third rail. I let the man with the camera take my hand until the white tiles of the next station glimmered ahead.

I went up the stairs and out into the street. Most of the other passengers did the same, not wanting to get into another subway. I didn't know where I was. Long boulevards, a gas station, factories, and I could see the edge of Manhattan in the distance. The man with the camera offered to walk back over the bridge with me. He had been on his way to Queens to photograph white gangs, he said, but I think now that he must have been on the wrong train or made the story up altogether. He was very sorry about my notebook and offered to buy me another, which was pointless. Some words he spoke with an accent, others not. He told me his name and said, *Look, I'll take your picture in front of the gas station*. I didn't have to go back to the comic office that afternoon, and wanted to know more about where the photographer came from besides out of the blue. He was very vague about a past marriage, but very exact about f-stops. He was vague about how long he lived anywhere, but very precise about how I should stand against the green side of the gas station. He was so thin, I thought he would break if he tried to run to the corner. I thought I was doing him a favor by having a drink with him in the middle of the day, but I was the one being told what to do. I never got to the Botanical Gardens.

I stood in front of a shop which developed and printed film. They advertised one-hour printing. Pictures studded a revolving drum in their window. It was someone's job to mind the drum all day long while an occasional passerby would stop to stare at an endless stream of private moments, the personal snapshots of people who were perfect strangers to me. The contents of the photographs were relatively repetitious: weddings, vacations, children. I stopped to watch. I was looking for coincidence, for my picture, although I knew Eamonn did his own printing and would never expose me in a window on a revolving drum on Thirty-second Street. I knew it, but I hadn't known him long, and so I watched the strips of beach, raised glasses, babies, eyes with red dots at the center, just for a few minutes before returning to work.

In a museum I had seen a photograph of Michael Rockefeller. He was sitting on the grass looking at his camera; it was 1961, and he was a very young man. Asmat tribesmen from Irian Jaya or New Guinea sat or stood behind him and looked at the photographer, who must have been standing about where I was. The Asmat smiled broadly at the photographer while Michael Rockefeller looked only into his camera, very white, in profile against their dark faces and legs. The braids, head-dresses, and penis gourds of the standing Asmat bristle behind him. He seems to ignore all of them, including the invisible photographer; he just examines his camera. Michael Rocke-feller eventually disappeared. Eamonn told me he was eaten, but the fate of the photographer remained unknown to me. I wanted to ask Eamonn if he would ever go to a place where to take a picture was to risk being eaten. Had he ever noticed that he did not go unobserved by his subjects? The answer seems obvious, but at the time, I wasn't sure how much he did notice. How was that photograph in front of the gas station different from the holiday snaps on the revolving drum?

And then I read about a photographer who was hit on the head with her own camera by an Israeli soldier on the West Bank. The gash was so serious it required stitches. I pressed my thumbs against the edges of Eamonn's camera.

They could easily open a woman's head. She had worked for an international wire service. The article was only a few lines in a newspaper. Just to have a camera, just to be in Hebron, you didn't have to say one word, you wouldn't have to show your passport. The trouble with Eamonn was that, with or without his camera, he wouldn't remain still, he wouldn't stand around asking innocent questions. I thought about not returning his calls, but instead I began to worry about places you could be shot just for having the thing around your neck.

One night when I couldn't sleep, I sorted through some old ink bottles clustered beside the telephone. Fantômes often allowed me to take work home, and when I worked at night, if Eamonn slept, it was almost as good as being by myself. A bottle of red left a ring on a note Eamonn had written. It said, *Look for Grace*. I didn't ask Eamonn who Grace was. I swept the inks into a bag. The tinkling sound of the thick bottles woke him. My insomniac's revenge affected him in the middle of the night and I was sorry for it later.

Eamonn stared at the ceiling and began to tell me about his high school in Brooklyn, petty drug dealing, the beginning of his life in crime. He wanted me to stop drawing and get back into bed. I was looking for a kind of matte opacity that I knew wouldn't reproduce. In a drawer I found the kind of thick paint that would dry in caked patches on delicate comic paper or bleed oily rings, haloing images. I squeezed a blob of veridian green out of the tube, much more than I needed. Light from the street lay in its curves, not enough light to paint by. His desire to sleep dwindled, and he insisted on talking, as if autobiography had the power to displace everything. There had been a place called the Sugar Street Club; small-time allegiances turned into gangs, a friend got murdered on the A train. His monotone voice made the whole thing sound religious. I tried to divert the talking, but resistance was useless. *Don't you remember I've heard this before?* He never sensed when someone was making a fool of him, and I often felt sorry for him. Occasionally he took all the parts in a conversation. He answered his own questions as if he were interrogator and respondent combined. Eamonn's speech often had a quality of self-consciousness, his narrations unfolded with a kind of dramatic distance. Each monologue could have been used as a voice-over for a film about his own life. When I spoke, he either looked away or stared at me in such a way I was sure he wasn't listening. (I was out of camera frame, tape recorder turned off.) When I first met him, the subjects he didn't discuss became something that might be continued next episode, and it was the information he withheld that convinced me one more drink, one more movie, one more night. Less and less did his inattention seem like a liability; less and less a clue to future books thrown against walls; to future fits, bouts of yawning, spells of lapsed concentration. I liked spending nights with a view of the park, even when I couldn't sleep, but the Möbius loop of stories bugged me sometimes.

I tore up a small piece of paper stuck to the lid of a paint jar, half covered with telephone numbers and movie times. Eamonn told me it was three in the morning.

"Delacroix wrote that once you get out of bed you shouldn't get back in until you're ready to go to sleep," I answered.

"Another screwball."

In the word *screwball* were traces of a man who left women. Absent from the word *screwball* were traces of the grandiose way he often thought of himself. If I were translating Eamonn's life into a historical cartoon, he would be Karl Liebknecht in Berlin in 1918. Liebknecht, devoted to Marx, one of the founders of the Internationale: a dramatic life. Eamonn's biographical tableau could be equally momentous. This is assuming everything he told me was absolutely true. (I know it's New York too many decades later for the analogy to be anything but farfetched, but remember, it's just a cartoon.) His high school in Brooklyn was the Charlottenburg jail which released Liebknecht in 1897 on the anniversary of the Paris Commune. In the middle of a riot he might decide he wanted only to return to Anhalter Station, to go to the *Rote Fahne* office. Rosa Luxemburg would be there. To Eamonn, City Hall could just as easily have been Wilhelmstrasse, but there the analogy fails: Eamonn would not have been tempted. I couldn't even pretend to have Rosa Luxemburg's convictions, so I'm not represented in the story. It was only persistent historical gossip that the two of them had been lovers. Bloody Rosa they called her, founder of the Spartacus group, author of *The Accumulation of Capital*, she had many admirers. Her body was thrown in the Landwehr Canal and remained undetected for four and a half months. Perhaps I would be cast as a printer or a messenger, in love from a distance, but only peripherally involved. A man who wavered over the assassination of Karl Liebknecht was found dead, shot twice in the back in a Lichterfelde alley. That might be my part in the end.

When Eamonn woke up, too, he'd go into his darkroom. He'd built one in the bathroom. He'd look into it in the middle of the night, the way some people go to the refrigerator. He was careful about arranging negatives and prints, so that when I used the bathroom, I rarely saw his work unless I looked for it. An enlarger, bottles of chemicals, and trays huddled around my feet, on shelves above my head, or under the sink. Occasionally he neglected to put prints away, and there were times when I did look. I would hold the edges of the negatives carefully with the tips of my fingers.

In the autumn Eamonn became interested in the case of the *Grace O'Malley*, an eighty-foot trawler which the United States Customs agents had seized on the Brooklyn waterfront. The *Grace O'Malley* was carrying seven tons of automatic weapons, hand grenades, explosives, and ammunition. It was supposed to meet another trawler off the Kerry coast. There were only two men aboard the *Grace O'Malley*. They were detained for questioning by customs agents, then released the next day. The newspapers didn't print their names. What had happened was that the *Grace O'Malley* had lain for several days in port, and a watchman had become suspicious. The ship looked abandoned. None of the boat's fishing gear showed evidence of use, nor did the boat appear ready for fishing. The windows were blown out of the pilothouse, as if it had just been through a violent gale.

"We believe," said the inspector to a reporter, "this is the vessel that shipped arms to the Provos. We found documentation aboard showing that it was in the area concerned at the time."

The area concerned, the pickup spot, was a few miles east of Mount Desert, Maine. Valued at $500,000, the *Grace O'Malley* was registered in the name of Freddy Driscoll of Staten Island, who said he knew nothing about any smuggling.

"The boat was supposed to be out swordfishing," he told United States agents. Driscoll owned a small fishing fleet and would say only that his boats caught fish, not hand grenades. They were designed as trawlers, not transatlantic gun runners.

Grace O'Malley, Eamonn said, was an Irish pirate who preyed on English ships returning from the New World. Sir Francis Drake's *Golden Hind* was counted among her quarry. Queen Elizabeth had brought Grace O'Malley to court in a diplomatic effort to stop the marauding. They met queen to queen. Elizabeth handed her a little dog. Grace O'Malley didn't know what the animal was for. She was told it was a lap dog, she should hold and pet it as they spoke. The pirate said she'd never sat down long enough to have a lap, and handed it back to Queen Elizabeth.

I filled in colors of my choice but didn't write the stories themselves. That was the job of the scripter, Mr. Loonan. If the obvious twist in plot lay right before him, he was consistently blind to it. In spite of his occasional ingenuity, I often grew bored with Electra, Mr. Loonan's dream warrior. Her carapace of bravado scarcely covered conventional femininity. There were more male power figures in the serial than you could shake a stick at. Sometimes they bailed her out; if not, they were there just in case. Neo-Nazi scientists with Russian names planned construction of the Ultimate Parent Entity. Russian names had been fixtures in the serial since the fifties, and the Ultimate Parent Entity, a threat that came and went over the years, was a term whose actual source, Mr. Loonan said, came from legal documents. It was a story of restricted themes: adventure, rescue, jailing, malevolent stepmothers who looked like post-Industrial Revolution Cyclopses. Electra hadn't changed much since the beginning of the series, on the premise that one audience grew up and was replaced by another. She was not phototropic; she thrived on dark space, which seemed ironic for a champion of good causes. But Mr. Loonan liked drawn blinds and often told me and Laurel Quan Liu, the inker, that he wrote best at night.

Fantômes studios were located in a building which looked like an imitation of an early Louis Sullivan building, Orientalist and grimy: cast-iron window mullions and lobby mosaics of Egyptian lotus blossoms were rarely cleaned. On the nineteenth floor the reception area and the corridors were gray and austere in comparison, but individual art rooms, cluttered with mock-ups, props, and storyboards, took on the character of whatever serial was being produced in them. The first door on the left was the studio which created a Camelot sort of knock-off; it was full of crenellated shapes, pictures of knights and chess monsters; the prehistorical serial, down the hall, typically had winged pterodactyls and other dinosaurs suspended from the ceiling, someone had copied a bit of a cave painting along one wall. The detective and police procedural studios were in badly lit adjoining rooms with scrappy yellow walls. Stacks of law-enforcement paraphernalia and movie stills lay in corners. These serials were scripted by a tired-looking man who wore a trench coat and kept bottles of rye in his desk. The Gothic studio was run mainly by women with inky hair and black-rimmed eyes who could be overheard talking about Poe and Victorian sexuality; they were intensely disliked by the scripter of the spy serial because they refused to lend him a back issue or a bottle of red ink, no one remembered the source of their particular cold war. I could never find the door to his studio.

The Electra story was the only Fantômes serial left which took place in space, so the studio had inherited some of the models from previous, phased-out comics. Spaceships which had been new during the McCarthy era lay in a lumpy row along the windows facing Thirty-second Street. No one knew what to do with them. The room was divided by low partitions separating the drawing tables of the artists from the desks of the writers. Although he worked in an alcove, the activities of the *Electra* room revolved around Mr. Loonan. Tacked above his desk were a few wrappers from hollow chocolate robots he had given out last Christmas. He had eaten some of them himself and saved the gold papers with their green and rose geometric patterns. They flattened into symmetrical abstractions. Each one was different. Propped beside one of the windows he kept a magnetic toy called a Wooly Willy composed of a man's blank face painted on a sheet of pink cardboard, covered by a shallow plastic box. Inside the box were powdered iron filings. If you waved a magnetized stick over the box, eyebrows, hair, or a beard would appear on the magnetic man's bare features. The clumps of iron filings stuck to the wand like wads of spinach Popeye might squeeze from a can. Loonan claimed Wooly Willy was over twenty years old. He played with the toy when he had trouble with what he called plot points. At first Laurel and I thought the toy was amusing, but the number of changes which could be made to Wooly Willy's face were so limited we soon found its presence annoying and tried to look away when Mr. Loonan played with it. Nearby on the floor were boxes of movie stills which were used as references for difficult compositions and camera angles. Once in a while an artist might look through them for an image of a cockpit or a body twisted in an unnatural position. Scattered across Mr. Loonan's desk were pages which looked like scripts with camera directions written between blocks of dialogue.

Over-the-shoulder shot, past the fat man in shadow. Highlight of Electra's face.

DR. K.

She came out of your image duplicator. That's all I can tell you, because that's all I know, and that's all anyone will ever know about her.

ELECTRA

What do you mean?

DR. K.

I mean the cipher for yesterday's duplications has been lost, perhaps deliberately obscured.

ELECTRA

That's not possible.

High-angle shot reveals another figure, the duplicant, in the shadow. On the top of the frame, Dr. K.'s words: **But I'm afraid it is.**

There were also stacks of layouts, trial sketches, inked drawings. Each black-and-white inked page was photocopied and reduced to the size it would be when printed. Until returned by the colorist, the pages looked flat and static, a cursory imitation, or at best a dry parody, of the final book. I filled the photocopies, lifeless pages of frames, leaving only the speech balloons blank. My colors gave the drawings the illusion of spatial depth and could imply dramatic content, while the stories themselves were very conventional. After writer, inker, and letterer had done their jobs, the colorist's territory was mood. A kitchen could be bright and cheerful (chrome yellow and cadmium), signifying security and good news, or it could be dark and ominous (sepia, Hooker's green), signifying an absent mother figure or household appliances discovered to have a life of their own.

It was September and Fantômes Comics, Limited, was busy producing the Christmas issues. Mr. Loonan needed new angles on catastrophe. The director, Mr. Regozin, said the Electra story was becoming too predictable, too repetitious, and they were losing readers. Readers always knew the end of the story, even if the end was nowhere in sight for the next ten issues. Each comic had to be set up as if the foretellable end might be imperiled in every other frame. Two fates, happy marriage and death, could be approached but must never actually be met. For anyone or anything in space to fall, even superficially, in love with Electra was useless. Love for Electra was doomed, and death a subject of close brushes, but never the big end. If ingeniously devised delays or obstacles in space ever turned fatal to Electra, they would be fatal for everyone else in the office.

I watched the two men talk through the dappled glass of the studio door. Loonan looked saurian in green or black turtleneck sweaters. Sometimes there were science-fiction books stuffed into his pockets. They were both short, but where the scripter's features were angular, Mr. Regozin's were round. Neither office intrigue nor comic flap would deter Mr. Regozin. He moved products out of the shop and never missed a deadline. Loonan, timid in the face of Mr. Regozin, marshaled us with the desperation of a wind-up King Kong facing a wall. Laurel said Mr. Loonan had the eyes of a poet, but a cathode ray shone behind them. He had dark hair and the pale skin of someone who, like Electra, rarely saw the sun. Regozin, flushed and unsmiling, wore red-rimmed glasses, loud ties, and lapel pins of cartoon characters. Krazy Kat days were usually bad. Mighty Mouse days were good. Felix the Cat, Mickey Mouse, and the Phantom were subject to interpretation. Through the bumpy glass of the office door, Mr. Loonan's nose looked increasingly beaky and Mr. Regozin's more bulbous, his glasses frighteningly large.

They're all children, Laurel said, as we lit cigarettes in the bathroom. She sat on the sink and looked in the mirror. She was wearing a black dress with tiny yellow pens and pencils printed on it, unbuttoned at the top and bottom. I knew without asking that she was probably going to Queens after work to visit her mother and was wearing this dress to irritate her. Dressing for antagonism was a sign of Queens days. I had seen Laurel's closet and knew that it contained boxes of clothes her mother used to buy for her: silk jackets with fastened frogs, dresses with high collars, sometimes she wore the black ones, but not to visit her mother. Then her mother seemed to give up. My own mother had divorced my father and I hadn't seen her in years. There was little I could do to antagonize her. When she lived with us and I happened to wear strange clothes or refused to cut my hair, she barely noticed. The idea of challenging her in any way was a futile exercise. To Laurel, my mother seemed like an impossible phantom of good fortune who appeared only in the form of an occasional letter or call from Los Angeles. She had another family, and I neither knew her address nor her telephone number by heart. This detail had always amazed Laurel, even now as she blew smoke at her reflection in the mirror. In spite of bitter complaints Laurel visited her mother often. When we first met, the antagonism took the form of colored streaks in her hair, and I now think the subject of my shadowy mother may have increased Laurel's interest in me. I was a curiosity, a person whose condition allowed a kind of advantage, but maybe somewhere lurking in Laurel's brain there was some small measure of pity. I only had a suspicion of this, but found it in itself a curious response, one Laurel would deny all the way downtown. No, she wasn't going to Queens after work. I was wrong.

Laurel and I met at art school. After graduation we often worked together at other studios. One of us would be hired, then she or I would suggest the other. Inker and colorist, we went together as a pair. Work in the comics had started out as a series of jobs, nothing more, but with *Electra* we became swept up into the story. Laurel wasn't in love with the heroine, as Loonan seemed to be, but if Electra was nothing more than a victim of circumstances imposed on her by Fantômes, so was Laurel. The restraints of design and layout, a scripter and director who appeared clumsy and blundering, were oppressive to her. Flat defenseless superheroines could be easily dominated, but Laurel didn't like to be treated as a busboy dabbling in inks. If this were ancient Egypt, she would say as she put a cigarette out in the sink, we would be royal scribes of Thebes, and they would be bricklayers.

I was only partially convinced of the buffoon aspect of the office. I also had moments when I felt like an intimidated prisoner of Fantômes. The target of Regozin's anger might be ridiculously trivial (a misspelled word had gotten too far along in the various stages of the printing process to be corrected) or reflect a case of misjudgment (Electra, he thought, was out of frame too often), but I still felt crushed by his weekly performances. Once, he walked into the studio looking annoyed, wearing a tie with glossy mermaids on it. Laurel glanced in my direction just for an instant. I pretended to look for a brush that hadn't rolled under my desk, and still burst out laughing. He was not amused, although I don't think he realized exactly what I was laughing at.

Regozin continually called Loonan into his office; then Loonan would repeat the director's injustices to his staff. *Too much emphasis on Electra's skills. Not enough risks taken. Retire the Orion character. Introduce a new threat. All kinds of things are terrifying in space. Write down your nightmares.* About once a week Mr. Loonan might wake feeling vaguely depressed or frightened, aware he had had a nightmare, but its images were elusive. He did say that. He had never made a practice of remembering his dreams and deliberately tried to forget them. Even if they didn't evaporate immediately, even if he remembered them during the day, I don't think he would have repeated the contents to his staff. Pursuit through unfinished rooms, corners occupied by ambiguous phantoms, the fleeting return of dead family and friends, whatever happened in dreams, these were not subjects for *Electra*. Mr. Regozin, however, believed all kinds of sources, once sorted, molded, and edited, were entirely suitable. Content was endless. He found what he called original material in mundane places. He was, at all times, all ears. The previous week Regozin had overheard two fourteen-year-old boys talking about jet packs, a space station, something about interlocking parts, reconnaissance probes, rotating hexagonal joints. "I should have hired them on the spot," he said. The director hinted that Loonan's imagination had grown plodding and pedestrian. *Electra* had lost all sense of intrigue. Electra never fell in love with the wrong man or woman, never underwent a personality change or had a treasonous crew member aboard her ship. I suggested to him that it was difficult to maintain intrigue in a story when people rarely went outside. Why don't you have them land on a planet? Laurel proposed that he plant a fifth columnist on Electra's ship.

Mr. Loonan rubbed his eyes under his glasses as if to say, Fifth columnist, this isn't Catalonia in 1937, this is Thirty-second Street, forget about the Unificacion Marxista and the Spanish Civil War. He returned to his desk, ignoring us.

There were rumors that Fantômes was going to phase out *Electra*, and Loonan began to plot each book with the resignation of a man who sensed he would soon be rejected. Fantômes might place him on another comic; *Red Sonja, She-Devil with a Sword* or *Dazzler* were weak substitutes, the inventions of other men. It was Electra Mr. Loonan loved, with her superhuman strength and microquick reflexes. His fascination with the Electra story was the adoration of the creator. Mr. Loonan lived alone. He had no other obsessions or interests, drank black coffee, thrived under fluorescent lights, and thought out loud with a passion that was probably inadvertent and sometimes shocking. Bits of *Electra* episodes floated past us, the tryout audience whose opinions didn't really matter. When Laurel turned up her radio, Mr. Loonan looked hurt. She got a Walkman.

As if close proximity to comic-book heroes lent him their tyrannical authority, he would hover around my desk, checking my colors constantly. He never seemed to understand, yet he surely must have known, that however saturated my colors appeared on the layouts, they always printed down to the same hue—cheap ink and cheap paper faded almost immediately. It was inevitable, yet he wanted to have Electra last. Even if we could have drawn her on archival paper, I don't think that was the kind of preservation he had in mind. Loonan was after the mythic.

Shades of blue stand for black and white in frames which have no colors—a long shot of Electra at the controls of her spaceship, almost pensive; there is no text. A close-up shot, the misregistration of color and ink make her eyes look even bigger. Eyebrows like Elizabeth Taylor's, like apostrophes. Tears are simple, Laurel does the outlines. When Electra demonstrates her test-tube-generated strength, her powers are signified by rays, sometimes arcing out of the frame. She's nearly naked in every caper, occasionally Mr. Loonan will suggest boots and gloves. Shock is simulated in their faces. *Ah, blam,* and *whap* aren't part of Electra's style. Expletives are suggested without being used too often. She isn't a borderline parody like *Wonder Woman,* not a parasite like *Spiderwoman.* No one at Fantômes would have used the word ideology, but Eamonn said they made Electra into the comicbook version of the Holy Virgin Mary, even if she didn't wear much clothing.

Loonan explained a frame split into eight sections as if divided by spokes on a wheel, Electra's head in the middle. In each section she tried to land on a random planet or comet and was continually turned away. Orion had spread rumors in the galaxy that she wasn't a heroine but one of the following: a scout for pirates, a cast-off counterspy, a psychobiotic polluter with minimal free will. The power and momentum of spreading tales intrigued Mr. Loonan. Orion's tales were easily launched, and each time one was repeated, it was altered a little and the implications for Electra appeared uglier. I colored a planet governed by a creature who looked like the wicked stepmother in Disney's *Snow White*. Blondes are usually good and gentle like Betty. Dark Veronicas are greedy and possessive. Loonan was a stickler on the symbolic, and he considered his directives on questions of color to be a reinforcement of classical thinking on aesthetics.

In the middle of his explanation, a man walked in, asked to use the bathroom, then came back a few minutes later. He was wearing a wrinkled black jacket. When I looked closer I could see faintly that it was plaid and I stared hard at his back as if picking out the blocks in an Ad Reinhardt painting. In fact, looking at him in general was like being in a dark room. Eventually your eyes get used to absence of light, and you begin to make out what's there. He had very long arms. He was reading Goethe's *Theory of Colors*. Loonan introduced him as Martin Chatfield, the temporary letterer, and told him that he noticed he was late. He was the tallest man ever seen at Fantômes. Curly hair fell over his forehead like a bunch of black grapes. Mr. Loonan showed him to his desk and told him he was trying to run a business, not a toy shop, and to get to work.

He smiled nervously at the scripter, said something about lost keys and sorry. He didn't yet know that no one in the studio took Mr. Loonan's threats very seriously. He looked at the pens Loonan gave him as if they were Loonan's own laundry. They did need to be cleaned, but Martin insisted he had brought his own. Loonan pocketed his special pens and muttered about authority figures and their problems in two-dimensional space. Laurel put on her Walkman.

Martin turned to me, saying he no longer read what he wrote. As a child he was told he had a lovely hand, but it's the twentieth century, kings' and bishops' scribes have long been out of work, so he ended up in the funnies. Martin moved slowly and seemed out of place in the little office where everyone suspected we might all be canned any minute. After his last job, he said, he had gone to Berlin to stay with an American woman who translated subtitles for films and lived near the Wall. I watched him letter:

YOU THINK SHE'LL BE A PROBLEM?

WE'LL ARRANGE A SHORT CIRCUIT.

ARIADNE LIFTED THE DECODER
FROM THE DEAD MAN'S JACKET.
SHE HEARD THE SOUND
OF A WINDOW BEING OPENED.

Listening to Martin talk about lettering, its history, and his own influences was like having a radio on in the background. I listened because I didn't have to think while coloring. He lined up his Ames guide on a T square. Not all comic lettering is the same. Some letterers can be identified by their style, but Martin was freelance and temporary. His interest in comic lettering was transient. It was a skill which required precision, and the precision lent professionalism to a man who felt amateurish about most things. I would later learn that Martin had enough interests and occupations, each held for a brief period of time, to sound authoritative if the listener didn't know any better. He knew enough about being an actor, and enough about writing scripts, to convince someone that with the donation of a large sum of money he could complete a project undoubtedly destined for commercial success. He collected all kinds of unusual junk in his apartment, but would describe the objects as if they were rare antiques, each unique in a special way and worth a small fortune. If he could concentrate and be consistent long enough, he would have been a great con artist, but he didn't go after serious quarry. In the studio, for the moments just after we had been introduced, he pretended to be an expert, not a scavenging dilettante.

In the fifties, he explained, letterers were always men who began in the comics and hoped to move on to magazines like *The Saturday Evening Post*. He spoke with an annoying sentimentality, as if he were some sort of noble relic no one really valued anymore. Lettering was a better job than coloring, he told me, and in the past, colorists had always been women because it was thought they had more patience. Hundreds of them worked in rows in large halls doing color separations on acetate sheets. That was before the morality crackdown on horror in the comics, before the Kefauver Commission swept away the severed limbs, and sales of Dr. Barton's red ink (carmine #26, scarlet #35) plummeted.

I looked up a minor character, a duplicant named Hermes, in my comic index. The character index includes such details as height, weight, and eye color: a strange alliance of factual statistics applied to creatures which exist mainly in boys' imaginations. Hermes appeared so many issues ago I could no longer remember his colors. He was a thief on a grand scale who wore a low, crowned hat. Rows of Dr. Barton's inks in their little glass bottles glowed fuchsia, orange, malachite, violet, and Yves Klein blue on my desk. I picked up Nile green, #20, for Hermes' hat and added a few drops of water to the ink.

Electra wore Prussian blue #17. The interior of her

spaceship was bluish black #38, except where she sat under a cone of light, chrome yellow #3, diluted 50 percent. It was always night in space. Under the yellow light Electra held a Payne's gray #10 gun and a Van Dyck brown #9 square which represented a photograph. Each subsequent frame was a close-up shot which brought the square nearer. It was a sepia print of a man dressed as a World War II soldier and he was tied to a chair. Something about a time warp beyond Mars and going steadily backwards, I wasn't paying close attention.

By the windows, near a corner, Mr. Loonan spoke to himself, in varying voices. " 'You're my kind of girl, sweetie.' 'That's what you think.' Door slam. Stupid thing to say. Orion causes everyone on Electra's ship to fall asleep. Even the image duplicator has Z's tracking across its video display terminal. No, the image duplicator is a machine and can't. That's what stopped O."

Beside me Martin read quietly out loud from his book:

221. Primary objects may be considered firstly as *original*, as images which are impressed on the eye by things before it, and which assure us of their validity. To these secondary images may be opposed as *derived* images, which remain in the organ when the object itself is taken away; those apparent after-images, which have been circumstantially treated in the doctrine of physiological colours.

At 5:30 Mr. Loonan left for a meeting with Mr. Regozin. He took things from his pockets so the objects wouldn't stick out: a little black notebook, his glasses case, coins. He combed his hair, straightened his tie, put the Styrofoam cups he'd been punching his thumbs through all day into the trash as if he were going to the electric chair. All those gestures that I never thought about twice suddenly seemed supportive of a hopeless case. Laurel was still humming along with her Walkman. Martin screwed the caps on all his pens.

We walked down the hall, and I motioned to Laurel to walk very quietly past Mr. Regozin's door. Through the bumpy glass we saw the smear of his long desk, and the two men were only gray blurs. We stopped on either side of the door so we couldn't be seen through the window. I thought I heard Mr. Loonan pleading that *Electra* kept Fantômes solidly in the black, and Mr. Regozin saying that was no longer true.

The elevator was packed, and as we waited for the next one, Martin caught up with us. He said he'd just seen Mr. Loonan walking quickly into the men's room. Martin had wanted to go in himself, but Loonan had seemed very upset and Martin wanted to avoid him. Laurel told him that if he took the stairs he would find another men's room up or down one flight.

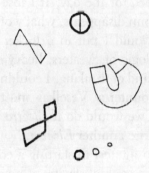

Laurel and I got out of the subway, stopping to look at the things, for sale, spread on blankets near the subway stop: toaster parts, car radios, answering machines without cords, used tweed suits with the pockets cut out, a pyramid made of tiny white plastic shoes—they even had bows and high heels—a secondhand copy of *The Thief's Journal*, old Patti Smith records, copies of *Life, Time, Look* from 1969, 1970, 1971; Richard Nixon on one cover, Patty Hearst on another. I saw black shorts over black sweatpants. Just for an instant, as those sweatpants leaped over a blanket spread with hundreds of fragments of glass and rhinestone jewelry, I thought of the kid from the roof, then the legs disappeared around the corner and he was gone.

We walked past empty lots filled with the winter shelters of the homeless. Constructions made of cardboard cartons (small Coke, Colgate-Palmolive, and Marlboro estates) cut into igloos; broken umbrellas stuck out like warnings or fake television antennas, sometimes real gardens sprinkled with empty amyl nitrate bottles, bags of cans and bottles that would later be counted by fives and cashed in. Soon a bulldozer will flatten all the paper and tin houses. A foundation was already being dug on the lot next door. Someone wrote on the plywood surrounding the pit: *Rich people will soon live here.* We looked through one of the holes, although it was dark out and construction had stopped for the day. If I lose my job, can't pay my rent, and Eamonn disappears, what would I put into shopping bags? What would I put in a locker in Grand Central Station? Even the logic of sweaters, heavy coats, and blankets reflects the wrong kind of thinking. I couldn't carry that much.

We sat at a counter at Veselkas and tried to eat dinner, talking about what we would do if *Electra* was phased out.

"We could write another *Electra*."

Laurel had no interest in starting a comic business, and she knew I would be content staying at home drawing Electra into spiraling obscurity.

We could make her do whatever we wanted her to do, and the whole enterprise would amount to nothing. Electra was depressing and ridiculous. Laurel didn't mind rewriting the story for her own amusement but insisted Electra have no political axe to grind. That, to her, made absolutely no sense.

We could get other jobs at other comics. Laurel was pragmatic, like Martin, one job followed another, you just had to spend a lot of time on the telephone. Serial comics were booming. There would always be an audience for them. A thin man in a blue raincoat approached table after table, trying to sell his photographs. The prints were scenes and people from the neighborhood, already become picturesque, already souvenirs. Nobody bought any photographs from him. He grinned at each rejection, but he reminded me of Loonan talking to himself about Electra's escape from Orion, desperate above the sound of Laurel singing along with her tapes.

Eamonn wasn't home yet. On the Brooklyn waterfront had he crept aboard the *Grace O'Malley* at the wrong moment? Arrest kept secret from the press; was the FBI or CIA detaining him in a house like the one in *North by Northwest?* Maybe the prison is in Forest Hills. They question and torture him. If he was simply in jail, he'd get one telephone call, and it wouldn't be to me, that one call. Eamonn was no more reliable than my job at Fantômes, flimsy, flyaway things. He would disappear after a telephone call or airmail letter. Meanwhile, Orion was chasing Electra, and her resources were getting thin, approaching zero; all of ours were. Loonan was flirting with the idea of rape by a superpower, and that would be the end of us all. In his rashness he would sweep away any concept of what ought or ought not to be in the book. There hadn't ever been a real need for rescue. Electra always took care of herself. Malcontents, inker and colorist, had no editorial voice.

Think of what it means to die hard, Mr. Loonan, the moment of death prolonged by a tangle of intravenous tubes, mercy killers banished to the hospital parking lot. Kids won't close the book thinking, Oh, what a wonderful world. You have to allow for resurrection, because resurrection can happen at Fantômes if someone changes his mind. You have only to hire Martin Chatfield for a week and he'll print the words.

There was nothing more to say about Fantômes. It was growing dark, and I knew Eamonn would still not be home. We stopped at a bodega to buy a quart of milk. A little boy sat on a crate looking at pictures in a body-builder magazine, pointing to one or another tanned, oiled body, as his father rang up the cash register. We walked to my apartment without talking.

Laurel laid cups and plates on the table, and I set up my inks, ruler, and paper between them. As we ate, we drew a version of the Electra story.

EPISODE I
Birth of Electra

K = the cube of any planet's distance from the sun divided by the square of the periodic time of that planet's revolution about the sun.

G = any constant M_s = the mass of the sun

Dr. Mary Atlas had been working for years in her laboratory under Sierra Madre del Sur. She worked alone. Unlike other scientists, she avoided hiring research assistants if she could do the work herself. She would name Madame Curie and Rosalind Franklin as examples of women who may have trusted the wrong people. Rather than risk trusting anyone, she kept to herself. Suspicious even of letters of inquiry, she held most other scientists at armslength. General letters, requests to publish papers or to speak at conferences went unanswered; letters from those interested in collaborating were left in a pile and finally thrown away. Each night she made sure her papers were locked in an old bank vault. She was very careful with her research, but at the same time didn't take it too seriously. *Don't swallow your own radium*, she would tell herself. Although misanthropic she proved her kindness by treating the animals used in her laboratory as if they were special children. For unexplained reasons, Dr. Atlas had no need of grants. The source of her income remained a mystery. She would say that she didn't want to become a dupe of the funding institutions that demanded results favorable to their industrial sponsors. In her rock-faced laboratory full of glowing minerals and chattering animals in cages, she created a human baby, Electra, whose scrambled genetic code endowed her with superhuman strength. The girl grew up in the lab. It was a happy if sunless childhood, feeding doomed birds, monkeys, and mice. One of their few connections with the outside world was the radio which they would listen to every evening. When the Secretary of State (futuristic in appearance, but not brewed from chemicals) threatened to begin bombing Leningrad, Dr. Atlas put Electra in a spaceship and sent her into space, thinking the girl would be less endangered beyond Mars.

$$G = \frac{4\pi^2 K}{M_s}$$

The Chrysler Building at night was a Tivoli sweet, partly ominous and Gothic the way he had photographed it. The woman on the Staten Island Ferry had her eyes shut as she kissed or was being kissed; the man had one eye open, and the one eye looked straight at the lens. Three-card-monte dealers, hands hovering over bent cards, grinned at the camera. These were some of his New York photographs.

A man made a call from behind a bombed-out telephone booth; jagged glass, splintered wood, his back to the photographer. Another picture; the ruins of a house. They looked like older ruins, not recent; perhaps the house had been gutted by fire or a bomb a few years before: a woman in a heavy coat looked out from what used to be a window. Two men with machine guns were painted carefully on a brick wall. One aimed at the sky, the other sat, stylized flags waving behind them. Thin men in masks carried a narrow coffin, the third picture. I returned to the woman in the coat. She didn't smile at the photographer. A dark line had been scratched over her eyes, but the negative remained clear. These were his Irish pictures.

It was about to rain. The picture sky was gray. *Wales*, it said on the back of the photograph. Before a stone bridge, a doll's carriage had been overturned. Six or seven children all stared at Eamonn's lens; curiosity, indifference, potential hostility. Short dress held a twisted doll. These were Eamonn's performers. A woman stared at her reflection between mannequins in a store window, white-painted dummies balancing Mexican hats on headless shoulders. Women in long fur coats stood next to their horses, men in bowlers on horseback beside them. I never asked him how he got onto their grounds in order to take these. The trappings of class sat more appropriately and with less jarring effect on the men. They looked so much less ridiculous even when they were old and obese and wore kilts or little caps. Perhaps Eamonn photographed them with more restraint, or maybe he would say that's just the way I looked at his pictures.

No crystal-clear scandal, no shock, no gun to the head. You had to come to these pictures with some information first. You might have to know geography and a little history. Eamonn had experienced the terror in the busted telephone booth and the racehorse. He knew his way around cities that imposed nightly curfews; he had hitchhiked to guerrilla encampments in mountains that still bore Indian names, but he often photographed the shards of glass from explosions rather than the bodies torn apart from the blast. He was reading Weegee's *Naked City*.

I hadn't been happy about having my picture taken, but hadn't wanted to give Eamonn a hard time. After about fifteen minutes of being told what to do and how to stand, what I should wear or should have worn, I did say that I felt like going home. It would be, he said, his picture. That seemed entirely unreasonable. It was a picture of a person, not a thing. He was behind the camera. He would give me a copy of the photograph if I wanted one, but the negatives, the contact sheet, the process, the lighting, the composition, telling me not to smile, all that belonged to him. Finally I got angry and walked away, leaving Eamonn with his camera. At about the age of ten or eleven, I no longer liked having my father take my picture, despite the knowledge that it gave him a great deal of pleasure. I found his pleasure, although innocent, suspect and manipulative. When he met me at the school bus, I would say, *No Dad, I don't want my picture taken*. Other children walked home by themselves, but I lost that small sign of independence because he was there. There was a sense of being used for a purpose that was beyond my control, like the Seattle man whose freakish, highly immune blood cells were taken from him, cultured and patented without his consent. I was miserable as I walked away from the school bus, not because he was there, but because he didn't understand why he should not be there. I didn't want to be admired when the admiration and attractiveness had nothing to do with me but with my father's idea of his daughter, a relatively good child. In the city, fifteen years later, it seemed to me that my father must have been hurt by my contempt and refusal to be a subject, but at the same time, I'm certain he expressed nothing of the kind and laughed at me during the whole incident. Eamonn perhaps only looked shocked and angry. There were hundreds of pictures of me as a child dispersed, lost. I don't know where they would be now. Maybe one or two lay in a drawer some-where in Los Angeles.

He took me into his darkroom and turned on the red light. Strips of negatives hung from the pipes, bottles of chemicals were wedged into tight rows. Odd lenses and a paper cutter he called the guillotine lay neatly stored under the bathtub. A negative was cut off, slid into the enlarger, and brought into focus. His hands were long and thin, and he handled every bit of paper or acetate as if it were a rare and delicate thing. My face was gray and small before shreds of torn posters stuck to a wall in the park. The writing looked reversed, but it wasn't. Set the timer for ten seconds; click. Slowly the print was taken out of the developer bath with tongs; the solution dripped off a corner and back into the tray. I floated under the stop bath for thirty seconds, then the fixer, next came the washer for half an hour, and at last the wet paper was hung up to dry.

The first time Laurel met Eamonn, it was an accident. He was waiting for me in front of the Fantômes building after work, although I hadn't expected him to be there.

It was the middle of the September Christmas rush, and it had not been a good day. Mr. Regozin had asked Laurel to re-ink a series of frames in which Orion tried to hypnotize Electra from a distance. Laurel had thought it was a weak scene, nothing really to visualize in it. Wouldn't creatures and meteorites get in the way and be hypnotized instead? Mr. Loonan told her narrative visualization wasn't part of her job and she should just ink, but then it was time to leave. The elevator was empty. Laurel tipped her head back and addressed the triangular mirror in an upper corner as if it were a video camera, and Loonan were watching her on a monitor at the reception desk. She called him the martinet of Fantômes and described the contents of her refrigerator: withered bok choy and half a ham sandwich. She felt too tired to go to the stores. She just wanted to go home.

Leaning against a cast-iron lobby lotus was Eamonn with his camera. I was glad to see him, but he wasn't interested in complaints about the pointlessness of hypnosis across miles of space. He asked Laurel about non-union sweatshops in Chinatown that exploited illegal immigrants as if that was something she might know about. Had he thought so rapidly: Liu, Chinese, exploitation, translator? Eamonn didn't enjoy prying and didn't think of his asking as a kind of needling. He only partly believed in the audience's right to know anyway. Depending on the circumstances, one's right to know could be swiftly scuttled. On the other hand, Eamonn could lock up secrets very well if he had to. When he was tired of being a photographic sleuth, he avoided situations that required middlemen. But it was rare when he wouldn't have to talk to someone. Usually he enjoyed acting, but I think even then, even when he first asked Laurel about Chinatown, he was getting tired of the range demanded of him: from subterfuge to sincerity, just to take a picture. He didn't really want to talk to anyone, he just wanted to snap the shutter and be done with it. We went downtown.

We watched fish in a tank in the window of a restaurant on the Bowery. The tanks were overcrowded. The scales of many of the fish were shredded or sliced to reveal white flesh and the thinnest red blood vessels underneath. As if drawn on, the vessels barely pulsed, and their gills fanned sluggishly in and out. Some floated nearly lifeless at the top of the water. Ordinarily expressionless eyes looked miserable and pained. There were pictures Eamonn wanted to take in Chinatown.

He might have had nothing but good intentions, but he was too quick to ask Laurel, again, about the sweatshops. The women who sew at home, who don't speak English, whom she saw on the N train with shopping bags full of cloth cut into sleeves, cuffs, pockets; he asked her to be his interpreter so he could speak to those women and perhaps take their pictures. He said it was all for the good, but Laurel wasn't sure. The women, if they could be persuaded to speak, would identify her with the American photographer. She would be part of what they didn't understand, part of what couldn't be translated.

Laura's mother hadn't worked in one of those shops, but she saw her mother in those women, and it disturbed her. Eamonn's good intentions translated into a mangled heap. She couldn't help him. Her mother dressed like the sweatshop workers, trousers and jackets of the same blue material, flat shoes. Her mother used to carry twin shopping bags on the subway, just as these women did, but now Laurel brought things home for her. Mrs. Liu didn't go out much, not because she was incapable, but because of many small fears, barely articulated, which kept her in her house. If she went out during the day, an occasion might arise in which she might fail to understand directions or a fine point in English grammar; single words with multiple meanings and words which sounded alike confused her. Puns appeared where none was intended. She would appear foolish or become lost. At the same time, it was part of her mother's vulnerability not to know anything about gambling rings or gangs whose names included words like dragon or jade. The women she saw on the subway knew, but her mother did not. She thought her mother lived like a child with its nose pressed against the window.

Laurel had the opposite disease. She couldn't be outside her tiny apartment enough. She often took dangerous late-night walks from the southeast part of Chinatown, past projects and remnants of an Italian neighborhood, past silver corporate skyscrapers to the Battery and, if the Staten Island Ferry ran at that hour, she might have taken it at the end of her walk. Although Laurel and her mother argued bitterly, each one asserted that she offered protection from what the vulnerable other couldn't possibly know lay outside the door. The subject of the women who sewed at home illegally represented certain doors which ought to be kept shut, even at the expense of those supposedly protected. Her mother was not an innocent, but she seemed to demand to be treated like one, or maybe it was just that Laurel assumed she had seen more than her mother, even though the only place she had ever lived was New York.

Eamonn left us looking at the wounded fish. He had a job somewhere farther downtown, photographing City Hall or Wall Street at night, he said, but I wondered if he wasn't really going to the Brooklyn waterfront or secretly meeting Driscoll on the Staten Island Ferry.

I had been out to Flushing once with Laurel. I hadn't wanted to go, because I was afraid she and her mother would argue, and I would have to sit by mutely unsure whether their arguing had reached the point at which it would be more polite for me to leave the room. On the other hand, my leaving (I imagined myself sitting on a curb, waiting) would only draw attention to their inability to get along. Mrs. Liu used to tell Laurel that she could never be anything other than what she had been born; to try would only make her look foolish, if not lead to trouble and humiliation, but by then Laurel was taking the subway into Manhattan to go to school, and she didn't want to feel she had anything in common with anyone else. Besides, her mother, too, in her own way, behaved as if she shared nothing with her neighbors. They came from other provinces, she was certain. She didn't want to melt into immigrantness. During her first year after leaving China, she didn't buy curtains, because she thought somehow the family wouldn't stay in that house. Mrs. Liu kept to herself, living mainly in the kitchen with the Venetian blinds drawn, steaming rice, brewing tea, reading Chinese newspapers and books.

The house was small and austere. Laurel unlocked the door with a lot of noise, yelling hello as we entered. Her mother was already there, smiling, glad to see her, it wasn't drawn swords from the start. Blue-gray jacket and trousers, Laurel had said, but Mrs. Liu wore a dark red dress, obviously western. I hoped she hadn't changed her clothes for me, but it was possible Mrs. Liu never wore the suits Laurel claimed she lived in. I expected to smell garlic, lemon grass, ginger root, and coriander but instead the close air smelled like overly boiled meat. A plastic orange tree tied with a red ribbon was near the door. I nearly knocked it over when we entered. Mrs. Liu frowned at Laurel's hair, which looked as though it was still wet. There was a photograph of Laurel's sister, who lived in California, and her father, who had died years ago. There were no pictures of Laurel or her mother. Laurel was taller than her mother and had very short, spiky hair that looked as if it would give your hand paper cuts if you ran it across the top. Her short hair was upsetting to her mother, even though Mrs. Liu's own was short and curled in a beauty parlor once a week. The trip was one of the few times she went beyond the perimeters of her block. She showed Laurel blue-and-green enameled sticks with which to put up her hair if she ever grew it again. Laurel had brought her a few books and medicinal herbs. I watched her mother soak spindly mushrooms in water, slice ginger, and steam bamboo shoots. Laurel poured tea into green cups and tried to make her mother sit down.

After college Laurel had to live at home with her mother, but soon got a job on *Spiderwoman* and was able to move into the city. Her mother didn't understand why she wanted to live in that bad part of Chinatown where families filled tiny apartments, and the landlord changed every few months as the buildings were sold.

Henry Street, Catherine Street, the part of East Broadway that hid shooting galleries. Laurel would go into stores, examine boxes of tiny red and green peppers glistening like tropical insects, heaps of cooked rock crabs whose halves were held together by rubber bands, tangled king crab legs laid out on ice, and red-eyed Buddha cookies. She spoke Chinese to the old women and young men hawking ginger root and oranges.

You could marry someone from Hong Kong for two to six thousand American dollars, you could get a fake passport in a basement in Queens, but all the networks started in Chinatown. She had returned to this neighborhood to live and could not imagine ever having enough money to leave it. She could leave if she were willing to live in her mother's house again, yet when she returned to the city after visiting her, she would walk around as if she were on a short vacation tour.

One night Laurel saw Eamonn coming out of the Hak Ng Fung Vocational Center and followed him for a few blocks. He stopped for tea at Hop Kee's on Pell Street. She went in and sat in a corner where he couldn't see her, pretending to read while watching him talk to a young Chinese man who seemed to have arranged to meet him there. Next he looked at turtles and frogs in the window of Sun Nol's Fish Palace. He went into an herb shop which was too small for Laurel to follow him into, so she didn't know what he bought there. She wondered how he, a non-Chinese, would know what to buy in such a place and what to do with the herbs once he had them. She waited outside, looking at the dried roots and seeds in the window, then moved to a newsstand across the narrow street for a better view. He left the shop and she followed him a few blocks, keeping sight of his head in the crowd. He went into an apartment building on Doyers Street. She went home. Eamonn could take care of himself.

Looking out windows on the nineteenth floor facing west, I could see a boat hardly moving on the Hudson. Fantômes Comics was a world by itself, and the rooms where *Electra* was produced were like a (nearly) self-sufficient medieval city whose gates were often locked. Food was brought up to the floor in the morning, garbage taken out at night, products sent to the engravers, to the printers, money distributed in the form of checks with taxes taken out.

Mr. Loonan was planning for the next comic convention in Philadelphia. He described his preparations out loud. We learned what he would wear and how, if *Electra* was successful, his life would become like a Vincente Minnelli musical. Comic characters would spring into life, at first popping out of the dreary corners of his apartment, then singing and tap dancing with him down dark halls and grimy elevators. They would follow him all the way to Fantômes where Mr. Regozin, feet on desk, cigar in mouth, would flee to Grand Central Station.

The world of *Electra* occupied three places: the office, Mr. Loonan's home, and the convention. The book existed in stores and in other people's homes all over the country, but for Mr. Loonan the audience was inconsequential. The story's popularity mattered, but the actual thoughts or personal interpretations of others were irrelevant to him.

What do people think about when they read *Electra?* When they can't sleep at night, do they project themselves into the next episode? Loonan didn't care. He had trouble imagining even a single reader except at the cash register. (Fantômes' surveys, done every two years, consistently reported that 85 percent of *Electra's* readers were boys, aged eight to thirteen, a group of excitable insomniacs whose bodies were transformed by what they thought about at night.)

At the convention he would sweep through rooms of oversized displays and toy knock-offs. He would give a speech to the other writers present, and he would declare that comics reflect technology within two months. Picture phones, space satellites, answering machines, computers, all appeared on cheap newsprint first. Comics, he would say to the camera, are not a utopian commentary but a legitimate mirror of society. Then he would give examples from *Electra*.

Electra was one of the epics, like *Spiderman, Sheena,* and *Aleta*. Mr. Loonan was not really her creator. A man named Rochester began the story in 1952. Another writer, Fasco Jr., took it over a few years later, and Mr. Loonan replaced him when he retired. An unknown scripter would follow Mr. Loonan, if the story survived. Rochester's version reflected the American Cold War; Fasco Jr.'s interpretation, we had heard, was coded with references to his turbulent personal life.

Loonan toyed with the idea of nuclear threat somewhere within Electra's orbit. Electra, he said, will discover war is imminent. Her attempts to arrest the crisis ought to occupy several issues. It seemed dangerous to me that the story which began and ended with nuclear threats had turned full circle. Martin interrupted him: "A multinational corporation, not necessarily a government, will know before anyone," he said. He suggested the scripter think in terms of establishing one in space. Mr. Loonan was not interested in planting ITT on Jupiter and told Martin to letter a series of frames along the left margin and top border.

Mr. Regozin entered the studio to discuss the advertising campaign for *Electra*. While he spoke to Mr. Loonan, Laurel and I debated the problem of whether powers of invisibility extended to a character's clothing and the degree of animation that duplicants ought to have. How should their state of duplicacy be rendered? The two conversations went on simultaneously and independently of one another.

"Television spots," said Mr. Loonan.

"The duplicants should look like grainy blown-up photographs," I said.

"Inside of bubble-gum wrappers," suggested Loonan.

"Done in the fifties and sixties," Regozin replied.

"Exactly."

"I thought so, too, but drawn photographs within a drawing are usually unreadable as photographs."

"It might work again," Loonan said.

"They can't bend, that's one thing," I answered.

"They can't run away, then. Can they move at all?"

"A little."

"How do you show that? How do you draw the small jerky movement of a duplicant?"

"Readers shouldn't miss a single issue because . . . some sort of prize."

"Prizes, no, not again, you can't con readers so easily anymore. Tricks like that don't sell."

"The prize duplicant, the really best one, is nearly as strong as Electra."

"Electra represents revenge. So do her copies."

"If she represents revenge to readers, then the timing of the ads is important." He whispered something about American hostages.

"Saturday morning would be all wrong, then."

"The duplicants could be rendered in a pointillist style."

"It's easy to draw their destruction."

"They just fold up like accordions."

. . . INTO THE MACHINE'S GAPING MAW

Martin lettered.

Mr. Regozin frowned over his shoulder and beckoned Loonan to Martin's desk. Wouldn't it be better just to draw the gaping maw rather than have the character describe it? Do readers of *Electra* know what a maw is? Why not simplify language and write mouth? And machine is misleading. It looks something like a machine, readers can see that; write creature or monster, tired words but reliable. Mr. Regozin preferred the obvious common choices at the expense of more suggestive phrases, and he would do away with words altogether if narrative evidence could be seen in a picture or two.

The top of a building near Fantômes was lit gold. As I walked east, the red and green lights on the top of the Empire State

Building appeared from behind the gold panels, seeming to move forward in the brilliantly colored fog. Like finding a badly lit cathedral with no visitors except a few faithful old women, you become a believer, even if it's just cold and raining on Thirty-sixth Street. In the misty and nearly empty streets at night, you could believe in androids, mutants, Dracula, Frankenstein, the nineteenth century, and the future. What wasn't making sense was the bit in the middle.

Mr. Loonan had a sound-effects library which he had sent away for from a company in New Jersey. He referred to the tapes for general inspiration or when he had trouble phoneticizing certain sounds. They were like audio definitions, a sort of dictionary with a voice.

Transitions & Cues (pips, bubbles, gongs, cymbals, bells, clocks, ticks, horns, music boxes, barrel organs, string and piano notes). Electra's ship is taken over by anaplastic life forms. That is, certain cells in certain individuals revert to a primitive, imperfect state, and gradually but inevitably, the anaplastic cells become the majority. As the behavior around Electra grows increasingly moronic, Orion has visions of rescuing her from the havoc caused by the invasion of the dissolute cells.

Backgrounds (Interior: cocktail party, hotel lobby, prize fight, laundromat, hospital, restaurant, bus station, concert hall, factory, bowling alley, skating rink. Exterior: garden, park, lakeside, pool, city streets, highway, racetrack, parade, playground, football game, buildings, seashore). Electra's ship passes through a storm of aerolites, each covered by signs of a demotic language. The fragments of writing are all the evidence that remains of an ancient planet now reduced to stony flying newspapers from an extinct society. Electra photographs the bits as they hurtle past, then tries to decode the lines which appear in the pictures. Her computer tells her that what she thought represented simple language in a popular format, something like a newspaper with large print, is really arcane and hieratic. Being an atheist since birth, Electra is disappointed, has the negatives destroyed, and locks up the remaining prints.

The sound-effects tapes were useful source material and they were an assault on Laurel's unfriendly Walkman, guarantor of obliviousness. Mr. Loonan often borrowed the tapes. He would take them home from the office, and in his dark apartment he might put on *Warfare & Guns* (21-gun salute, revolvers, machine guns, rifles, marching, naval battles, torpedoes, depth charges, sonar, destroyer siren, air strikes, bombs, tanks, grenades, pistols, mortars, cannon, rocket launch) while he made his dinner. He behaved heroically as he snapped his opener onto a can of beets. He was the first on Normandy Beach as he defrosted french fries. He rescued children during the bombing of London. He anticipated Pearl Harbor and survived.

Period Effects (horse-drawn traffic, mail coach, paddle steamer, railway, monoplane, streetcar, movie organ). He floated down the Mississippi; shadows from trees darkened his face as he lay on the deck of his small boat. He drank local beer and danced in local dance halls. He was bitten by mosquitoes. He had his back to the movies as he played the organ. He pleased or disappointed the men and women on his mail route as he drove through the New England countryside delivering letters, packages, and postcards, which he always read before placing in the box. He would shiver as he drove through the same barren landscape during the winter.

Electric Home & Office (food processors, smoke alarms, ice maker, microwave oven, garbage disposal, corn popper, blow dryer, paper shredder, word processor, photocopier).

With these sound effects playing, he led an ordinary life. This was the tape that most confused the neighbors because of its duplicity. It sounded like an echo, a disturbing echo which had been taken over by something demonic. They knew Mr. Loonan was not the kind of person who would own a food processor or an ice maker. The mimicry of the smoke alarm caused genuine panic. Down the hall, doors slammed. The neighbors told each other that they didn't smell smoke, and the sound of the alarm, though clearly coming from a certain apartment, was muffled and far away. Perhaps the man in 5E had set it off accidentally. Finding themselves together all at once, they would take the opportunity to complain about the furnace or the roof; then feeling vaguely satisfied and communal, they would go back to their own apartments. It was all triggered by the invisible tenant in 5E.

Laurel asked if she could borrow some of the more eerie and ambiguous tapes, but Mr. Loonan refused unconditionally and began to play *Work* (factory ambiance, whistle, time clock, loading-bay crane, forklift, telephones, switchboard, coffee break, miscellaneous machines) at a high volume.

"What does he think this is?" Laurel asked. "*Modern Times?*"

What we would say about Loonan was that he was the kind of person who wanted to see a man commit suicide on television. I hadn't seen the live shooting but knew about it. So early in the morning, yet it was the first topic Mr. Loonan wanted to discuss. A borough president had called a news conference, began to speak, and then, *wham*, Loonan said, *he shot himself*. A woman put her hands over the lens. Loonan was annoyed and changed the channel, but it did no good. Lenses everywhere were blacked out. The aftermath of the pulled trigger had been denied to him. His voyeurism was morbid, but there was some glee in it, a bit of rubbing the hands together, and aren't I glad it's not me. Everything spilled out of him in the office: how he watched the broadcast, how the cameras were turned off at just that moment when everyone knew what would follow. He explained his watching as if Laurel, Martin, and I were sitting with him on his couch, as interested as he was.

Laurel had already turned away and begun to line up the storyboards on her desk. The inker whose figures were so fluid her hand appeared to waltz across the paper behaved as if she had been transformed into a drudge by the sound of his voice. Loonan did give Laurel extra work. She spoke to him infrequently. She treated him as if he weren't there, weren't in the story, and I could sense his annoyance, his thinking it was his story, *didn't she see?*

Martin had glimpsed the broadcast at a friend's apartment. He'd had a television, he explained, but it had been secondhand to start with, and in a short time the picture grew impenetrably grainy, and the sound faded in and out. Finally it croaked, he said, and he never got another. At the friend's apartment he remembered hands nervously placed in front of an empty screen, gray and soundless, but only for a few seconds. Loonan thought Martin talked too much, especially to me. He would stroll by my drawing table while Martin was bent over it. Martin had been drawing a picture of himself in half-empty discarded frames. His face was pressed against the glass of Electra's ship. He drew features which vaguely resembled mine over Electra's blank face. Mr. Loonan leaned over him and told him there were such things as deadlines at Fantômes, and Martin should return to his desk. I was afraid that once the Christmas rush ended he wouldn't hire him again, but at the same time, I was embarrassed. My distant and, I admit, condescending attitude toward the scripter was upset by his knowledge of the suggestions contained in the drawn-over frame. I didn't like to think Mr. Loonan had the upper hand in any way. Laurel thought he was blind to connotations of romance, but I couldn't believe it.

"Citron yellow would be a good color for this scene," I said. A strange illness; Electra would look jaundiced.

"No, chalk white," Loonan said. He must have known there was no such color among my inks and chalk white would not reproduce. There was only one white, that of the paper on which the serial was printed, a fragile paper which yellowed rapidly.

Loonan went into the alcove where he had his desk and looked through the sound-effects library without finding what he wanted. If he was still thinking about television suicide, I wondered what he could be looking for among the tapes. When he wasn't looking, I took the torn bit of storyboard Martin had drawn over and folded it into a large notebook. I could imagine Mr. Loonan ransacking the trash after we'd left, looking for evidence of what had been going on between letterer and colorist. To watch an office drama unfold at a distance through overheard conversations or relics found in the trash was similar to his watching television. I threw the frames away when I reached the subway. Martin was oblivious to Mr. Loonan's surveillance and thought I only imagined I was the center of his observations, his constant looking. He never seemed to hear the scripter mutter out loud along with sound-effects tapes.

I began to hope Martin Chatfield would be hired again as a letterer. When there were three of us, the office seemed less oppressive. Each morning I gave him until 11:00 to come in late.

"Did you see the first page of *Ms. Tree* this month?" Mr.

Loonan was in a good mood. Ms. Tree was Electra's rival in popularity and it was to the detective that the space traveler would be sacrificed if there were cutbacks. Loonan felt Electra was much more sophisticated, more truly heroic. The first page, had we even looked at it?

No.

"Ms. Tree is standing over a dead body in a high-angle shot and she says, 'Sid was deader than polyester.' " Loonan often wore those kinds of clothes. He saw no humor in that first page quoted from Eclipse Comics.

He asked Laurel about steamed egg rolls and kung fu. Could she show him how to eat with chopsticks? As long as Electra's rival looked silly and made jokes that were no longer funny, as long as he could stay with his comic-book test-tube child, he was full of Christmas spirit. Otherwise Laurel was Shanghai Lily and I was Clytemnestra. He was right, too. If he should be locked out, peering through the window, his suspicions would be confirmed. He would characterize us as adulterers, cosmopolite spies, renegades, revisionists. We would soon be out of work anyway, but as long as he could grasp at straws, he would hand out chocolate robots and be great friends with us.

Loonan called Regozin into the studio. Krazy Kat tie and pin, red nose and hoarse voice, the signs indicated Regozin was not going to give out Christmas bonuses in September. Laurel whispered to me, *Where does he find those things?* Martin had been called in and he lettered *les enfants terrible* in the margin of an empty frame. It wasn't half funny. I could see the two men as line drawings, without any color, caricatures of politicians, but didn't draw them and silently filled in Orion's space suit a watery manganese blue. All they argued over was a comic. Underneath the scripter's sincerity and underneath the director's speeches, which began, *In the best interests of Fantômes,* lay hostility and competitiveness, which were exhibited indirectly but often acutely. They couldn't stand each other. Loonan wasn't consistently obsequious, so when he did try to curry favor, it was painfully transparent. Mr. Regozin was not impressed by silliness in a rival. He smiled weakly at Ms. Tree, looked at all of us coldly, then returned to his office; Loonan deftly humiliated in front of his staff, again.

By Friday, Mr. Regozin had decided not to put any more money into advertising for *Electra*.

I put *Electra* aside and drew a pair of shapes, labeled them *Etta Cone* and *Ed Rod,* gave them arms and legs, hats and briefcases, then threw them away. It was turning colder. The next time I looked out the window, the bag men had left their park bench. They had probably gone a few blocks farther south to gather in lots or near curbs, huddling over fires started in old drums.

I was often given photocopies to work on at home. At my desk, away from Mr. Loonan's preference for cool colors, I painted Electra Rose Lake #8 as she endured a blast of light from an artificially induced meteor shower. The whole scene was done in reds. Eamonn would say Electra's redness when she fought was the mock red of a bloodless revolution. In the comics, I would say, color is never an entity by itself, color is never a message without a sign. I looked out the window at the clusters of bag men in the park. There was no conflict between word and image in Electra's bit of space. Artificial and highly stylized, there were no contradictions between what was said and what was seen.

Here's Eamonn again:

When any single color or hues of a color are isolated or given special status in a social context, the color becomes connected to ideas or becomes symbolic of a set of ideas. Color is more than an optical phenomenon, more than masses of rods and cones in your retinas.

Martin would quote:

Goethe thought yellow was the favorite color of children and savages, capable of enraging educated men. Red-blue was a disquieting color and therefore appropriated by the Church. Red was at the apex of his system of colors. Yellow is active. Blue is passive. Color induces mental and emotional states regardless of the nature of the object itself.

Laurel rang with newly inked frames. I threw her the key, but when she came up, we put Fantômes' *Electra* aside.

EPISODE II
THE ORION AFFAIR

As the teenage Electra hurtles past Mars, Orion catches a glimpse of her silhouette against the thermaglass win dows. Bewitched beyond reason, he pursues her across space. His obsessiveness manifests itself immediately (he can talk of nothing else, he grows jumpy, yet doesn't really listen to anyone or thing on his ship), although jaded crew members tell each other they have seen him behave this way before. He is undaunted by Electra's lack of interest, even when indifference turns to anger and then to violence.

Dr. Atlas had coded Electra's genetic material to pro duce remarkable results. She could do vast sums in her head, repeat piano concertos perfectly after having heard them only once, and read *Robinson Crusoe* in a day, but her aesthetic acumen was often faulty. Dr. Atlas had given her art books for her education and amusement during the long ride into space. When Kandinsky wrote of spirituality she drew no conceptual link between that word and his triangles and tornados. Electra traced his colored prints and asked the absent Dr. Atlas why she had given her these books. The idea of having a mother was nearly as confusing as the art books. Growing up under a mountain with only one other human being available, Electra was not socialized. She had read about mothers and fathers and decided that somehow they flew together, like the bits in the Kandinsky abstractions. Gender identification also confused her. Pursued by Orion, she always sped away from him without confiding to herself or anyone else exactly why she found him revolting.

The only way Electra's brain could be tampered with was if her spaceship was intercepted by radioactive lasers. An accident of this kind would result in amnesia. Dr. Atlas had given her one weapon: an image duplicator. Using the image duplicator Electra could create copies of herself like animated Xeroxes, phony trick women who crumpled under Orion's embraces. The duplicants were like shadows, mirrors, reversed images. They were right-handed, while the real Electra was left-handed.

There had been telephone calls from Driscoll, and Eamonn left for Mount Desert, Maine, the pickup spot for the doomed *Grace O'Malley*. I couldn't imagine what was left to photograph since the boat had been impounded in New York, and he said, No, you're right, there was nothing left to take pictures of, but as always, he did take his camera, film, and a telephoto lens. Someone in Maine may have informed on the trawler and that led to the trouble in Brooklyn, when the boat was unexpectedly seized. Driscoll smelled a rat and wanted Eamonn's lens to somehow catch the suspect. It involved another boat and watching the man Driscoll suspected. I could half believe his story. As I sat alone late at night painting Electra in a black suit, it seemed plausible.

He had been gone for three days when his mother called. It was the first time I had ever spoken to her. "Hello, dear, this is Mrs. Hanratty. Is my son there?" Her accent had resisted years in Brooklyn. Hanratty, not Archer. I assumed she had remarried. She didn't pronounce his first name during our brief conversation. She was going into the hospital for another operation. She was very ill. Eamonn had told me she had cancer, but was vague about how invasive the disease had become. She didn't want to meet new people who hadn't seen her when she was all in one piece, was all he had said. The drugs, he claimed, made her short-tempered and forgetful, although she sounded perfectly calm on the telephone. I said I'd try to reach him and hung up. He hadn't left me a number where he could be reached. Either he didn't have any numbers, or he just didn't want to leave me one. I looked through his papers for telephone numbers in Maine, area code 207. I found his passport and another one ten years out of date. Dark green, a little moldy, it was for fourteen-year-old Eamonn Hanratty. Same long eyes, same brown hair in the same shade of gray that black-and-white photography renders. Did they call him Ratty, Rat-face, or Ratzo in high school? When did Archer come in?

A friend told me she didn't care when she found letters written to her husband by an unknown woman. Even the marginally pornographic parts describing what the woman would have liked to have done if there had been enough time, even these she had found somewhat entertaining. Eventually she found herself obsessed by the idea of the letters; not the letters but what they represented made her shake. The person with whom she had lived had another identity that she had always been ignorant of. Infidelity, faithlessness, she had said, seemed like archaic words, the language of criminality.

Archer/Hanratty's affair was with himself. The Archer I knew canceled out the Hanratty I certainly didn't. When he did call from Maine two days later, I said nothing about the old passport or that his mother called herself by another name. He told me that before he left he had gone to Brooklyn to photograph the *Grace O'Malley*. I hadn't known. On the telephone he described the guards on the boat. He struck up a conversation with one of them and made up a story about a brother who had been in the Coast Guard. The man asked him what paper he worked for, and even when Eamonn said syndicated press (not true either), he asked him if he'd like to take a look around the boat. The customs agent followed him about but seemed to have no sense of how the cameras worked. I mean, Eamonn said, you would think he would have found it strange that I would take a close-up of the control panel, but while I was taking the picture he told me how the trawler had been found, how barely seaworthy it was, never stopping to consider that the distance between lens and object made no sense as a newspaper photograph.

I knew there was something Eamonn wasn't telling me. Perhaps when the guard wasn't looking he found a bit of paper with the addresses of American gun merchants or safe houses for exiles in northern Scotland, perhaps scratched in the unseaworthy wood he found Gaelic obscenities or a pair of familiar initials carved in a heart, perhaps he had stolen the captain's log, hidden under the control panel. Instead, he described dirty seaweed and deserted beaches he would like to follow up to Nova Scotia. He didn't believe his mother was that sick, but said he would call her.

In Eamonn's absence the darkroom retreated and was just a bathroom again. There was still something ominous about the trays and chemicals, reminders I wasn't entirely at home, and then I fought back, leaving my things around. If lipstick could leak onto negatives, images would have been invaded by red grease, but even in my carelessness, I was cautious. I imagined Eamonn falling through rotting floorboards on the *Grace O'Malley* and drowning, or being shot at by anxious United States Customs agents, and felt sorry for him, alone, poking around an old wreck and staring north. That much I think I did know.

I was late for work, but the office was nearly empty. Only Martin Chatfield was there. He was looking at some typed pages of *Electra* script laid out on Mr. Loonan's desk. Laurel had phoned in sick. He had been called to replace her, to do her inking as well as the lettering for a few days. The Christmas rush was ending. All the scripters were in meetings or at the printer's. We would be alone all day. Mr. Loonan telephoned twice to check if we were following the directions he'd left. Thinking he wouldn't call a third time, we left *Electra* only half colored, her speech balloons blank, and went downtown.

No one knew who owned Martin's building. The absentee landlord has disappeared, hadn't paid back taxes, heirs couldn't be traced, or something to that effect. Martin thought the city would take over the building and tear it down. Part of the structure was boarded up. A narrow slice of the ground floor was a store which sold a variety of objects, the character of which changed every month. Sometimes auto parts, Martin said, sometimes bits of old appliances, and you can always get pet food there. As we looked in front of the store Martin stood very close, elbow knocking mine. I squinted, trying to see quick shadows in the back fetching cans of liver parts and chicken scraps. The glass was too dusty. I gave up trying to see. He lived alone in two rooms filled with furniture found on the street. Books were stacked in columns, without shelves. The walls were probably white, but I remember them as dark olive green, Rousseau colors. If Rousseau had painted urban detritus instead of tropical plants, he would have loved this room. The objects crowded in corners and along the walls were as densely arranged as trees in his landscapes. A single fluorescent tube hung from the ceiling. Martin had a lot of lamps of different styles and sizes: a matador with a frozen cape who held a bulb instead of a sword, office lamps from a city auction, lamps arching on stems behind parchment-yellow shades. In the two which were functional, he had put low-watt bulbs. I felt as if I were in a ruin and the only light available was the one attached to my head. The floors slanted dramatically: here was a permanently listing boat or a lopsided chamber unearthed in Pompeii, relics intact; Martin and I were the only survivors.

Martin showed me some storyboards, plans for a movie about an out-of-work actor who drove a cab. One day he picks up a woman on the corner of Forty-ninth Street and Broadway. He drops her off in Chinatown. A few days later, he picks her up again at the same spot. Though she barely speaks to him, the driver becomes very interested in her, almost obsessed. Like magic she is on that same corner every time he passes it in his cab. He suspects there might be two of them, that they are twins. He ignores other fares and tries to tail whichever one he can. Relentless in his pursuit, he is drawn to the conclusion that the twins are involved in a midtown ring of some kind, whether the object of the ring is smuggling (dock scenes) or murder (alleys, empty parking lots), he hadn't decided. That was as far as Martin's storyboards went. I could see him looking at me as he drove an imaginary cab down Second Avenue, hands on an invisible steering wheel, demonstrating the part of the out-of-work actor. Was he identifying with the man who gets the girl? The story was unfinished. When he stood very close, I looked away. I have never needed to take a cab from Forty-ninth Street and Broadway, and as far as I know, I have no twin.

Suddenly Mr. Regozin put a stop to the practice of coloring and lettering at home. All work had to be done at Fantômes. There had been a leak. A plot resolution, a character twist which had been little more than an idea, a wisp of conference discussion had turned up on the cover of another comic. Regozin was furious. He issued memos suggesting a guard be hired to search employees who might attempt to leave the premises with stolen cartoon frames in their pockets. Laurel and I had occasionally drawn our own versions of *Electra* while at Fantômes but could no longer risk it. If we were searched at the door, our rewritten *Electra* might be mistaken for the legitimate serial. A week passed, but no guards were hired and the receptionist was disappointed. A guard would have been someone to talk to during the dull periods when the telephone didn't ring. A sense of mistrust grew in the studios. Since one could no longer take work home there were more employees present at any given time. Lines formed at the drinking fountain and duplicating machine. Colorists, inkers, letterers couldn't come and go as they had in the past. Mr. Loonan became agitated at the slightest question. He was reading a book called *The Talisman*. A lurid stone engraved with primitive-looking glyphs blazed on its cover, while small figures, presumably the book's characters, chased each other around the margins. If the Icas or Celts had had floppy disks, he said, they would have looked like this stone. With an unusual show of defiance, his response to Mr. Regozin's censuring arguments was to sit at his desk and read. Since we had to work at the studio, we were always there. He probably missed the afternoons when he had the empty room all to himself.

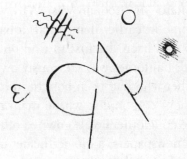

I wanted to ask Mr. Loonan if he thought readers were armchair Peeping Toms. Did he imagine readers arguing whether characters' actions were the results of repressed sexual desires, while others believed a straightforward haunting was all that the story involved? Did he imagine groups or pairs of them taking sides, arguing as to which narrator was the most credible? I had heard the scripter say the reader was extraneous marginalia, insignificant. His/her interpretations were unknowable, and if learned, they would surely be disturbing. When the printing press with movable type was invented, when copies began to be dispersed, anyone who could read, and therefore (pretend to) interpret, could also become a scripter. Mr. Loonan mourned the loss of the original and the appearance of the reader(s). Audience and printing press provided him with a job but detracted from his sense of omnipotence. Regozin argued that readers' sympathies were there to be manipulated. They root for one side (aggressor or underdog) over the other and then, when their expectations are disappointed, they feel jerked around. Forget about what readers will think, he had wanted to tell Regozin, if you consider every reader or group of readers, you will end up with an impossibly opaque serial.

I asked Laurel where Mr. Loonan was. Why was his desk so neat? She had come in earlier than usual, a half hour before I arrived, and so had been the first to find out. The rumors had been realized; Fantômes was previously owned by a large New York publisher who had been bought in turn by a larger media/entertainment corporation whose main offices were in Los Angeles. The conglomerate also owned other comics and magazines, a few newspapers, a movie-theater chain, and one or two amusement parks whose themes involved cartoon characters and figures from American history. Regozin had been making short trips to Los Angeles for months and had leaked information about a takeover attempt. It was not supposed to affect anyone. All the other comic serials—prehistoric, Gothic, splatter, mystery, and so on—would remain as before, at least for the time being. The real problem was that *Electra* didn't make enough money. Laurel explained that *Electra* had been terminated.

Regozin had probably known about the completion of the deal last week but didn't tell anyone. He had told Loonan last night. His arguments with Loonan were not really about character or plot, only cash. Loonan had packed his belongings well into the night. He would not be back, and Regozin could write the last chapter. Electra was either going to be killed or surrender to Orion. The latter fate seemed to signify termination was serious, beyond hope of a nostalgic resurrection. Electra, like Red Sonja and many others before her, had a long tradition of celibacy. This was something scripter and director agreed upon: avoiding or never quite getting the man, even if the various shes wanted the hims. The reader, intrigued, left hanging, would hope for a resolution which would never come about. It was a strategy they believed would sell comics.

Regozin came in with the end of the story and the roughs to be colored and inked. The director's office had been planning and drawing this last chapter without telling Loonan's staff. His iguana cheeks were red from either embarrassment or hurry. Here it was: Electra marrying Orion on the cusp, almost a morganatic marriage, she would get nothing from the transformed brute when he kicked off. He might seem an uxorious mate at first, but in a few episodes he would take over the story, keeping Electra out of the picture whenever possible. We could see her dwindle out of frame and storyboard; only an echo, an occasional oblique reference to her would remain, but Electra herself would not be murdered, however, because someday Mr. Regozin might want to bring her back. "Make her look happy," he said. White boots, long gloves, lots of hair blowing around, but no dress, because a white dress signifies, if not virginity, a lack of experience. He insisted that Electra had never worn dresses, and no one ran to the microfilm archives to check if this had always been true. (*Electra* was an epic with an archive kept under lock and key and turned into microfilm. Early issues from the 1960s, crumbling, yellow, and very thin, were worth a great deal.) Accurate or not, the director's idea of Electra's wedding was that as she wore very little, she should be married in a lot of white streamers blowing around, covering most of her. Mr. Regozin let me know that he had noticed I was late and told me what he had already told Laurel. We were both laid off indefinitely. When Laurel finished inking she packed her things, waiting for me to finish coloring. She put an old biology textbook which had been used for reference and a few old *Electra* comics in her bag. Regozin had insisted on so much white, indicated by empty space, that I had very little to do. I used the most diluted yellow, pink, blue, and brown; by the last frame there was very little color left at all. Mr. Regozin wouldn't see the frames until tomorrow, and by then, if he didn't like the way I had faded out, he would have to hire someone to change it. Laurel took the biology book and the old comics out of her bag. She decided she didn't want to take anything with her. We put the storyboards on what had been Mr. Loonan's desk, turned out the light, and left Fantômes.

I found it painful to imagine Loonan's depression and took it for granted he sat alone at home, his voyeurism turned inward. There were other comics. Regozin had promised to recommend him for another job. *His conscientiousness borders on the ardent* . . . Regozin might write. Loonan had put all his eggs in one basket. When he unlocked the door to his apartment, would it seem dark and empty to him? Unread newspapers piled in a stack, half-eaten meals put back in the refrigerator, tickets from suits forgotten at the cleaners: signs of abandonment and things left as they lay. He may think of applying for another job, but he doesn't make the calls. Instead, he will sell his furniture piece by piece and the telephone will be disconnected. Living on instant coffee, radiators sputtering out, he fades away without television coverage, without an audience either prurient or indifferent. I don't know what actually happened to him. I never heard another word about Mr. Loonan, so this gradual end, tying his fate to that of Electra, seemed logical.

Jane without Tarzan, Lois without Clark, Lady Jaguar

without Johnny Hazard, Copper Calhoun without Steve Canyon, Maggie without Jiggs, Spiderwoman, Batgirl, Modesty Blaise. When I read cartoons after grade school, they were all my characters. I didn't see odious teachers or classmates in villainous roles or victims of comic treachery. I identified with no character or situation. I read the stories in spite of the fact that I found them disturbing. Most, except for the shrewish Maggie and beanpole Olive Oyl, looked like pin-ups, and it seemed to me the artist in charge didn't care a fig for even the slightest verisimilitude. I didn't know anyone who looked like Ms. Marvel or Claire Voyant. It was a style intended for another audience, not for me, not for my friends. Tight clothes and muscle-bound voluptuous shapes were too fantastic, too unrealistic, and probably reflected the tastes of scripters, directors, and boy audience. They weren't really dressed for motion. Intrepid qualities and vision clashed with those display bodies. On any real street they would be harassed and teased Of course, there were no hard, concrete streets in the serials, that was the whole point, but real lessons could be culled from Red Sonja or Dazzler. A drop of reality took the form of advice. In the comics I found a cautionary tale or two. When Hu Shee was surprised by a Japanese spy or Batgirl was recognized at her librarian's job, these scenes posed a definition of the idea of risk, and those circumstances were a model which seemed, if not realistic, to present a definite possibility. Those possibilities were not all that farfetched. Even at Fantômes, when Mr. Regozin used to insist that anything might happen, I knew he was right. The man on the roof might find me again. Coloring might be taken over by computer and I would be destitute. All kinds of fears were given a voice, and in each solution lay superhuman heroism, and at the core of that heroism was the heroine's solitary existence. The scripters would use words like hook and (potential/denied) romance. Colleagues were more like sidekicks than complicated equals.

Each woman had to be unattached for the serial to continue; I kept this in mind until the incident on the roof of the building in which I lived alone. You can have two identities (why not one hundred?), the comics seemed to say, go ahead, do it, but watch out. One might peek around the edges of the other, and it's just those hints that give you away: the monogrammed cuff links you forgot to change, the accents that slipped out on certain words, the telephone number written inside an illegal book.

The Electra Laurel and I drew at home bore little resemblance to Fantômes' collection of mascara and boots. She was sometimes a vague black shape with a beaky face; sometimes we drew a more anatomically accurate figure in baggy clothes and lace-up sneakers. Her spaceship was a simple box with a checkered floor. My disapproval of Fantômes' Electra wasn't based in prudery but in childhood boredom. I'd been coloring over that image since I was a little girl sitting on the kitchen floor with the funnies. Then it was over. There was no work, and the only Electra that remained, the version which would always be the most recent and the one to be most trusted, was the serial Laurel and I made up.

The other Electra, invented and full of deliberate misquotes, was to Eamonn just a long private joke that went on between myself and Laurel. He saw comics as an ongoing tease, that *TO BE CONTINUED* and *UNTIL NEXT WEEK*. When he returned he had pictures of Mount Desert. They seemed useless. The story was no longer in the papers. He wouldn't discuss the guns bound for the Kerry coast. He said he had eaten lobster in Maine and made the trip sound like a vacation.

I stood behind Eamonn in the darkroom/bathroom and put my hands in his front pockets. They were empty. His legs didn't tense, didn't move at all. He just stood there. He took my hands out, his fingers were wet. There were no secrets in his pockets, no dollar bills or apartment keys. He just stood there pushing glossy prints around in the bath. I wanted to leave, to walk out, but opening the door would let light in. I didn't like the way he just stood at the sink, the way he removed my hands with bored fingers. I wanted to open the door, but the red light was on. I wanted to ruin the picture but was afraid to. Eamonn, the photographer who concentrated, held the camera up to his eyes, turned rings, to the left, to the right, f-stop up or down, I told him he put a spell on everyone he photographed. (If I wasn't spellbound, why didn't I open the door?) He said that he wished that were true. How is taking a picture like casting a spell? He thought I spent too much time in the comics.

Clothes left in piles made an isthmus from the closet to the bed, my inks leaked and accidentally dripped onto his books and papers. I left things as they lay for days. I was the tenant of a feudalist who didn't believe in private property, and it seemed all right to endure spells of lethargy and inertia. I consolidated the piles without ever really cleaning. We did manage to take the garbage out, and he kept his own work neat and precise. To Eamonn my personal sloppiness represented an exploitative personality taking advantage of his goodwill, while his represented a casual approach to the position of household objects.

He had left a couple of empty boxes of film and cigarettes on the table. It was already two in the afternoon and his box of shredded wheat was still on the table, too. My complaints may have been essentially narcissistic and in the interest of sloth, but I wasn't simply acting on a bratty impulse either. His shredded wheat, even left on the table, had the aura of moral authority, and that was what bothered me, that aura, not the box itself. On the floor lay the single-volume encyclopedia open to C. It had sat there for days. Last week Eamonn had looked up Fletcher Christian and the story of the mutiny on the *Bounty*. He had been reading about the fate of the descendants of the Tahitian women and the mutineers left on the Pitcairn Islands. He asked me what kind of amalgamated culture I thought they might have made up in their isolation. When I read over his shoulder, he told me I was like a shadow sewn to his heels. No, I said, it's the other way around. I couldn't find my keys and so had to stay in the apartment until the idea seemed more ridiculous than offensive, if not entirely forgotten. I could always take his keys, I could have just walked out. I put the box of shredded wheat on the floor, and dropped the one-volume encyclopedia on top of it.

The crumpling of cardboard and smashing of cereal made an odd noise. Eamonn didn't look angry, just stunned by the collision of two objects which ordinarily would have had nothing to do with each other. We both stared at the blot on the floor. I was curious about the state of the shredded wheat and so removed the heavy one-volume encyclopedia. Completely crushed—only crumbs remained.

I wanted to put the radio on when it was already on. I wanted to put the television on while the radio was on. I wanted to go to the movies when I was already at the movies.

Martin called me from Spector Comics, there was work on *Agent 998*. The regular colorist was on vacation, so I got four days of work. Spector Comics did shorter books, and they came out more frequently than the various Fantômes serials. Martin did the lettering on another floor, so I only saw him a few times. *Agent 998* was done in shades of black and red, that was all. It was a mechanical sort of job.

I saw him coming out of a newsstand and called after him. He didn't hear me, and I didn't run after him, I just watched. He stopped to read a series of posters peeling from a brick wall. I caught up with him, and he walked me home. It was late, but a car alarm went off down the street, and when we got to my building, although most of the lights were out, a dog barked from an upstairs window. The entrance was a short hall with a dozen mailboxes and buzzers divided between two walls. The buzzers signal someone is at the door, but you can't buzz them in. You have to go downstairs or throw a key. Martin said goodbye to me in the hall. A few days before, I had been awakened by a prolonged press on the bell. It was six o'clock in the morning, too early for the mailman, but I got dressed and ran downstairs. In the hall a prostitute was with a man and they were leaning against the buzzers. The man had a broad back. The woman was wearing a knitted beret and a suede jacket, stiff, as if things had spilt and dried on it in long patches. Their breath misted in the entrance over the mailboxes. The man seemed barely alert enough to pull up his pants, but he did and they shambled into the street. I was careful not to lean against anything and not to let Martin.

Sometimes I think I'm too old for this. Martin in a doorway, desperate calls to comics, Eamonn who comes and goes. I heard about a woman who was in my class in high school who has two children, life insurance, and a rich husband who sees other women when he can. She's way ahead of me. She lives in a big house that looks like a prison built by Louis XIV and it's next door to the house she grew up in. The east side of the avenue near Seventh Street is a series of five-story buildings and at night they look entirely like a *trompe l'oeil* painting;

a false front stuck in a landscape where real-estate values make the idea of its falseness absurd. I know it's not true. From the street, people can be seen in their apartments and you can walk around to the back. It's not painted on. People live in those (not) *trompe l'oeil* buildings, and they probably don't consider themselves living according to *trompe l'oeil* inclinations. The woman in the Louis XIV prison who waits for her husband until early in the morning, as she looks at her neighbors' houses, does she think they're a painted setup, fakes staged to make her feel miserable? I don't feel tromped on or watched by my fakes, and this is the reassuring part.

I have tried to assign definitions to my fakes whether reproduced Electra stories or imagined meetings with Martin. I ask myself where the heart of fakery lies. It's the kind of thing I tend to forget when it's raining pleasantly outside; Orion's obsession is in remission, and Electra appears content in her spaceship. But there are situations, dramatic and easily dreamed up, which give the fakes a nudge, send them spinning into a troubled frenzy.

EPISODE III
ELECTRA RETURNS TO EARTH

Electra shut the book on Kandinsky again. Dr. Mary Atlas hadn't coded her against claustrophobia or homesickness and longing, by-products of a good memory. Orion was pelting her with intergalactic valentines, but his offers were annoying, dangerous, and offered no companionship. She suspected that if he was in love with her, he would still appear a kind of pest, another (space) chiseler who, instead of spare parts or a lift, might want only a little sympathy. She felt sorry for him but wished he'd glom onto someone else. She was curious about Earth. What had happened to Kandinsky and Cocteau?

To her mother? She turned her spaceship around. Orion went numb. He couldn't follow her. On Earth he'd be a mammoth, a freak with an ursine cast to his features. No privacy, no secrecy, no subtle way to plead his case. He'd be seen from miles away. He couldn't function on the planet of Electra's origin. As far as he was concerned, that whole galaxy was a Palookaville, nothing more. The disappearance of the object of his desire turned the universe into a dull, barren place inhabited only by early life forms, evolving slowly. He watched her ship grow smaller, until only a faint light remained hundreds of miles away. His gorgon-like assistants clutched the buttons and dials of the cockpit in terror of Orion's violent depression. In his frustration he pounded the controls of his spaceship, and a fragment of an amnesia-inducing ray pierced Electra's thermaglass window. It was only a small bit of a ray, but it erased the part of her brain that stored the memory of Dr. Atlas. The spaceship still headed toward Earth. It was too late to change course. Though slight, the laser beam did more than just alter Electra's memory. Her spaceshift disintegrated as it fell through the Earth's atmosphere, and Electra grew lighter. She landed beside Cleopatra's Needle in Central Park, clutching a microchip from her image duplicator.

Eamonn frequently sold his pictures to newspapers. We lined them up on the table in chronological order, and they read like a nursery rhyme before I swept them into a pile. One jumped in front of the R Local, two shot a teller and a bank guard, three escaped from prison and were found already dead in a Williamsburg basement, four were threatened by white gangs, a family of five living in an abandoned car in an abandoned lot. None of the pictures was in color, and in their black-and-white harshness I found no clues as to his foolhardiness or bravery. I had no desire to say to him, *Did you really see that, were you really there?* It was his job, that was all.

Blue-and-white roadblocks crossed Fifth Avenue. A bomb had gone off in an embassy. The avenue metamorphosed from a street whose history had always been one of order, expensive clothing, and jewelry to one of police sirens, ambulances, fire engines, and camera crews. In the chaos, what had been valuable, even priceless, suffered the displacement of archaeological relics uncovered at a location where their original context has been rendered impossible to guess. A neo-Baroque façade shattered, angel body parts were found five blocks away, flying slivers of glass blinded tourists on their way to the Metropolitan, credit-card machines smashed on curbstones, bloody cuffs on mannequins. People who passed by or ran to the site from unaffected blocks had two choices: to watch or to walk away. They stood behind the cordons, some of them, and struggled to see or to be recorded by a television camera or by Eamonn. Later, at home, witnesses could repeat, *Today I saw . . .*

City crime, accident, murder, domestic crisis, emergency, suicide, double suicide. Scenes of death in photographs are compelling because they satisfy morbid curiosity and people have that kind of curiosity, Eamonn said, because they wish violence upon bosses, family members, former friends. Also, they are afraid these horrible things will happen to them. Car collisions, plane crashes, gang war, turning to the pictures first, trying to see the unseeable anatomy, the violence that eludes illustration in medical textbooks. Because it happened to strangers, or someone unknown, not even an acquaintance, the anonymous corpses could take on any identity. Eamonn sometimes hated the pictures by which he made a living. The photographer of victims and perpetrators looked for victimizers who acted from a distance, too; the ones for whom the subtext of their lives was exclusivity: certain clubs, certain tables at certain clubs. He listened as he photographed them. They spoke of their childhood visits to the White House, where they were introduced to Calvin Coolidge, and their recent trips to Johannesburg, where black waiters refused to serve them cordially. He couldn't gain entry to the golf clubs, yacht clubs, and parties. They might want *Life* magazine, but they suspected Diane Arbus, and they were right to.

The firebombed pub, the gutted row of flats, the police with their transparent shields made from NASA surplus spacecraft windows. Some pictures Eamonn couldn't take: the faces of those who packed crates aboard the *Grace O'Malley*, those whose plans, conversations, and faces depended on anonymity. Eamonn thought of the frozen faces of executed Communards, a daguerreotype taken as they lay in a heap in 1871. There were those who had wanted to have their pictures taken, not necessarily out of vanity, but to provide a kind of evidence, and they were later identified and done in. He didn't know whether he would have agreed to take portraits which he suspected would later prove damaging, but he also felt the temptation to snap at everything, to let no face escape documentation. To do portraits of the men and women who met on the Shankill Road after curfew and to label the prints put them all in danger, and to document what? Here in New York he could lock his pictures away for thirty or forty years, but there are few guarantees strong enough and no photographs so neutral they could not engender risk and still be meaningful. When is a camera not like a gun? The Blanket Men in Long Kesh had wanted their pictures taken.

Even as the American, Archer, he hadn't, at first, been able to gain entrance to the H block. He had had to leave his camera at the door and the guards confiscated his film. Later he worked out a way to take the camera apart and smuggle it in piece by piece, to be reassembled once inside. The prisoners wanted their pictures taken. The camera, Eamonn's Nikon, a relic from life on the outside, must have seemed foreign and yet an ally, or potentially so, unlike the metal detectors and instruments of torture used by the screws of Long Kesh. "Had you really helped the Blanket Men?" I asked. "Didn't you make things worse for them by publishing their pictures?" Eamonn said, even if that was true, the idea was to make public a kind of brutality that had been private and whose existence had been denied. *Couldn't you see that?*

When Eamonn accidentally saw someone without clothes on near a window, he assumed the open curtains were intentional. What was accidental was the presence of the passerby audience. The dead in the embassy explosion might have wanted privacy, but it was denied them because they worked in an embassy. Eamonn was there with his camera and so their wish for privacy was violated a step further. (*Did you ever feel embarrassed?* I would ask him. "The kind of accident which occurs when a guest falls down a flight of stairs because someone yanked the carpet, would you be there to photograph everyone's awkwardness?" "It's not the same thing," Eamonn said. "Why are you so concerned with the privacy of strangers?")

I heard an announcement on the radio asking for clothing to be brought for homeless men and women who lined up each night near Grand Central Station. Don't bring your camera, the radio announcer said, they don't want their pictures taken.

The camera never lies, you know, Eamonn had said when he first showed me his pictures. It had been a few days after he had taken my picture in front of the gas station. *They also tidy up, make accessible, and establish distance because they remove the firebombed pub from its context,* he admitted. I remember looking at pictures of rolls of barbed wire; they became a black abstraction, an endless concertina. Eamonn examined negatives, prints just back from the lab. No captions, no titles on the margins or on the back. These were disassociated from printed language. The power of specific site and circumstance was lost.

Movie posters: green, blue, black, plastered one over another, and then the same one in a line in sequence, like film frames themselves. A face was partly torn away. *First Blood, Part II*. A man standing with his legs apart and a Uzi between them, an image repeated eight or nine times, making a zigzag pattern along the west side of Union Square. I went into the subway.

French rockets
Korean hand grenades
Israeli submachine guns
West German automatic rifles
Thirty American handguns

What the police were looking for on the *Grace O'Malley*. In photographs the boat looked battered and harmless. When I asked Eamonn about it, he gave me an evasive answer, telling me about the woman the boat had been named for.

The *Golden Hind* entered the Irish Sea on its return from the New World. They were nearly in sight of the Isles of Scilly when Grace O'Malley and her crew appeared silently, from nowhere, and boarded the ship. Sir Francis Drake fought back. He was wounded by the pirate queen herself. Many were stabbed to death and fell into the sea. One managed to swim to the island of Saint Mary's. Grace O'Malley returned to Howth, Ireland, with Aztec gold Drake took from the Spanish at Valparaiso, which he had intended for Queen Elizabeth.

A few hours after he spoke to his mother, Eamonn took a crumpled manila envelope which I'd never seen before out of a drawer. It was full of pictures, some very worn. Eamonn usually treated his photographs carefully. Prints and negatives were wrapped in glassine and handled with bits of paper he called clackers. He spread old photographs of himself and his parents on the table and told me about this one taken on Long Island or that one taken in Derry. His mother was beginning to give things away. Eamonn was disappointed about the order in which she dispersed her possessions. Photographs ought to have been the last to go, instead of the first. They should have been saved before summer dresses and teapots. His mother explained she didn't need those pictures because she knew he would visit her in person. It was a trap to be sure he would stay, but he was going to leave again. Before he left, he sent a handful of photographs back to his mother, writing that she would now be forced to remember and not die quite yet. Here, he was sending the photographs. (Eight-year-old Eamonn sitting in the driver's seat of his father's truck. Fifteen-year-old Eamonn on the porch in Brooklyn.) He was reversing the trap.

I found a new passport for Eamonn Hanratty and asked him about it. He didn't think I needed to know, and if I did know, I might tell other people who certainly ought not to know. I had no idea what he was talking about. He put the extra passport away. The telephone rang. It was Laurel, and I told her I'd call her back. Eamonn said he couldn't understand why Laurel had to know everything I did. It wasn't that Laurel demanded this, but he thought I spoke to her whenever I was discouraged or depressed, and I was that way too often for him to risk telling me that he changed his name to Archer in 1979. His answer to the double passport question was evasive; he had no idea what Laurel and I talked about. He had reasons for wanting to appear more American when he went to the North of Ireland. The border guards might search his bags, but they didn't confiscate his film. That was the main thing, getting the film through and out again. He had been in countries where he risked his life just getting off the plane carrying a camera. The name was supposed to be only temporary, but he had kept it, at least for a while. He still said nothing about the source of the name Hanratty.

Eamonn left for Maine again during the week between Christmas and New Year's. He accused me of being like Dreyfus, as if I were so timorous that I wouldn't be on my own side if I were falsely accused of treasonous actions. That wasn't true for me or for Dreyfus, but it was the kind of betrayal I'd been waiting for since the near-murder on the roof. I told him there are a lot of men in a lot of apartments. There are a lot of women in a lot of apartments. Sometimes they are in the same one together and it doesn't amount to a hill of beans.

"You could be useful, a photographer could be useful," Freddy Driscoll had said. "Go as Hanratty to Boston. On Tremont Street go to Sunshine Rent-a-Car and then drive north to Maine." *Grace O'Malley II* was being launched.

He was on a train going to Mount Desert, Maine. Amateurs think only in terms of content, professionals think about light just as much, and when he thought he had a parasitic relationship to his subjects, he remembered he was also the kind of photographer who thought about light before anything else. You see, I had once told him, you do think about photographs as photographs with nothing to do with history.

A woman on the platform waving goodbye. A woman boarding the train waved at no one and didn't turn around. She was wearing a gray raincoat and a man's hat, and she looked as if she had stepped onto the train from another decade, although certainly she had not. A woman sat across the aisle from him and deliberately put all her bags on the seat next to her so no one would sit there. No one would talk to her or try to buy her a drink in the café car. All the signs read that she wanted to be left alone. The image of a woman alone on a train leaving one city at twilight, due to arrive in another at night, was almost sentimental. Eamonn looked out his window and saw another woman across the platform waiting for a train. They all, each of them, seemed romantic images and compelling, but they were not photographs or even potential photographs. The click of the shutter meant or might mean reducing them to playing cards. It wasn't that he had no desire to exploit them as photographic images, in fact he did want to, but often he felt paralyzed by self-consciousness and would have trouble focusing. When I first met Eamonn, I noticed he rarely photographed women by themselves or as models for the sake of a pretty picture. As the photographs increased in number and fell into categories, it was an obvious omission. Eamonn felt the women on the train compelling because they excluded him. Everything about them excluded him. They wouldn't listen to him. They would say the click of the shutter is not the shot heard round the world, dummy, and anyway, I want to be left alone. He was unwelcome in the next seat, they didn't want to share an armrest with him, they weren't interested in the dangers of his work. They wouldn't trust him, and he was no good at appealing to their vanity.

How is being on a train like being in a movie? The answer

has something to do with linear motion and a finite number of characters. The journey comes to some sort of end, just like a story.

The train pulled out of Penn Station. The women were left behind. The one across from him opened a book but wasn't reading it. He was Archer. He was Hanratty. Driscoll had wanted more pictures taken at night. He made Eamonn feel he would become a hostage, although a slippery one and not all that valuable. Driscoll would pay for his ticket to Shannon, and he had told him over the telephone he had business for him in Ulster. He did not say he wanted Eamonn to be seen in that town in Maine first, but that seemed to be the idea. He wouldn't return to New York right away, Driscoll had implied. The photographs of the boat would be mailed to him.

I finally got my last check in the mail from Fantômes and Company, Ltd. Before he left, as I was idly drawing, not even aware of his imminent departure, Eamonn had said that if I insisted drawing her on Earth, I should at least have Electra learn the value of currency immediately. He advised that she should try to blend in as much as possible. To have her wandering around Manhattan would only cause trouble. He thought I was going to make her into some kind of holy martyr.

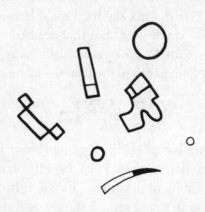

He would call up from the street at exactly the moment I least wanted company. I might have just gotten in, might be sitting at my drawing table drinking a cup of coffee to go, sitting in front of a page of black-and-white frames, Styrofoam or paper cup in hand. Staring at an unfinished drawing, I don't think about money, Eamonn, or my old job. (What does Electra see as she falls through space? Is her fall in any way similar to Alice's drop down the rabbit hole? Between Mercury and Venus, she might as well pass by cupboards, bookshelves, maps, and pictures hung on pegs, stick her fingers in a jar labeled *Orange Marmalade*.) I made faces at myself in the mirror, imitating Martin's offhandedness, calling me from the street as if nothing were easier or required less preparation.

The American representative to the UN was on television. I heard her say very distinctly that no aid was being sent to Central America. She said zero quite emphatically, her lips remaining in an O shape a few seconds longer than was necessary. She also made a circle with two fingers and held up her hand. So if you were deaf or had turned down the sound you would still know. Zero. In the seconds between throwing the key and the knock on the door I thought about the possibility of believing lies were true because a supposedly higher purpose is served by telling them. The range of creative lying was limitless. If she could do it, so could I. In light of these assorted means of getting to the truth, I was uneasy about having Martin here. Maybe my responsibility for his presence didn't count, because I really felt more like sitting in the bath than trying to think of what to say to a temporarily storyless letterer. I didn't have to answer the door. Nobody forced me to throw the key. She didn't have to go on television. The zero shape of her mouth and fingers left a longish afterimage.

He seemed to ignore the bottles of chemicals, basins stored under the bathtub, the dry-mount press, the enlarger, the guillotine. At the same time, I'm sure he didn't look at the drawings of Electra engaged in scenes which bore no similarity to the serial produced at Fantômes. The evidence of the apartment's tenants presented hints which were either invisible or inconsequential to him. He was so sure of himself, even naked, even when he looked ridiculous, mimicking Mr. Loonan, for example.

Martin had been a child actor in television commercials. He did them locally in Michigan for a car dealer who wanted to emphaisze a family image, and for a large bakery with several branch stores in the county. Adorable, with freckles, he was embarrassed by his roles but was saved from doing many of them by the fact that he grew too fast and didn't retain cuteness into late childhood. His parents thought he might go to New

York, study acting, perform in real commercials, but Martin, as he grew up, was no performer. He was frightened by an audience; even in school, he never spoke unless called upon. It seemed a terrible thing to be an old actor. The grandfather in the car-dealer commercials really disliked children. Between takes he would roughly remove the little girl from his lap, get out of the station wagon, and have a cigarette alone, away from the lights. He had probably wanted to do Ibsen, Pirandello, Beckett, and ended up performing for the local Dodge dealership and living in a hotel in Detroit. Martin's part as the disillusioned man's grandson, who only wanted to go for a ride, seemed, even to young Martin, mealy-mouthed and dumb beyond reason. His parents told him the money he earned would send him to college. They couldn't understand his lack of interest. Martin's mother thought that as he grew up he was always acting, always pretending to be someone else. Years later, Martin told her that he never acted, he was only playing. The reason she didn't recognize the difference between acting and playing was because she thought celebrity conferred authority status and that's what she wanted for her son. I couldn't tell the difference either, but my expectations of Martin were not what hers had been.

The evidence Eamonn left behind was all flat. I tried to give a picture, a list, or a shoelace a poke and have the object pop into remembered life. Memory was a vacuum, my ability to pretend was limited to the borders of a cartoon frame and I couldn't, for the moment, urge myself out of foggy amnesia. Addiction to the present initiated Martin's transition from a temporary letterer I used to work with to something more electrified.

"To a microbe your ear looks like the Guggenheim Museum," he said abruptly.

Beside his bed Martin had a photograph of the American translator who lived near the Wall. She had short black hair and was sitting on the edge of her Steenbeck editing table, her black shoes on the chair as if it were a footrest. Martin described a movie he'd like to make about life in a prison. He had read a newspaper story about a jail in Brazil where a prisoner was being murdered or forced to commit suicide to protest conditions. One suicide/murder happened each week. There was a leader, but the prisoner who would be murdered was chosen by lottery or by drawing straws. He cut the story out and tacked it above his desk. I wondered why Martin picked this story rather than any other story. Did the boy actor left behind in Detroit really want this part? *Carcerate, carnage, carney, cancer*, I said, you could get a lot of writing done in jail. There were so many men in each cell, he explained, that he could put any combination of characters he liked in one of them. In each cell a hierarchy of power and authority was established based on physical strength and cowardice. Each character, he held up three fingers, had three lives. The actual life he had led outside in the world, the life he led in prison, and the life he imagined was continuing outside. He ticked off each of his fingers. The only absolute in the huge overcrowded cell was the random system of death which the prison guards, in his script, did nothing to prevent. Martin saw Genet's *Chant d'Amour*, and because he had a friend who was a projectionist at the Museum of Modern Art, he was able to see it twice. A man inhaled the cigarette smoke of his lover through a hole in the prison wall. Men dancing in their cells, feeling engulfed by a person who wasn't here, who sent signals through a wall that might be an ocean. Touching themselves alone in their cells, they remember each other until they remember so repetitively and so intensely that memory veers off course and grows violent. Martin described *someone who might . . . or someone who used to*, a kind of comic abyss in his script. I told him if he looked out the window he could see men in the park dancing alone to their radios and touching themselves. He made up foreign-sounding scenarios while foreignness lay outside his window, and he saw strangers dancing in the park as nothing out of the ordinary, part of the nightly landscape, that's all. He'd have to have himself incarcerated to find out what jail was really like. He couldn't imagine it.

One Sunday afternoon Martin and I were out of money and so we visited a cash machine in a small enclosed cubicle near Broadway. The glassed-in room was ankle deep in garbage: green and brown beer bottles, aluminum and plastic containers, remaining shreds of takeout food, newspapers, drugstore ads, things passed out in the street, and huddled in the corner was a solitary old sock. I wondered how or why it was there. Someone had painted the President's name near one of the cash machines, and the name was followed by the statement that he was a liar and a drug dealer. A very thin man who looked like one of the Senegalese umbrella salesmen, but who spoke without an accent, opened the door for people so they wouldn't have to use their bank cards to get in. He shook a plastic cup, the rim bitten into small flaps. A line of customers snaked around the room. A few minutes after we arrived, a chinless blond man in his twenties stood in the door, holding it open, depriving the beggar of his job. The blond man said to another black man, *It will take a while but it will come;* then he took out a piece of paper and listed the four different kinds of prayer. The black man said he had been a POW in Vietnam, he had been there three and a half years. The proselytizer looked condescendingly surprised and told him it would take a long time to learn how to pray. People continued to get into line as he spoke. He was preventing the man with the cup from opening the door for people, and the beggar looked crushed and defeated. Martin asked the chinless man if he was going to get into line or just stand there all day, and he finally got out of the doorway. A Jamaican wearing several sweaters instructed the man with the cup what to do if the police attacked him. *If it was just a bit of a poke, forget it, but if he look crazy, sitting in his car, and like he is going to run you through with his night stick, then you run.* The beggar barely responded. A large woman with curly hair signed a check with relish, saying, *My last check from the lab,* while another talked about shopping. When we got to the machine Martin scratched an **N** after *withdraw* with a dried-out pen he had found in his pocket.

Outside, it was bright and cold. Early Christmas decorations, bits of Christmas music floated past us as we walked east. Someone had removed parts of sentences painted on the side of the bank. *Stop the   in El Salvador*

Homeless

South Africa

= Death

Somewhere in the garbage was *Murder, House the, U.S. out of, Silence.* I turned around and saw the blond, chinless man a few yards behind us. I told Martin he might be following us, looking for converts. Martin looked back and said that when he saw repulsive characters like that he was afraid one of them might be a relative. I stared. Martin looked nothing like the man who seemed to be following us. We stopped and let him pass. He went into the subway, and I asked Martin what the physical resemblance might be. I didn't see it. Martin was not blond and had rather a large jaw.

As we approached Martin's building, he told me about his family. He had described them at length when we worked at Fantômes. I knew about his stage mother, was not very interested in her, and didn't see how he could ever dream about being related to a random stranger who made selected speeches in a cash-machine line. The story Martin told me sounded like one of his scripts.

When Martin's father died, he discovered he had an older half brother no one had ever mentioned before. His mother knew the woman's name, her family came from Chicago, but she had married since, and Martin's mother couldn't remember her married name. His father had met her when he was stationed in New Orleans, where she was working in a school for the blind. It was just before he was sent to Korea. They didn't marry because Martin's father didn't think he would return. He wrote no letters; he had always been lazy about writing even postcards. By the end of his assignment he had sent only one letter to his parents. In spite of his belief in his own bad luck, he did survive and went to Detroit, where he met Martin's mother. A few weeks after their wedding he got a letter from the woman in New Orleans, forwarded to him by his parents. By that time she had married the man whose name Martin's mother had forgotten. She suspected the woman's mail must have gotten lost, because she couldn't believe Martin's father would have abandoned her in that way. If he'd known, he'd have done something.

What about the telephone? I asked. It had been invented. He could have called. Martin said he had asked the same question. His father had always seemed to have a conventional, uneventful past. I mean, Martin said, when I would ask him to tell me a story about when he was a little boy, there was nothing to tell. Martin looked shocked when he described the rake his father had been transformed into a few days after he died. A man who had no memory of any personal event before the Korean War was replaced by a scoundrel who abandoned women. I asked if his father had ever gone back to New Orleans, and this too he had asked his mother. She hadn't thought so but couldn't be certain. She knew no more than she had already told him. His older sisters were surprised but not very curious about their half brother. A few days after the funeral they went back to their respective families in other cities and the discovery of the half brother born in New Orleans was a story they told their friends over the telephone, but no more than that. Just before he left, his mother remembered the other woman's name. *Montessori, Montesquieu, no, Fortesquieu*, that was it, she had said. The key to her remembering the name, he said, was that she still thought of him as a child.

Martin returned to New York. He had written the woman's name in a notebook, but he wouldn't have forgotten it. Before he unpacked, before he did anything, he called information in Chicago and New Orleans. The telephone calls were unrewarding at first, and he felt ridiculous. Wrong numbers, dead ends told him he was cracked, said, *You're kidding*, laughed, hung up, or said no so coldly he grew suspicious. When he finally found his brother listed in the Manhattan telephone book, he laughed at the simplicity of it, but his good humor was short-lived. He agreed he was the person Martin had been looking for but refused to meet him. They might pass each other on the street, ride the same subway, have the same handwriting, but they would never know it. The half brother might have tried very hard to be different from Martin without ever having met him to learn what those differences might have sprung from. His address was on the west side in a nice neighborhood. For an hour or two Martin sat in the lobby at night and looked at young men's faces: eyes, nose, mouth; who looked or walked like him? Martin's opposite: a student who spoke in class, an actor who had never known a minute of stage fright, who confidently memorized monologues and got along well with directors, co-workers, family, and friends. Martin was certain his half brother performed in the kinds of plays his mother and stepfather could attend and appreciate. His own family knew little about his life above a fence who also sold pet food.

I suggested that for a few years he had probably enjoyed his mother's undivided attention, and perhaps he hated his stepfather. Martin was convinced the other family was harmonious and respectful of each other, while his had not been. His half brother was a person who could concentrate on a problem to the exclusion of everything and everyone else, who read three newspapers every morning before nine o'clock, a man who finished every book he ever started and never felt personally threatened by what he read. Maybe the half brother was the kind of man who didn't like the irony in the idea that the sibling recognized by their father turned out to live at an address too far east to mean anything, but that he was penniless or a gouging real-estate developer. Maybe the half brother thought he would ask for money.

The half brother may have been the religious fanatic we had seen on the street, might be anyone. I told Martin I was skeptical that just anyone at all, especially opposite sorts of people, were candidates for half-brotherhood, but raising the issue of the lost man gave Martin the idea of using me to find out more about him besides an address and a telephone number.

He wanted me to call him, to say I ran an apartment-cleaning service. That way Martin could get into his apartment and learn about him. There would be books, letters, photographs, college yearbooks, bills, partially eaten food in the refrigerator. I made the call, but the half brother wasn't interested.

"Tell him you're bonded. You won't steal anything. You have credentials. He sounded like the kind of person who cares about that sort of thing."

"He doesn't care, Martin. Give up."

"At least," Martin said, "I know he's neat." He switched off an old office lamp. The half brother was like one of Martin's scripts, begun feverishly but eventually forgotten.

He listened to *Jailhouse Rock*, but Elvis Presley presented no conclusion to the movie about men in jail. He talked about another script which involved the translator who lived in Berlin.

She is asked to subtitle a film studying feline and canine response to high frequency noise levels. At first she refuses, then decides to smuggle the film to a member of the Baader Meinhof gang. A survivor exists, living underground in the city. Martin will play this part. For a film shoot he will conquer his stage fright.

I asked him how she would be able to get a lab to make a copy of the sensitive film. Such films (I knew this from Eamonn) were not things you could just photocopy around the corner. How could a member of the Baader Meinhof gang still be living in Berlin, even underground? Martin explained: The man had had an operation to change his face, as Humphrey Bogart did in *Dark Passage*. During the first part of the movie the camera was where his head should have been. Actors looked at the camera, spoke to it, offered it cigarettes, recognized the face of an accused murderer. The audience never saw his face until, following plastic surgery, he removed the bandages and emerged with Humphrey Bogart's face. The camera backed off, returned to its normal place, and nobody offered it cigarettes anymore. *Plastic surgery, that's the answer.*

I put my head under a pillow as if I didn't want to hear any more about his films.

From a doorway, in a room full of broken bits of furniture, a sort of Seventh Street Orion, Martin lived in misdirection, awash in quotation and borrowing. Eamonn claimed and consumed, if only for the moment a print was left up to dry. Some kind of purpose lay behind every photograph. Suppose they were to meet, accidentally caught in some tedious situation, waiting in line at the post office, sitting next to each other on a long train ride. They would be forced to talk to each other out of boredom or confusion. Eamonn would find his conversational feet stuck in the mire of Martin's descriptions of his projects, but stuck implies there's glue at work somewhere. The nature of that glue is Martin's ability to keep his audience interested. The *what ifs*, the *and then supposes* pile up. The accretions grow entangled, and you become mesmerized trying to sort them out. Because of this, Martin would learn little about Eamonn. Reserved, secretive about whatever he might be up to, that's Eamonn's trick for staying in control. If Martin catches on to the trick during the long train ride, he'll become annoyed and feel ridiculous. Eamonn will get off the train as if nothing extraordinary had happened at all.

I often had trouble falling asleep. I might hear a radio from across the street. At such times there seemed nothing more inert than a sleeping man. I wondered what I was doing in his apartment, if I had made a mistake, and how I might be made to pay for that mistake. What is the insomniac's revenge on the man who sleeps and in that sound sleep is blind to the light creeping into the room, deaf to the people drinking in an empty lot, ignorant of my chimeras, which are partly about him? Leaking sesame sauce from last night's dinner's bowed white cartons still sitting on the table. I might pick fruit flies from a glass of wine left out and drink the rest. The first thing he said when he woke up was hello, which had some truth to it. In sleep he was dead to everything.

Do you know what this is like? I asked Martin as he slept. I had looked at his photograph with a magnifying glass. He was smiling in the picture, and I couldn't find a trace of the sort of contempt I'd seen when he mimicked cabdrivers, Mr. Loonan, or me, but I was sure it must have been there at the moment the shutter snapped, because I saw it even as he slept and didn't understand how the clues of his smirky expression escaped fast film.

When he woke up he said, "Sometimes I think there must have been a fork in the road and I picked the wrong branch. I don't remember when I had the choice, where, or what the alternatives were, but I'm sure I made a mistake." When he said this, I pictured Martin in a Grimm brothers' wood confronted with several choices, but instead of picking the path which led to fatality, poverty, hopelessness, or simple bad luck, Martin would sit in the middle of the crossroads, have a cigarette, a nap, and never get on with it. Like his father, ordered to the Korean theater and sure he would never return, Martin at least had the option of choice no matter what premonition of inevitability he was stuck with. The image of him at some sort of crossroads used to settle over him as he slept, in my imagination or in fact.

I never knew when he wanted to leave or when he wanted to stay. The only way to avoid being made a fool of was to barge on ahead anyway, to risk being more foolish, as if deliberate intention could cancel out inadvertent ridiculousness. I got sick and tired of the act of seduction being some kind of trial.

What am I supposed to say? What am I supposed to do?

I spoke into the telephone, and then it occurred to me I didn't care all that much about the answer.

Even a kiss can be mistranslated. I thought it meant Martin would turn up again. It was a sunny day, on a busy corner, with witnesses passing by. I thought I would see him again, and then I changed my mind. I didn't return his calls. I wanted to forget about the whole thing.

A movie seen so long ago I remembered nothing about it except one bit. It was barely even a narrative in my memory anymore; there was just one scene, one joke, one mystification. Jack Lemmon or Walter Matthau, I couldn't remember which, was in bed with a blonde woman. His wife walked in. She screamed, "Who's that woman?" "What woman?" her husband asked. He and the blonde got out of bed and began to get dressed. "That blonde," his wife said, and she pointed. "What blonde?" the man asked again. He and the woman began to make the bed. "That one." "There's no one else here." The other woman walked out the door as his wife watched. "What do you want for dinner, dear?" she asked, defeated.

The point of the disturbing comedy was the demonstration of the deniability of visual evidence. What woman? What long kiss? I could erase the whole scene and tape over it. There was no proof. Witnesses couldn't be found. I passed that corner many times. There were no plaques, commemorative statues, or lingering afterimages marking the spot. If there had been, I would have returned in the night and removed them.

Even a kiss can change meaning, be misread. It had been a forgery, a practice kiss, a simulation of a kiss meant for another. I finally called Martin.

"I admit to seduction, but I draw the line at deception,"

I said, and I was partly right, but I refrained from answering that I agreed: I had betrayed myself. We'd both had a hand in it.

He answered that if a long kiss doesn't mean what you think it means, then what does anything mean? If a kiss means nothing, then the handshake, the accidental knock on the street lose their definition also. Why not kiss instead? The definition of a kiss grows vague and blurred. (You think only of bits of chocolate wrapped in silver.) Perhaps it means nothing and we're all better off for it. When a kiss has no meaning, then related activities also lose their meaning in light of the meaningless kiss. He felt left in a blind crowd; each sightless, inference-less, connotation-less word or gesture stumbling into the next. No definitions, no significations, no if you do this, it means . . . I love you or I hate you. Fog, soup, nothing. This is not an apology for the puritan streak, nor does it mean you can kiss the concept of otherness goodbye. We hung up.

How close did Dreyfus come to breaking, to giving in? His accusers said: You wrote this note, you wrote it, we have your confession in your own handwriting. He knew he'd written no treasonous note and signed no forged confession, but Devil's Island is a horrible place to be, and he had no conception of the identities of the real traitors. Ground and sky turned upside down, gravity reversed, and the fixed pinnings of your life seem undone, useless. What is the meaning of a kiss in comparison?

Don't feel trivialized, I imagined saying to Martin. Public betrayals have parallels in private affairs. A rotter on a global scale can be a small-time cheat as well. His personal life might be just as exploitative; at the same time, a stolen kiss doesn't make me a potential member of a future Gang of Four. I didn't say any of this to Martin. He hadn't asked for an explanation.

When we worked on *Electra* he only touched me as if it was an accident, and although he seemed to arrange the when Laurel and Mr. Loonan were out of the room, prolonged the accidental into the intentional while at work. Now there were no more accidents. The oblique gestures disappeared, but Martin remained just as obscure to me. We would say that he thought about me when he was alone in his badly lit rooms, but I didn't entirely believe him, and in his absence, I can't separate regrets from an obsession with absence itself. When loss seems nothing more mysterious than habit, desire for the missing disturbs me far less.

Then Martin disappeared, his image swallowed up in the vacuousness of an empty kiss, nothing but a blur. I had nothing of his, no pictures, no letters, no borrowed book, no caricatures of Mr. Loonan passed to me at work. Martin vanished. I felt embarrassed about the mornings at Fantômes when I'd asked if I could work at home because he hadn't been called in. I had gotten involved in his schemes and discussed how he might resolve his half-baked plots. (The women in the cab perform murders on a contractual basis. The men in prison put on a play which is followed by a spontaneous riot. The Baader Meinhof character earns a living as a stand-up comedian performing for American servicemen stationed in West Germany.) Then I forgot all about him, reassuring myself that since I hadn't a shred of physical evidence, it was as if nothing had ever happened. Even if a relic could be produced, I refused to remember the details: the child actor having powder brushed on his face, the lines drawn under names in the telephone directory which may or may not have belonged to his half brother. Laurel rarely referred to Martin, even if she saw him on the street or in the hall of a floor where they both happened to be working. I no longer spoke of him. It wasn't amnesia, deliberate or accidentally induced, but Martin had only ever been half there anyway, so he was easy to deny. He had seemed to matter so much because there was so little there, and then he didn't matter at all.

He did appear occasionally: in a chart of different types of lettering displayed on a counter in the store where I bought my colors, or in a conversation overheard in an elevator between a woman and a little boy obviously on their way to an audition. When I thought about Martin I thought about unfinished business or imagined stories which dwindled off when he reached the end of the page, vague and wanting little. These reminders were only small sparks. His afterimage was weak. Whatever opportunism he had was buried under all kinds of stops and starts, and so coasting along until I came to one of his stops, my memory abandoned him.

I ate cold sesame noodles and reheated leftover coffee. I no longer went to the laundromat, but washed my clothes at home in the bathtub, hanging them to dry across the room. I did not realize how much water even wrung-out shirts and socks hold. They dripped onto a stack of drawings stored nearby, ruining the top ones. At night the clothes hanging across my apartment looked like a child's idea of ghosts, but during the day the lines of sheets and socks made it look even smaller and more cluttered than before.

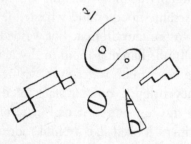

I received one postcard from Eamonn. It was from Ireland, an aerial view of the Rock of Cashel, rows of Gothic arches in gray sponge. The cathedral had been a ruin for centuries. He wrote only that he had arrived and was traveling by train, visiting friends in Roscommon. There was more information on the printed part of the postcard than in what Eamonn himself had written.

The Rock of Cashel, a remarkable outcrop of limestone rising 200 feet; it was the seat of Munster kings from A.D. 370 until 1101, when King Murtagh O'Brien granted the Rock to the Church. St. Patrick visited Cashel in A.D. 450 and baptised there King Aengus. The buildings on the Rock include a tenth-century round tower, Cormac's Chapel, the Cathedral, the Hall of Vicars Choral, and St. Patrick's Cross, as well as some modern tombs and enclosing walls.

I tried to interpret what Eamonn might really be doing based on the printed description, but the clues were vague and interpretations contradictory. He was staying with a man named Aengus or on a road called Cormac. He haunted one of the towers. He was pretending to be choir master, camera hidden in his robe. The ruin of the cathedral, a clump of buildings simultaneously falling apart and being preserved, was overburdened with enigmatic signs. I carried it around with me for a few days. Not because it reminded me of Eamonn; it didn't really. He was gone and the aerial view of ancient limestone buildings suggested no memory of him. Even his handwriting seemed remote and unfamiliar. Before I noticed the specks of gravestones, I thought the ruin was a castle and parts of it would still be lived in. The glassless arched windows would look inviting to someone just fallen from space. Electra, homeless, sleeping in a box, could live here. Perhaps Eamonn was camped in the ruins and never got farther north than County Tipperary. I didn't expect to hear from him again.

EPISODE IV
ELECTRA DOESN'T KNOW WHAT TO DO

Useful on Earth in some places, the package said. It had been zippered into her suit. Inside were hundreds and thousands of dollar bills. She had read about dollars, pounds, and francs but didn't really understand what money might be; its purpose or value was unclear to her. A picture of a house, a picture of a man, a signature, numbers; there were so many bits of paper but no directions as to what they were for. She left the package on a rock in Central Park.

She had to live on the street and grew ragged constructing her possessions from what other people threw away. Because inconspicuousness seemed desirable, Electra drifted to the southeast side of the city. A rush-hour crowd pushed her through a subway turnstile, and the hurtling motion of the trains reminded her of a primitive sort of spaceship. When the streets ceased to be numbered and stations were named she got off. The cars were packed full of people, and she felt claustrophobic, as if she must certainly be rushing toward a fatal accident. She asked people who stared at her questions about food and sleeping. Her system was to avoid pepole who looked away, but she had no guarantee that those who politely looked away would have been less anxious to explain the city to her. Even if other citizens treated her with equanimity, as if she were just like them, she suspected her slipups, she sensed they were being polite and not mentioning her mistakes in social behavior. Memories of a life of privilege, extravagant intelligence, and faintly odd looks served to give her away to herself, if not to others. Only vague childhood memories resisted erasure. A laboratory whose walls were uneven rock, a little girl splashing soapy water from test tube to petri dish, domes of suds in the sink, a recording of Glenn Gould playing partitas (although she didn't clearly remember Dr. Atlas, who had been in love with him). Parts of the city looked familiar, but the familiarity was grounded in mistaken identity. A stone-faced tunnel near Police Plaza bore little resemblance to rooms hollowed under the Sierra Madres. Nothing to jar presence into the absence created by Orion's chance ray, touched off in agony.

Her glassy, translucent skin grew dirty and cracked,

but the dirt concealed the fact that Electra had the look of someone who was born out of a tank. Layers of clothing found in the street; jackets, trousers, skirts made her a shapeless Père Ubu; hair matted and greased stood up straight. It was summer and she could wash under the hydrant at night after the children ran away, but she began to like it, thinking smell was like a thumbprint or the sound of voices, each peculiarly idiosyncratic. She had no concept of what it might be to appear offensive.

Language had a chancier aspect on the streets. It wasn't entirely neologisms she hadn't learned due to her isolation in space but a combination of idioms and slang, and the local habit of aposiopesis and metonymy, which confused her. Spoken sentences never seemed finished, although she suspected the thoughts behind the broken phrases were.

Few of Electra's companions on the street were charitable or magnanimous about distributing whatever they might have scavenged. The concept of surplus didn't exist. One's body was a savings bank, a storage vault, interest cumulative depending on market value. Rubber bands were among the utilitarian rarities coveted by the homeless. Incapacity didn't eliminate the imperative of committing crimes, and there was a gluey nastiness to their fights. In the aftermath of a fight between two men, as one lay unconscious and bleeding, the other rifled through his stiff, ligneous rags. They did this to the dead as well. Useful objects—bags, safety pins, rope, rubber bands—were of value and had degrees of preciousness. Down along the line, everything changed hands, was transformed. A belt became a handle, bicycle tires became trouser suspenders, a paper bag became a hat. Possessions, bits of objects were piled into supermarket carts. One had to maintain a balance between accumulation and mobility. They filtered through the garbage like the *houilleurs* of nineteeenth-century Paris.

Electra lived in an old cardboard refrigerator box. The manufacturer's emblem printed on the box reminded her of her spaceship. Electra knew other citizens on other avenues looked and behaved differently, so she stayed on her street, rarely going more than a few blocks in any direction. Sometimes she moved with clots of homeless men and women, settling for a few days on the corner of a busy intersection. The men might wash cars. When her box disappeared she slept by herself on a traffic island in the middle of Allen Street, learning to ignore the sound of cars and trucks. Electra's clothing was made up of what she found, but she was selective as well as eclectic. Another homeless woman had painted her face so she looked like a Bengali princess: her eyes were ringed with black and green from makeup found in a discarded stolen suitcase, her scalp was painted red at the part, beaded silver key chains were linked together and pinned across her forehead.

One night an unhappy woman alone in her car mistook Electra for her lost sister. Electra was leaning against a chain-link fence; she had turned away from a basketball game, which made no sense to her. The car slowed down, came to a stop, window rolled down. "Hey, you," the unhappy woman shouted. "Come here, please." Electra ignored her, not out of antisocial instincts, but because salutations and requests confused her. The woman walked toward her. She was wearing a large black coat and a black fur hat. One or two of the men playing basketball yelled at her, and she said to Electra, "I wish you hadn't made me get out of my car." She held Electra's face in her hands for a few minutes without saying anything, then asked, "Can't you see that we're mirror images of each other, but I can't take you home me?" Electra's unsuitability and their similarity seem connected, at least for the woman in black. It seem logical that her missing sister would have turned into the kind of person she couldn't have in her home. When she had imagined the lost woman she imagined someone utterly rebellious and unconventional. That had seemed as predictable as their physical likeness would be. One of the basketball players who'd stopped to yell noticed a glimmer of recognition on Electra's glassy face. Electra initially mistook the woman in black for one of her own duplicants, but she was too well adjusted, too comfortable, and had too much self-confidence. Unless a duplicant had somehow escaped Orion and had managed to precede Electra to Earth . . . Such a woman, although a paper tiger, would not have figured the planet out by now with the apparent ease of the woman in black. She extended her left hand to Electra. The dupes were right-handed. She reached into a coat pocket and handed Electra a wallet, her husband's. She'd abandoned him at a party, in a car, anywhere, and she'd taken his wallet by mistake, or because she had no money of her own. Electra hugged her, because if this woman was a duplicant, she would fold up like an accordion. She didn't. She remained standing. She handed Electra the keys to her car, said she was very sorry, and walked away toward Stanton Street, which she crossed before disappearing into the night. Electra was utterly confused. She screamed, but the street was deserted, no NYPD, not even a Fantômas appeared on the Boulevard du Crime. In the middle of the night, nobody would have looked twice. She stuffed the wallet into her pocket, it was warm and curved like a hot clamshell. She guessed the keys went to the car. Electra had seen bodies rifled through on the street before, although it wasn't clear to her what the objects were for. She drove down Allen Street to Pike, parked the car, put the microchip for the lost mimetic device in the glove compartment, and fell asleep in the back seat.

Laurel drew close-ups of the money left on a rock in Central Park and the silver key chains strung across Electra's forehead. I lettered *UNHAPPY* in the frame just above the woman in black, that was what she was as she sat in her car. The car was blue. I took out a dollar bill to be sure I was painting the money accurately, even though Dr. Atlas probably wouldn't have given her such a large amount in singles. Laurel agreed, but she concentrated on the eye hovering above the pyramid. We had no scripter looking over our shoulders checking each color, each line. It was difficult to leave all that money just sitting there in Central Park.

Laurel had intermittent temporary jobs as an inker at Fantômes since we had been officially laid off. There were more cutbacks after *Electra* was terminated, and Mr. Regozin called her less often each month. When I tried to get work as a colorist again, I was told, "We'll telephone you when there's something to do." They never did call. Once in a while there would be a job on *Red Sonja*, *Dazzler*, *The Thing*, or *Spiderwoman*. The latter was terminated in a special double issue.

I applied for a job painting backdrops behind exhibitions at the Museum of Natural History. The offices were remote, on an upper floor, and I wandered around the museum studying the backdrops. Blown-up painted bacteria and bits of root ends surrounded a greatly magnified night crawler that looked as if it had been inspired by ribbed plastic pipe; steamy fern forests lay behind dinosaurs; hapless, nameless fish behind a model of a hammerhead shark; pine trees and mountains behind a grizzly bear. I could paint plants and animals naturalistically, and some of the microbes looked like objects encountered in Electra's bit of space, but every backdrop appeared entirely finished. It didn't look as if there would be much to do beyond the restoration of a leaf or a fish once in a while, but I thought it would be a quiet place to work; painting in a window surrounded by stuffed animals and bones, watched by an occasional audience of grade school science students. I went upstairs and showed my portfolio to the director of the art department, a gray-haired woman in a lab coat. She gave me a brief tour of her studio. It was a large, cluttered room with windows facing the park. Tables were laid out with plaster models of extinct species, and she showed me a cabinet full of the records of backdrops used for the Hall of Asian Peoples: deserts, tundra, equatorial jungles, she waved at the flat shelves. I explained that although I had worked only as a colorist for comics I could paint forests and microbes on a large scale. She looked through pages of Electra and Dr. Atlas under Sierra Madre del Sur without smiling. I imagined the laboratory looked inaccurate and dated. She told me they were looking for someone with more experience; a man who had been with them since working for the 1964 World's Fair was retiring, but she would call me if anything came up. She closed my portfolio, and I wanted to ask her if the man had painted the whole fair by himself, but didn't. I knew she wouldn't call me.

I stood in line at Veselka to buy a lottery ticket, but passed by Gem Spa newsstand. I had a system. I would pass every other newsstand or candy store that sold tickets. Laurel did the same in Chinatown. She broke the system when she went to Queens to visit her mother, because she neglected the third newsstand, the next one according to her route. It had sold a winning number the year before and she thought the odds were negligible that another chance millionaire would come of it. We knew this was an example of the Monte Carlo fallacy, in gambling lightning does strike the same place twice, but what seemed to matter was that we stuck to some kind of system.

As long as I could get Unemployment and my landlord remained confined to a wheelchair, I felt safe. He'd had a stroke in the middle of the summer and was partly paralyzed, knew little of what went on around him; food fell from his mouth into the chair.

It was Easter. The brightest colors in the city were purple and yellow. They far outdistanced neon blue, subway-worker orange, and the fragments of pink and rose in flower buckets in front of Korean groceries. The saffron yellow looked Oriental, the purple simultaneously aristocratic and parvenu. Green, the pale but logical choice, seemed left out of the iconography.

Eamonn sent money for his half of the rent, but it arrived in erratic installments. Although the postcard had come from Ireland, the checks were mailed from England, so I wasn't sure where he was. The amount varied, as if he'd forgotten exactly what we paid. Eamonn wanted to hold on to his share of the apartment, but the haphazard checks seemed an indirect way of telling me not to depend on his presence in the near future. The apartment was his. I was its caretaker. I had managed to get Unemployment but my twelve weeks were running out.

One Thursday morning at Unemployment I was sent to Section C. Something had gone wrong. Each week I glanced quickly at Section C, a group of folding chairs set into warped lines facing double rows of desks, most of which were empty. This cordoned-off area was for people who wrote the wrong social-security number on their forms or got caught having a job off the books. Two men and a woman sat at their desks looking seriously occupied, as if preparing for a play before an audience they knew to be fractious and captive for up to an hour. Belligerent, nervous Section C felons knew this was where you fought for your checks or gave up. The lines at Unemployment were long, but the wait in Section C was even longer. Counselors were impuissant civil servants who might have started out with vague ideas about social welfare, but by the time they worked in Section C, they had turned cynical and self-righteous. They tipped back in their chairs, astute and sophisticated. They really had only a small bit of power over individuals, but they posed questions like amateur sleuths, as if the problem of the federal deficit would be solved by apprehending petty frauds, even where no fraud existed. My counselor, Mr. Belvilacqua, thought of himself as perceptive and smooth, ignoring the dirty beige walls and lack of a private office; all that really drove him was the desire to nab another cheat.

I told him I had been looking for work and I listed the jobs I'd applied for, the advertisements I'd answered, the inquiries I'd made. Mr. Belvilacqua didn't know what a colorist was, thought it had something to do with dyeing hair, and comics were a feeble excuse for adult employment. Couldn't I work at any magazine? Hadn't I even tried? Mr. Belvilacqua wrote down everything I said on a folded four-page form like a little book, and everything he wrote was in the first person. He read the statement back to me.

" 'Last Wednesday I called Spector Comics, but they said they weren't hiring any illustrators.' "

"I'm not an illustrator. I do coloring. I'm a colorist."

He looked at me as if I had said I was a professional loafer. I gave up. Mr. Belvilacqua made my search for a job sound as if I never got out of bed. His handwriting was neat and round, so different from mine, fast and jerky. His text was a procrustean narrative, had nothing to do with what I said, and was stupid to boot. I refused to sign the statement. He gave me a date for Unemployment Court in two weeks. In the meantime, my checks would be cut off. If I won my case, I would receive the back checks and be entitled to another twelve weeks. I wouldn't need a lawyer, Mr. Belvilacqua said, just show up in room 1209 and talk. It seemed hopeless. Room 1209 was another day wasted. I decided not to even try it.

My landlord was moved to a nursing home. A sharper sister managed the building now and demanded a late fee if rent was paid after the fifteenth. Her English was good, and she made a point of being sure she was understood.

As the date approached, I began to be a little curious about room 1209. I might go, after all. In a grand sweep of humanist eloquence that would appeal to the judge, I would reveal Mr. Belvilacqua as a petty termite. I would reduce his fiefdom, his corner of Section C, to bits of twisted paper clips and eraser dust. The judge would grant me triple back compensation and a trip to Rome. Room 1209 had no connection to any mental construct about grace, or winning an imaginary vacation. Court room eloquence fell on deaf ears. 1209 might have no exit. I would be the one reduced to confessions of unimagined crimes: cheating the crippled landlord, haunting Off-Track Betting joints, turning tricks on lower Third Avenue, lying to the government. Room 1209 meant waiting, listening to other claimants who didn't have a leg to stand on either, who pleaded they'd end up living in the tunnels under Grand Central Station. I would listen to story after story, and as I listened I'd draw pictures of Electra on my forms. Electra lands back on Earth, lives in an abandoned car, sells the art-history books originally put in her spaceship by her creator, and begs for change at subway stations. Her carefully engineered genetic code goes haywire because her special talents are of no use to the disenfranchised, and in the last frame her nostalgia for the test tube is impossible to draw.

We were just short of grasping at straws. On the telephone we were told it was a slow season, when we brought our portfolios into comic offices we were told comics were being phased out in favor of video and computer games, which earned higher profits. I couldn't visualize what these things might be. "How does the video game work?" I once asked. "Chase and target," was the answer. I felt ready for a retirement home. I called Laurel, but she was in Queens.

I had kept a little folded pamphlet handed to me on the subway which I found almost articulate and convincing.

There was a section at the back which discussed the nature of desire and the absence of its object. Miss Rose didn't directly address the subject of affairs of the heart or predictions about the future. Her approach was oblique. She used phrases like *the scars of the unconscious* and *the terrority of shades*, all of which were bound up in one's skittish and unreliable memory. Miss Rose wrote that she had, over the years, noticed how language stumbles when we speak or write of certain things, and she wanted to know why. "We often find ourselves addressing those who are no longer with us, rather than those closest." Was she advocating the abandonment of psychic healing? "Desire seems indestructible but has its limitations. Through changes of perspective and by recognizing points of view which are at variance, desire can melt away. Notice I wrote *desire*, not *pleasure*." Laurel and I were going through help-wanted ads. When I read this out loud, she

You no longer believe in God
and can't remember when you did.
Your silent prayers have always seemed useless.

BUT

By finding this paper your prayers have been
ANSWERED!
MISS ROSE
HAS FOUND
YOU!

A spiritualist . . .

A psychic reader . . .

who has been bequeathed with the power to help
those in need.

Are you often at a loss for words?
Do you feel fate has swept you along,
that you've no control over your circumstances?
Do you succumb to wayward influences
in spite of your best attempts to the contrary;
in short, resiliency fails you?

QUESTION:

CAN FALLIBLE HUMAN BEINGS RECOGNIZE WHEN
WE'RE BEING LED ASTRAY?

THE ANSWER:

MISS ROSE!

Fill in the space below with the three most difficult life
problems you need help with:

1. _____

2. _____

3. _____

asked if Miss Rose had cited footnotes. Laurel was not taking
her suggestions seriously. She told me she was sick of the
word *desire*.

I continued to read aloud. "Do you feel yourself to be the target of petty deceptions and, what's worse, self-deception? As a result, are you driven to traumatic despair? Life is not a dream. Forget about those cloying, aggravating aphorisms and maxims that leave you out in the cold."

Laurel pointed out the irony in this. "She feels she needs to tell you *life is not a dream*, and then instructs you to ignore that expression because you've probably heard it a million times before."

But Miss Rose could be practical. As I read on, the tone changed. "Do you scan the want ads and job notices on the odd bulletin boards, not knowing what you're capable of accomplishing? Are you beleaguered by tyrannical bosses and unresponsive co-workers?"

I suggested to Laurel that Miss Rose might be a psychic labor organizer. She told me to wake up. I hadn't been serious about going to a reader, but like the pattern of buying lottery tickets, any system was better than our random pinball-like way of bouncing off one situation and sliding toward the next. Why not Miss Rose? The little paper was full of signs in her favor. Influences were wayward. Wayward had less incriminating connotations than evil, and lacked a theological ring. It had a softer, more forgivable sound. There was no mention of any specific religion, no description of damnation other than punishment which might be self-inflicted. Laurel didn't understand, it wasn't Miss Rose that I was attracted to but the idea of Miss Rose. I found it encouraging that under "Question" Miss Rose included herself among those capable of being misled. She did say "we." " 'Life problems!' " Laurel said. "What other kind are there? And look at how little space she allowed for life problems." Laurel took the pamphlet from my hand and threw it away.

Laurel would not be caught watching a block of frozen carrots, for example, melt in a saucepan. She would always be too busy and too alert. I was the one to become spellbound by watching ice melt. I would be caught reading both sides of an advertisement for a psychic found entirely by chance.

I had once seen Laurel daydream at work, and it had been very jarring, like glimpsing a moralist in a moment of obsessive philandering. Mr. Loonan, Martin, the others who came and went, I had often seen them staring into space. The appearance of vagueness was almost a requisite for the job; with very little concrete evidence at hand, one was constantly having to imagine how an episode might look. Laurel concentrated, inking with matter-of-fact disdain while everyone else appeared sincerely interested in whatever episode was being produced. To watch her stare in an unfocused way at nothing in particular represented an abyss of unpredictability. What might Laurel have witnessed that would, hours later, cause her to stop inking, leave figures half drawn, and stare out the window, headphones dangling around her neck?

Coming home very late, Laurel had seen a man's body on the sidewalk on the corner of East Broadway and Pike Street. She guessed he was from Hong Kong, about seventeen or eighteen, a new immigrant recruit from one of the gangs. She guessed this because that's what she'd heard. At first they lived in buildings like hers, she could hear their voices spilling out into the halls and stairwells. They would soon change their haircuts and smoke more American cigarettes. The new recruits, she had been told, start out small—running rinky-dink clubs with Korean prostitutes and a little gambling, kung fu arcades; then they might buy into a restaurant. They don't kill for pleasure—sometimes for revenge, more often for cash. As long as it's within the neighborhood, the police leave them to themselves. There are no stray bullets. In the morning the body was gone.

She had told me that she hurried around the corner of East Broadway and Pike. She no longer thought about the murder when she walked past. Had she been watching from a window when it happened, she would have turned away. *She devoured him with her eyes. The creature devoured her with its eyes.* Martin had lettered those words over and over at Fantômes and at other comics, and certainly Laurel had read them. To look, in the case of the dead man, was to become ashamed.

A letter arrived from Eamonn. Between Mount Desert, Maine, and checks mailed in envelopes bearing the North London postmarks were several missing chapters, then a few were filled in.

Eamonn managed to stay awake through most of the bus ride from Shannon to Dublin, turning his head to look at half a castle in the middle of a town or ruins of buildings in another. He had made this bus trip many times before but no longer took the landscape for granted. There was no reason to feel more like a foreigner this time. The vagueness of the circumstances of his trip (a couple of telephone calls, the photographs of the *Grace O'Malley*) contributed to foreignness. He should have relied on the familiarity of the landscape. He fought against sleep. Small-town stores reminded him of bodegas on East Houston Street, with bananas and balsa-wood airplanes in their windows. He finally fell asleep near Roscrea. When he woke in Dublin, three old women had boarded the bus, followed by three high-school girls. He heard one of the girls talk about how a man in the movies had reached over and stroked her hand. She'd loudly told him to piss off.

The bus finally arrived in Dublin, and he quickly found the small hotel where Freddy Driscoll had told him to stay. He left his camera in his room and went for a walk. He also left his address book in the room; he made no telephone calls. O'Connell Bridge was covered with rose sequins, an ad for Scotch. He'd last seen a splash of metallic pink on a torn dress abandoned on a curb in New York.

The next day he left his camera in his room and went out again. He took another bus to Dún Laoghaire, a neighborhood of Georgian houses, apricot and green, with gardens of lilacs and fuchsia. He walked past the pink and gray houses to the Martello tower. The GENTLEMEN'S BATHING ONLY sign was still on the beach and obeyed. Although it was cold and Eamonn shivered in a sweater and leather jacket, people were swimming; even an old woman who pedaled past on her bicycle went in on the side reserved for women. The sea was clear green-gray seen close up. Marlboro wrappers clung to the rocks. He ignored the magpies' squawking, which was supposed to foretell a bad day. *Have a bad day! Have a bad day!* Shopping bags with faces on them. There was New York again. Only by the third day would the random things which crossed his path no longer remind him, even vaguely, of the city he had left behind. He wrote on a postcard that the rocks to the north near Howth looked like Easter Island statues turned on their sides. When I would later tell him that I never received the postcard, he would say he hadn't mailed it. He walked farther down the beach, then got a bus back to Dublin, and from there he would go north.

He walked through cars with NI TABAC signs because he wanted to smoke. "Is this seat taken?" His accent sounded like Dublin, but he would want it to sound American again when soldiers searched his bags at the border. A strange woman sat opposite him, but his stranger on the train only vaguely resembled Miss Froy. She alternated knitting with chain-smoking and looking out the window. If she had appeared diabolic, if she gave any hints indicating a prelude to scenes of chaos, he might have been distracted. When the train lurched suddenly, he felt no panic, only boredom. In that moment, there seemed such a thing as a happy death.

His passport was a picture of innocence. This was his American passport, not the Irish one. It was new and bore no stamps other than the oval recently acquired at Shannon. When he reached Ulster, the guards would find no evidence he'd been in Spanish-speaking countries. For them, he was just an American with a camera and a name with a rolling sound. He was a tourist. See, he'd take postcards out. He'd been to the Joyce museum. He had postcards of the *Book of Kells*. He had seen a map of Hibernia and England drawn by Ptolemy. It seemed surprisingly accurate, although Caledonia was bent out of shape. He had been to the Museum of Natural History and seen trilobites in long tubes of ether, tiny wood lice, opossum shrimps, and livid crabs in glass thimble jars, translucent in their preservative baths. He'd seen a book of Dublin corporation reports in which layers of bullets had been concealed during the 1916 Easter Rising. He heard a woman in a pub ask another how she liked the cut of a certain man.

They might have been brassers, and the man in question might have been himself, but he wasn't sure. He'd seen men with little gold-colored pins attached to their lapels. The feet were supposed to be the size of those of an aborted fetus. He had seen women waiting for the ferry to England at the Dún Laoghaire pier. The guards wouldn't be interested in his postcards.

Eamonn wasn't sure what he expected to find in the North. He and Freddy Driscoll hadn't much use for each other, really. Driscoll's plans were too deliberately vague. A *photographer could be useful.* Driscoll had given him a number to call in Dublin, but though he dialed it many times over several days, no one ever answered. He had only recently written ahead to Belfast. His letters might not yet have arrived. No one was expecting him. He called no friends. Each time he rang one of Driscoll's useless numbers, each time he entered a telephone box, he almost made one of his own calls, but then he didn't. A sense of powerlessness put him on the train traveling north, and this was new. He hadn't ever felt like Electra, sent successfully all over someone's idea of space and finally assigned by the colorist to failure on earth. Now, on the train, he did. The last time he'd been in the North, he'd gone specifically to Long Kesh, but even as Archer, he wouldn't be allowed back in.

The Blanket Men in Long Kesh were rationed three squares of prison toilet paper each day. Some used only two squares and saved the third to write letters on. Eamonn had smuggled one out. Tiny words, sentences in long lines; there were eight consecutive ragged bits which composed one letter. The writing looked like Celtic script. The pages described a brutality which relied, in part, on modern methods of degradation and on a cruelty which required no special equipment. Each detail was crucial. When words faded at the end of a line, or if a bit accidentally tore off, there was no way to retrieve those words once Eamonn was outside the prison gates. He couldn't ring back and ask, Was this what you really meant? The eight squares described dirty food and cells so cold breath misted in the air, as if you were out in the bog. All the beatings denied would resist denial when these bits of paper were reproduced. Far from Long Kesh, Eamonn put the eight squares in a thick envelope and had them photocopied in a shop where he could work the machine himself and not have to hand them over to a clerk. He gave the original eight squares to the man's brother, who lived in the Divis Flats, but was reluctant to let go of them. They belonged to the prisoner's brother and were addressed to him but had become precious to Eamonn. He had the copies blown up and sent the enlargements to New York.

Eamonn had one series of the letters with him on the train traveling north. He didn't know if it was dangerous to be carrying them years later. He would watch the faces of the border guards if they went through his papers. The photocopies might be too difficult to read, and the guards wouldn't bother to examine them, but one might come along who was a real stickler, who would remember that every document was potentially important. As the one guard peered at blurred lines photocopied from prison toilet paper, one or two words might glare out at him: *Blanket, maggots, disinfectant in the tea*. He wasn't at the border yet. He could leave the papers under his seat while the nearly Miss Froy look-alike was asleep, but he did not.

They stopped at Newry at the foot of the Mourne Mountains, just over the border. From the window Eamonn could see UDA graffiti and British flags painted on walls. Usually the border crossing was casual, but this time guards in flak jackets boarded the train. They took his American passport, asked where he was going, how long he intended to stay, who was he to stay with, what was the nature of his visit? He'd been through this before, played the tourist, gave the address of the hotel in Dublin. Down the corridor he could see more soldiers carrying machine guns and checking baggage. Out came every article of clothing and every pocket was felt. Film was opened, cameras taken apart. Books were thumbed through and shaken.

Miss Froy, just ahead of him, had yards of knitting wool in her bag. The soldiers squeezed each ball to be sure there was nothing hidden in the yarn. A young man with a thin mustache dropped an armful of them and the balls rolled across the floor, gathering dust as they unraveled. He started to untangle the strands and rewind the yarn, then clearly believing he looked foolish, shoved the lot back in Miss Froy's bag. The old woman looked distracted, as if all that mattered was getting to her destination, dirty yarn was part of the trip, and the soldier must know he was in a silly position. There was no need to tell him so. He was now quite annoyed with himself and therefore Eamonn was sure he would be given a hard time. The soldier opened Eamonn's bag, rummaged through the folded clothing, didn't examine books or open envelopes which contained the blown-up photocopies of smuggled letters. He stuck his hands in the compartments in a cursory way, then waved Eamonn through. He didn't want to appear ridiculous a second time.

Eamonn slept through the rest of the trip to Belfast. Miss Froy poked him when they arrived at the station, telling him if he didn't wake up he'd be sent back to where he came from. Belfast was the last stop.

He wandered around the station like someone who had missed his train, although he had arrived at exactly the location he'd set out for. He bought a paper and looked for signs of people who might live in Central Station, like the homeless people who lived in train stations in New York. Eamonn would get arrested if he tried to sleep on a bench, but he had friends in Belfast. He could still call them. He didn't have to pretend he was desperate although he felt he certainly was.

A woman's voice announced the departure of a train for Londonderry. The day had turned so sunny it seemed to Eamonn he might get on another train, go farther north, and take a boat to one of the remote clusters of islands, the Hebrides, Orkney, or Shetland. He sat on a bench and played with his camera, holding the viewfinder up to his eye, turning his head and focusing as he turned. A soldier crossed the frame and came toward him. He told Eamonn it was illegal to photograph military personnel. Eamonn explained he had wandered into his frame, Eamonn hadn't been looking for him. The soldier replied no, Eamonn had been deliberately aiming straight at him. His American accent was difficult to control; it abandoned him altogether on some words. While listening to the soldier's Ulster accent, Eamonn also found it difficult not to imitate him. The soldier told him that loitering was illegal and he should move on. Eamonn left Central Station, walking until it was out of sight. He found a telephone booth and tried one of Driscoll's Dublin numbers. This time a woman answered and asked him if he might be Eamonn Hanratty.

The woman said she'd been expecting his call. She gave him an address and said he should get the key from the landlady, Mrs. Malone, she'd be expecting him, too. He would have a room overlooking the corner of Cliftonville Park Avenue and Cliftonville Road. What she wanted him to do was simple: he was to photograph whoever met on that corner, by the phone box; he would see the place as soon as he got there. He could ignore couples who walked by, but must photograph two individuals who would meet one day this week. She didn't know who the two might be or what they looked like, so he should photograph all who met at this corner, even if one of the two was a child. There was enough film and food to last a week. He could go out at night if he wished. At the end of the week he should return the key to Mrs. Malone. The woman asked where he was calling from and was very glad he was already in Belfast. She told him which bus to take to Cliftonville Park Avenue. Then she described seven boxes Eamonn would find on the kitchen table in the apartment. Each box would be labeled for each date. At the end of the day, he should leave the negatives in the box labeled with the appropriate day. He was not to have the prints made himself. If he used less than thirty-six shots on any given day, the woman told him, he could finish the film in any way he liked. A new roll should be started each morning. Obviously, she explained, they didn't want dates to be confused or overlap. What should he do at the end of the week? Whatever you like, the woman replied. Just leave the room as you find it, with the film for each day in each box. Their conversation ended.

Mrs. Malone lived in the ground-floor flat between a grocery store and a fish-and-chips stand painted pale blue. She was a thin woman with a square face, didn't ask him many questions or appear to want much to do with him. She said, Oh, you're Mr. Shutter, yes, here's the key. You'll find everything you need upstairs. Whatever you don't have, just ask me for. It was difficult for him to keep from laughing. Eamonn thanked God Driscoll hadn't told her that his name was Mr. Thirty-Six Exposures or Dr. Sprocket.

He had expected a broken-down squat with graffiti on the walls, but Mrs. Malone showed him to a neat quiet flat which smelled of fried fish from the stand below. After she left him, he looked in the closets and drawers. They contained the clothing of a middle-sized man, shorter than Eamonn. The middle-sized man had a small shelf of books which included maps of Europe and Africa, a North American nature atlas, some reference books, the complete works of Flann O'Brien, and a book of crossword puzzles. It looked as if the middle-size man had gone on vacation for a week. There was no name on the mailbox, no old letters, bills, or initialed objects lying around which might hint at the identity of the flat's permanent resident. All Eamonn could conclude was that the man liked to travel.

The corner he was to keep under surveillance was empty. According to the dates written on the seven boxes, his watch would officially begin the next day.

In the morning he sat on the floor and studied the corner with the phone box on it. He got up to turn on the radio and returned with his camera, film, and a chair. Childen went by on their way to school, individual men and women passed, then it began to rain. It rained steadily, which Eamonn rather liked because he felt safe in the flat and saved from carrying out his ambiguous job. He didn't have a strobe flash. In the dark afternoon, little would register. When two black umbrellas met on the corner, he decided to play dumb and photograph the twin bumps. Driscoll or whoever received the final prints might think he was making fools of them. He was just doing what they asked. Soon it would be completely dark. Eamonn took a chance that no further meetings would occur on that rainy corner and used up the roll of film by taking pictures of the flat. It was more documentation than the three small rooms ever needed, but Eamonn wanted them to know he was following the rules.

Tuesday, Wednesday, and Thursday were bright and sunny, and Eamonn used an entire roll of film each day. He nearly missed one meeting because he got up to make a cup of tea. Afterward he kept food near the chair by the window. The fifth day was dull. Eamonn watched the corner until he felt hypnotized, until he felt the only afterimage he would ever see was that intersection. He could have gone out at night, and did once, but the neighborhood was unfamiliar to him. He couldn't find the local pub, didn't know anyone, was afraid of running into one of his friends. Afterward, even at night, he stayed in the little flat.

On the fifth day he remembered the telephone. There was one near the radio. Although it hadn't ever rung, the telephone did work. Making a call was like going out and he didn't use it, didn't want any of his calls to be traced later. It would be nearly dawn in New York. That day had brought only a few contacts. He noticed several of the contacts had also met each other on other days. A woman with short black hair in a denim jacket met a man in a long sweater. It was warm weather for wearing a sweater. He also saw a middle-aged man wearing American sunglasses, although the rest of him didn't stand out as foreign. It was he who had the encounter with the heavy sweater this time. None of them looked up and saw him as he snapped their pictures. Perhaps they were informants that Driscoll or the woman on the telephone from Dublin expected might meet on this corner. Human watchers are fallible and have their axes to grind; a photograph can be more concrete proof than reports from the naked eye.

He didn't know what to do with the extra film on the fifth day. There was a mirror above the mantel. He put his camera on it and took his picture looking into the mirror. Too late, he realized whoever printed the film would have a record of his face and his camera in this flat overlooking the corner of Cliftonville Road. He could take the entire roll of negatives with him when he left, but that would leave no film at all for the fifth day. He'd followed the rules so closely up until now.

On the sixth day he neglected to photograph two school-children who met on the corner. A few hours later, when the short-haired woman met the heavy sweater, Eamonn had left the camera in the kitchen. He had no idea whom he was working for. It had started with the *Grace O'Malley*, but by now his employer could have had any number of motives. The people he photographed on the corner could have been innocent neighbors who just crossed paths by chance. Driscoll might be selling guns to anyone. Eamonn could be traced and shot as he walked into a pub, a telephone box, down any street, and all he'd been was an innocent eye, a hired camera. Boredom came and went in waves. He looked at the nature atlas, studied a few of the maps. Why had Driscoll wanted an American to take the pictures? He had led Driscoll to believe he hardly knew anyone in Ulster. Driscoll thought Eamonn came out of nowhere and would return to nowhere, but that wasn't true. He wasn't anonymous in Belfast, and he had taken his own picture in the flat. He could have been an informer without knowing it. When he walked down Cliftonville Road and waited for a bus, he felt as if he had a spotlight on him. He left before the seventh day, taking the undeveloped film with him. The job wasn't finished. He still didn't know if he had fingered a pair who only happened to be in the wrong place at the wrong time, but no one would ever find out. The rolls of exposed film were packed in his bag. He left the key under Mrs. Malone's door.

It had been a dreary corner. Maybe that had been what he wanted to look at after he left Maine. He took a ferry to Stranraer, Scotland, and from there an overnight train to London.

EPISODE V
Electra Meets her Match

Electra had, by now, learned how money is used. The woman in black left her about $100. She was very hungry and tried to go into places where people were able to eat in exchange for money. She had watched transactions through restaurant windows: first food is served and eaten, then money given to a person who delivers paper and coins to a machine with a drawer. The meaning of small plastic cards surrendered and returned at the end of a meal was unknown to Electra. When the meal was finished these would appear, but first the man or woman who served the meal would bring a piece of paper to the table, and many hands would grab for it. Finally one would win and take out this small square of plastic. At first she had thought food was free and given in exchange for a signature. The ritual also involved taking small sticks and books of matches from bowls kept near the machine with a drawer. Sometimes when people left these places they gave her coins, as if she had been begging, when all she intended was to watch.

She was very hungry, but even having dollar bills and showing that she had them wasn't enough to get her into some restaurants. In a large one with broad windows on Broome Street, smelling of narcissus, red wine, and meat barely grilled, she was shown to the door. The same thing happened on Spring Street in a long, dark place full of dwarf palms, potted ivy, and plants she'd never seen before. On Mulberry Street; pink neon, coral-colored tiles, she smelled fried garlic and limp whorls of artichokes lying in pools of olive oil; a man with tattooed arms showed her to the door. Either she was losing her strength, or she sensed knocking the man flat still wouldn't get her anything to eat, and so she passively let herself be thrown out. On Pell Street, she passed steamy windows full of glazed ducks with crackling skins, dripping in red rows. She was so hungry, but even her tears and money wouldn't get her a table or a bite of food. People didn't want her in their restaurants. Finally, on Canal Street, she was allowed to sit at the counter of a small place which was very crowded. Nearly everyone was speaking Spanish.

It was by now very early in the morning, but Electra

ordered red beans and rice, pork chops, a cup of coffee, which she had refilled three times.

Most of the men ignored Electra, except one who came in by himself and didn't speak Spanish. He watched Electra pour hot sauce on her red beans and rice. Watching her was more interesting that eating. He pierced his eggs so the yolk spilled out and let the runny part cool sticky yellow around the edges. There was a Spanish man between them who yelled insulting greetings to the cook, and the American gestured to him. They changed places so the American was sitting next to Electra. He slid his plate of eggs next to hers so that they knocked together. "Excuse me," he said. "Have you been up all night?"

Under her layers of clothing and transparent raincoat the man with the eggs could see she was very tall and beautiful. Although she had the proportions and features of an overstated cartoon caricature, he guessed she had escaped from a private sanitorium, probably in Connecticut. He told her his name was Lenny Roper. She introduced herself as Electra, and then he was sure of it. No one had a name like that unless they made it up themselves. She might have been a sedated fugitive, or an heiress with a few screws loose. She had lived on the street long enough. It was clear whoever had been tracking her down had had trouble doing so and had perhaps given up. He asked her if she would like to go home with him when she was finished eating. He was a photographer, and he'd like to take her picture.

Lenny Roper looked like a character from the book of Bible stories Dr. Atlas had given her a long time ago. She had given it to her reluctantly, as a reference book, not as a theological text, but all Electra remembered were the pictures. Lenny Roper's hair looked as if it had been cut with a bowl on his head, and he wore gold jewelry like one of the illustrations of the New Testament version of a Pharisee priest. He led her through the rain to a warehouse building as far west as one could walk in the city without falling into the river. In between awnings spread over loading bays, he put his arm around her.

His loft was full of theatrical props and scenery, which appeared assembled and half arranged but still partly in storage. The whole warehouse-like space was sporadically lit and broken up into corners of incomplete settings. His bed, a shower, and a kitchenette were in one corner. He photographed Electra as she was, with all her clothes on, in front of a brick wall in the loft. She watched him hang lights from beams, sometimes covered by pink or orange gels. He disappeared, then brought out silver umbrellas and more lights on stands. He took off her clothing piece by piece and photographed each change. She remained passive and let him do whatever he liked. When he got down to the shreds of her original space suit, the smell overwhelmed Lenny Roper. He made her take a shower. Something was changing almost imperceptively. He wasn't quite as nice as he had been in the restaurant on Canal Street. He had all her clothes. She couldn't leave. The shower was the only place she had any privacy and she stayed in it as long as possible. She stayed in the shower until Lenny Roper reached in and turned off the water. He took pictures of her while she was still wet and drying off in front of his lights. Electra thought if she could enjoy taking her clothes off, or having them taken off for her, she might get some pleasure out of being photographed, but she had only a glimmer of a sense of what being an exhibitionist might be. She found it difficult to resist him, and she detected some contempt in the way he asked her to move this way or that. She was no longer as strong as she had been and didn't entirely understand what was going on. Perhaps the food had made her sleepy, but she had had to eat it.

She saw none of the photographs he took of her. Her will ebbed away, and she felt half awake most of the time, as if she were drugged. She did whatever she was told. The shower was the only place she had any privacy, and sometimes she was not even left alone there. Another character could walk in at any time. Escape was a difficult, almost impossible project. The loft was wired so she couldn't touch the main door without setting off alarms. Even so, Lenny Roper had a German shepherd, as if intruders or captives might slip past electricity but not dogs. In case of blackout, he said.

He brought in a friend, Lolo, who was often in the pictures, too. Lolo did Electra's makeup before the photography sessions. One day she cut Electra's hair very short so she could wear wigs. No one asked her if she wanted her hair cut, but she did as she was told. A place to sleep, enough to eat, it was as if the fulfillment of those two necessities compensated for the confusion she endured in Lenny Roper's loft.

He photographed her in scenes he arranged with his prop collection. As in the Fantômes version, she wore very little: a red-and-white checkered apron when she posed as a waitress, a blue cap when she worked in a cardboard gas station, a stethoscope when she was a doctor, and Lolo was a nurse. If she could have gotten each bit together at once, she would have had enough clothing to escape from a window, decently covered in a costume of non sequiturs, but she was never able to do this.

In one series Lolo painted their bodies with gold paint. They were supposed to be on a spaceship Lenny made out of stacked video monitors, fluorescent lights, and fish tanks. She liked the way Lolo's narrow sable brushes felt against her eyelids and cheeks when she painted her face. For a scene with large Japanese fans, Lolo painted a fish from her collarbone to the small of her back. Electra lay on a table and shut her eyes. The lights had been set up for the picture, but Lolo was still painting turquoise and yellow scales spiraling around Electra's waist. Lenny Roper didn't like the fish, so Lolo had to wash the painting off. He put orange fly swatters in Electra's obi, which made Lolo laugh. There were also Moroccan settings with coppery backgrounds and Turkish ones with artificial smoke from a machine which gave Electra a headache, but she said nothing about it.

When Electra posed by herself Lenny occasionally talked about how he had started his business. His monologues were delivered partly as if he was talking to himself.

Anyone can take a photograph, but Lenny had a way of composing shots so that ordinary neutral objects appeared lascivious. He could turn a pile of paper clips into something lewd and winking. His friends and associates called him a provocateur. He was offended if anyone used the phrase dirty pictures.

People would tell him he had an eye. He was always looking around. No view out any window, no stroll down a west side street was too ordinary or predictable. Everything interested him. All kinds of people and things ended up in his photographs, from Styrofoam hamburger boxes to rare automobiles. He was able to seduce men and women into working for him because of promises of exposure, a future in the movies, and there were those naïve enough to call scenarios eccentric and nothing more. An innocent might pick up an object, ignore the setting, and call the thing cute or nostalgic. They often volunteered willingly, without realizing they were going to be made into menacing tableaus or potentially humiliating *photo romans* which they would never see. If he discovered a particular neon clock from an old diner or pharmacy, if he spied a shell of a thirties-era gasoline pump specially shipped from the Midwest to a New York antique store, he would snatch the things up, take them home, and arrange the shots. He made so much money from his photographs he could continue to acquire anything.

When he began his work, he laughed when people called him a pornographer, but eventually he agreed with them: yes, that's what he was. The title had a subversive sound to it which he had liked, and then he began to deny he was a pornographer. To call his photographs pornographic, he explained to Lolo, was to reduce them to one thing, and they were not that one thing. In a moment which Lolo called bombastic, Lenny claimed he was an artist. Lolo said, *Oh, please.* Lenny employed her because, although she was cynical, she took little seriously and was not very analytical. If he asked her whether an arrangement was in bad taste, she would answer that that dress or that pose might have been considered tasteless at one time, but viewers might not bat an eyelash now, or maybe they would. She didn't really care, she would say. She set up scenarios, painted actors' faces, and sometimes posed herself. He had found Lolo when she was working as a waitress. She had just arrived from Maine and had never heard of Lenny Roper. He told her she looked nice in black and white, the color of her uniform. Whether she actually did look nice in her uniform hadn't ever occurred to her as she dressed before work, but her feet hurt and the man offered her a job. She was embarrassed that she'd never heard of him but later learned his name was very far from being a household word and that was partly what he preferred. Later when Electra found herself forgetting his name, Lolo was usually there to remind her.

Sometimes he brought in other men and women to perform with her in various scenes. Lenny instructed the men to put their hands on her and Electra went numb. It didn't matter to Lenny whether she actually felt anything or not, but he grew angry if her face appeared blank. He instructed her to look at Lolo and mimic her expressions of pleasure. Electra managed to imitate Lolo. "Think of something else, while he's taking your picture," Lolo suggested. What else? Electra's memory, never very reliable, deserted her. The men and women who also posed for Roper touched her when told to, but they only made conversation among themselves. Except for Lolo, the other characters treated her as if she were deaf and dumb. They might live lives chained to columns in another part of the warehouse, but they moved with a freedom that suggested they came and went nearly as they pleased. Electra tried to speak to them, but they would barely respond, except to mimic her. Some seemed to like the work, others were indifferent. Some men felt like sandpaper to her and made no noise when they posed. Lenny would give them directions from behind the camera. Some women felt powdery or secretly muscular. One was almost too old, Lenny said. She didn't want certain parts of her body to be visible and liked to be shot lying down. Some got paid. Electra saw Lenny give them money. He offered her nothing and took what was left of the hundred dollars given to her on Allen Street.

Electra tried to become friends with Lolo. Lolo constantly laughed at her. She made fun of Electra's simpleminded obedience and her resilient ignorance. No matter how degrading Lenny's scenes, Electra never complained about them or asked him for money. She clearly got no pleasure from the work but resisted understanding why the pictures were taken or what they were for. Lolo didn't want to give Electra ideas which would make him angry, because he, in turn, might turn on her. Ask for money, she might have said, or tell him you don't want to be handled like that. Tell Lenny you need to go outside or at least take a break once in a while. Lolo teased Electra about her fastidiousness. Since her first day she took showers every two or three hours when she could get away with it. In spite of constant bathing, the gold paint would not come off some parts of her body. Lolo also looked after Electra in a small way. She noticed when Electra stopped eating and tried to get her to start again, or at least drink some tea or orange juice.

Electra got thinner and thinner. Soon she was too thin to be of any real use in Lenny Roper's photographs, but he continued to take them, even when Electra's partners were so horrified by her emaciated state they refused to touch her unless he paid them at least twenty dollars more. When Lolo or Lenny Roper called out for Chinese food, Electra put only very small amounts on her plate, one or two bamboo shoots, half a shrimp. Food was the only element in Lenny Roper's setup which she could control.

Finally Lolo noticed Electra was no longer breathing. It wasn't easy to tell. She had been passive and nearly lifeless, for three days; still the shutter clicked away. She finally slumped under a silver umbrella and couldn't be roused. Lolo got angry and asked him if he was going to have Electra taken to a taxidermist and stuffed like a pet parrot. Roper told her she'd never work again and shouted that someone should call the coroner or an ambulance or whatever you're supposed to do when someone dies.

A man dressed as a French sailor said they shouldn't call someone who might raise their eyebrows upon entering the warehouse, someone who might ask questions and whatnot. The sailor picked up Electra as if she were a shovelful of cinders, put her in a trash bag, and brought the bundle to a dumpster a few blocks away.

In the years following Electra's death, Lenny Roper became very successful in his business. When he sold his loft on Saint John's Lane, he was a millionaire and bought an island off the southeast coast of Florida. His household staff was made up of Cuban refugees and he had friends flown down from New York in his private plane.

We could have had Electra kill Lenny Roper. She was so brilliant, aside from her great physical strength, we could have had her rebuild her image duplicator from parts bought at CK & L Surplus and Lafayette Electronics, but we didn't. Laurel didn't want Lenny to be a photographer. She accused me of writing about Eamonn and I wanted her to leave. They weren't alike at all. Lenny was a sleazy caricature, there was no comparison.

"How about just a small-time hustler or a real-estate developer," she had persisted. We had no context for Electra as a hustler's right hand, that would have involved too much of a personality change. We had painted her into a corner. Once she landed in the city, I thought, it was inevitable that she should be reduced to a sort of a breathing mannequin. I crossed off circled want ads, lying on a chair next to my drawing table. Laurel could be impossible to argue with, sulky if she didn't get her own way, but Lenny Roper had too much history to be axed as a failure.

"Revenge and resurrection seem completely unrealistic solutions," I said.

If I had her martyred off and Fantômes had her married off, she was not symbolic of forgiveness but of its opposite. What she represented was antipathetic to the idea of dying for someone else's sins. Avenging unnamed innocents or acting in the name of abstract innocence itself; by doing this, the martyr seems to get revenge. We didn't know what else to do with Electra. Laurel swept up the last storyboards and put them still wet into her portfolio. Electra posing as Cleopatra bled into the space heroine staring at a plate of food without eating any of it.

I hadn't spoken to Laurel for a week and called to see if she'd found work. She'd had one day, but it wasn't enough. I could hear a newspaper being folded beside her.

She was on a boat on the Pacific Ocean in which the dried salted fish had run out, and Malaysian pirates in motorboats might appear at any moment to rob them of the money they hoped to take to America. She was crossing the Cambodian–Thai border on foot, she was working in a sweatshop in Singapore, she had no time for my hesitation, for my alternative plans. She wasn't working as a dancer in Bangkok balancing Coke bottles on her head for American servicemen; not even her cousins had actually worked in those sweatshops in Taiwan or crossed the ocean in rickety fishing boats, but sometimes Laurel was obsessed by a personal idea of history. The personalized horrific stories (deprivation, exploitation, murder), combined with saturation by the heroics of the cast at Fantômes and Company, Ltd., was, for Laurel, a volatile mixture which hinted revenge was possible. Laurel was not Rouge sprung from *Terry and the Pirates*, but she could see herself as tough as nails, full of those received ideas about buying and selling, about not being a victim, no matter what. I don't know if other prostitutes thought along those lines.

When I was in school one of my teachers read a line to the class from Mayakovsky. In the line something was *like a naked hooker jumping from a burning building*. She could barely read the words through her laughter. The class laughed, too. "This should tell you something about poetry," she had said to the class. "This should tell you that people find humor in degradation," I said to Laurel when I described the class to her. She seemed very desperate. I wasn't sure she could suspend Laurel-the-inker for one night, become someone else, then never think about it again. She told me I was naïve and hung up.

A man of indeterminate age told one of the women that as she spoke, she wasted time, and time to him was money. He screamed at her that she was wasting time. It was a mistake to think streetwalkers came out only at night. I passed them on my corner at all hours and often stared, not out of hostility, but from curiosity. The rangy or squat pimps were usually not too far away. If I saw them I would stare at them as long as I could while walking past. Although they must have recognized me from the neighborhood, I was afraid to stare for too long. They must have known I wasn't an undercover policewoman. That was too farfetched for even a jumpy crack runner, but the prostitutes did not want to be stared at, and neither did their pimps. I couldn't help it. They always looked as though they were waiting. Women sometimes fought with the man leaning against a car. This was when I most wanted to ignore a traffic light that had long been red and watch the pair, but fights were the most intrusive time to watch. I saw a man hit one of them, and I yelled at him, automatically, without thinking. The woman turned toward me with a big grin on her face. They were just joking around. All his moves were the false moves of a genuinely bad egg playing at everyday violence. Some days the slaps were real. He told me he didn't get any respect, and he and the woman laughed. I ran home. I felt not quite a complete fool but close to one. My watching was neither prurient nor moralistic. I continued to stare at one or two women on my corner as they waited. I almost couldn't help it.

(Loonan's Electra was for show, like the women who stood on my corner, but she was a colder, more remote version. She would never get into cars. Loonan himself would drive past. More cars stopped when summer began, but Loonan would not be one of them. Cover her in tinsel, he would direct. He would admit silvery threads are difficult to render in comic books, but he would want an image to contradict Regozin's white streamers.)

I read that, according to Balzac, a courtesan is not a radical. She is always a monarchist. He believed a man could be despised, but not his money. Laurel said she didn't know what I was talking about. She didn't want a king. She needed the money and it seemed easy; she had been told that it could be easy and paid well. I drew a string of dollar bills with sly faces, wearing suits and ties.

"We can't do anything with those."

Laurel heard you could make more than $500 a night. A woman who lived in Laurel's building had told her. They often met in the laundromat and acknowledged each other, because neither was an immigrant Chinese. They spoke of mundane things at first. In the winter there was not enough heat. There was no lock on the front door to the building. The mailboxes were smashed in. Both complained about the noise of radios and children in the halls. The woman had decided to leave New York. She was going to Los Angeles and she offered to sell Laurel her black book for $10,000. Laurel only wanted it for one night. The woman asked for a flat rental fee, $400 in advance. When Laurel told her she didn't have that much, they negotiated an arrangement whereby the woman would take a percentage of whatever Laurel made in one night. Her generosity wasn't without threats as to what would happen if Laurel were delinquent. Opposite each name in the book was a description of what she should expect to do and how much each usually paid. When Laurel called she was to say she was a friend of Janet Ling's. The name meant nothing to Laurel. It wasn't the label on her mailbox, but Laurel folded her laundry and didn't ask the woman who used Janet Ling as a professional name, why she did so.

A. Ray—$275.00. He wanted to drive to Long Island which was a very long way, and I wondered if he really did have a house out there as he said. I told him I always go to hotels but way out beyond Babylon, New York, we couldn't find one and ended up at a drive-in movie. I refused to get undressed. There were cars on three sides, and I would have been arrested on the spot. He argued he must pay me less. Next time charge more, no matter what.

K. L. Pearsall—$325.00. Always takes you out to dinner and may want to spend the whole night in a hotel ($600 plus). Make sure someone knows where you're meeting him and when you expect to return.

H. Naples—$150.00. All you have to do is talk to him as you undress and dress again. He will give you cues. For example, he might have you speak to him as if you're his mother. The pattern in this role is scolding and for-giveness. In another tableau he might want you to play an animal trainer (ridiculous, I know). This pattern is about reward and punishment. The cues are usually simple. You will always be an authority figure of some kind. No props needed. He's an hour, tops. A gem when you're in a pinch.

Laurel barely read the black book. She only vaguely cared about personalities and preferences. She was interested in prices. Personal desires, aberrant or conventional, adjectives not even thought of, all could be reduced to a simple exchange, a thing taken for granted, sold many times over, twenty-four hours a day. The Rays and the Napleses represented every man ever thought about, every pedestrian solicitation or telephone arrangement. Laurel thought none of it had anything to do with a dusty orange tree, trips to Flushing, or a dead boy found on East Broadway. A temporary condition, with no afterimage; when it's over you are yourself again, not a woman who once or a woman who used to. Part of Laurel's ruse was to say yes, she would use the black book for one night, to believe it for a few hours, one complete shift. Janet Ling wouldn't care, she was leaving the city. I asked Laurel about disgust. It was an unpredictable experiment, she might become paralyzed by revulsion.

I agreed to help. Laurel had no one else to ask, and she would give me part of whatever she made. She wanted me to hide in the closet in case anyone got violent. I wasn't sure what I would do and imitated a feeble karate kick, knocking over a plant in true sight-gag form. Laurel was serious. She found a crowbar in the basement of her building; I put it in a portfolio case, but this would be one more object the desk clerk might remember if he was called upon to describe us. Laurel had heard a story about a dancer who taped a ruler to her back to keep herself very straight during ballet class. Laurel taped the bar to my spine with heavy silver duct tape. Under a big jacket it didn't really show, but I couldn't sit down, and if I slipped and fell, I was certain my spine would be severed. I walked carefully. It was useless. I would come if she wanted me to, just in case; I wasn't sure what I would do, but I'd go with her.

We took a room in a place off Gramercy Park, which sounded like an impressive address, but once you crossed the threshold, it became increasingly shabby. That the hotel had not been gutted or turned into luxury apartments like other tenements and SROs was the curiosity of the block. It was almost a museum piece, representing tawdriness in a context of newish glamour and old New York prestige. In the lobby there was a long, wavy desk made of red Formica with gold flecks swirling it in. We went up two floors in a cranky elevator, down a hall papered by a geological map of stains, to 14D. There were actually few transients in the hotel; several tenants had lived at the Metropole Arms for years. 14D was bigger than I expected. The size of the room was the only sign we were at what was, traditionally, a nice address. It had a leaky air conditioner stuck into a window which faced a brick wall but was near enough to the street so that green flashes from a neon sign below lit a triangle of bricks every five seconds. An unemptied ashtray lay on the table near the bed. Laurel sat in the middle of the monogrammed chenille bedspread with Janet Ling's book and the telephone on her lap. The monogram was from another hotel. There was a Loonan in the black book but not the Loonan from Fantômes. Laurel turned the pages and read aloud.

A. Astor—$1,000.00. He will describe a scenario, often for two girls, and generally he will just watch. If he does get involved, ask for more money. You should always be paid first. I can't stress this enough. Be sure to do nothing until you are paid, because if the session has been one of those times when all he's done is sit on the edge of the bed watching, then he'll claim he was cheated. You weren't so great, he'll say, he might just as well have gone to the movies and for less money, too. He'll say it was your fault and argue in his chintzy way until you want to pay him just to leave the room.

Laurel made the call. For a long time there was no answer. When his service picked up, she left the hotel number and Janet Ling's name.

L. Carne—$1,000.00 The arrangement with Carne is similar to Astor's but with different warnings. He is even more of a watcher but will ask for props which could be dangerous. I never got to the point where these things were used, they were just there. He will pay a lot for what seems like very little, almost complete passivity on your part. The woman who traded him to me said he never touched her, but she had grown increasingly frightened and wanted to be rid of him. He's okay at the beginning, she said, so assume the first few times are safe. He'll sit in a chair, hat in hand, like a ventriloquist without a dummy. Don't be fooled for too many sessions. I mean it. He works for the city, I think. He starts off undemanding, but when he gets short-tempered and offers more money, it's time to cut out, unless you're really desperate.

I made the call this time. He had the voice of an old man, which I hadn't expected, a voice too carefully modulated, like that of a retired actor. In white makeup, black-rimmed eyes, and too much rouge, he would pose as if he were still before a camera, although none was focused on his sagging skin, slack muscles, dyed hair. He said he'd be over in an hour.

I stepped into the closet, and asked if Laurel could see me through the slats in the door. It was a deep closet and a stuffy one. The question of props of violence made us nervous, but according to the book, he might only allude to them the first time. If he did bring them, he would surrender the props because, Laurel reasoned, he would be paying for Laurel to use them. In little less than an hour, Carne knocked on the door. He didn't look all that much like a retired actor, but through the crack in the slats, I narrowed my eyes and, by squinting, carried on the illusion of watching Mr. Carne on film. He paid Laurel in cash, then undressed. Laurel took his jacket, shirt, trousers. She wouldn't let him hang them up but threw the clothes at my feet. Laurel wasn't exactly sure what she should do with Mr. Carne. She waited for his cues. Where's the other girl? he asked. He knew that someone else had called him. She'll be here any minute, Laurel said. She went on talking, but she wasn't sure what he wanted to hear. He got undressed. Carne had once been a strong man, he still had the dents of old muscles in his ass, but he looked unfortunate, ugly, and pathetic seen naked from behind. Helpless-looking, alone in a dim hotel room, he could easily be taken for a lost outpatient. He sat in a chair, then stood up and walked toward the closet. I felt him look at my eyes as I peered through the slats. Carne turned his back. He hadn't seen me. Laurel's voice grew shaky. She looked toward the closet. Perhaps she wanted me to come out and hit Carne, to end her performance, but he had seen the look and walked toward the slatted doors. I could see him coming through the slivers of space. I wanted to watch what would happen as if it were happening to someone else. It wasn't even a matter of a missed cue. I was entirely separate from the roles played out before me. I just watched. He smirked in a numb sort of way, as if even his suspicions of a voyeur in the closet were as routine as his performance. Then he stopped, took off his glasses, rubbed his hands against his sides, turned around, and told Laurel to get undressed. She turned off the light.

In the dark I slowly and soundlessly lowered myself to the floor, like a terrified child. Sweating, huddled in a corner in the closet, I strained my eyes to make out the hands of my watch. It was an activity, a job to concentrate on. Laurel made no noise. Grunts and garbled words were coming from Carne, but I couldn't make any of them out. I stood up again, careful not to jangle hangers, remembering that when it was over Laurel would have to open the closet door a little to retrieve his clothes. They were lying in a heap a few inches away and I wondered if I had gotten any footprints on them. Sounds of a heavy man sitting on the edge of an old bed. Light went on. The door opened a crack, and I saw Laurel's hand reach into the closet. She must have been crouching on the floor. I gave Carne's clothes a slight, invisible nudge with my foot. She took them and the door shut. He dressed and I heard him leave. I leaned against the closet wall but stayed inside until Laurel whispered it was all right to come out.

She went into the bathroom and dressed more quickly than I would have thought possible. Laurel wanted to get out of the place immediately. Whether she had stolen his wallet or it had fallen out as he left, I never knew, but she had it. Inside was another thousand dollars, a few credit cards, a social-security card, and a driver's license, which said he was fifty-seven. As we picked up our things, the telephone rang. We could hear it as we locked the door behind us. Perhaps it was A. Astor.

We didn't use the credit cards, just took the money and dropped his wallet on a park bench. Someone might find the cards and use them. We walked to my apartment. Laurel fell asleep, but I stayed awake.

Mr. Regozin would have the story properly finished. You can't just leave us dangling, he would tell the scripter. We don't believe you when you say you don't remember what happened afterward. The alternative, the excuse that the story is entirely true, and the outcome was out of your hands, that won't wash either. *That's the way the plot actually wound up*, you suddenly recall. *The fate of the characters is absolutely the complete truth as it happened*. The reader may never believe it, but what really happened is ordinary and credible. Mr. Regozin would cut the advertising budget for the story because it couldn't possibly sell as it stood, but this, the scripter will say, is the truth. He wouldn't want me to get away with nothing more than a few nights of insomnia, and Laurel to suffer no more than narcolepsy.

I thought about leaving, and if I had been anxious, I might have left or I might have confessed. If the memory of L. Carne made me feel guilty, I might have walked into the Ninth Precinct house or any precinct house and just blurted it all out but I didn't. There are scenes in movies, from *Vertigo* to *Star Wars*, scenes so familiar they are almost clichés: characters on the edge of a window or a rocky ledge, and you know they are going to be rescued, but the degree of anxiety is such that I've always imagined, if that were me, I'd get it over with and jump to end the sick feeling in my stomach. In the week after the incident at the hotel, it was as if the ledge was extended and I had no vertigo, no need to jump, to confess and get it over with. I didn't worry about L. Carne catching up with me in any legal way. We behaved as if we lived in a marginal, unmapped, or at least rarely recognized part of the city, where no one would look for us. Our buildings didn't have intercoms or lobbies. The halls hadn't been painted in decades.

Some pages, especially toward the end of Janet Ling's book, contained lists of shopping errands, calls to be made, letters to be written, and small caricatures of male and female faces which she must have drawn while waiting for someone to pick up the telephone. Ordinary lists had different implications when framed in the black book. Notes to remember to call her landlord or to return library books were no longer simple reminders. Why did the woman who worked under the name Janet Ling have to call her landlord, and what books did she take out of the library? I tried to look at the black book as if it were a notebook for a writer. The names were fictional, made-up characters for a novella. That characters were traded like baseball cards between different "writers" was a demonstration of inventiveness. Janet Ling was a pen name. But L. Carne had answered Laurel's telephone call, he had traveled downtown to the Metropole Arms. I can't pretend it's just a story, any more than I believe Janet Ling had a job just like any other. Was I desperate for a fairy tale to explain away these notebook entries as being nothing more than a series of oddballs made up by a woman with a lively imagination? Not only did I want to rob the entries in the book of their actual lives, but I wanted to transform Janet Ling as well. Maybe, Laurel said, she's all right as she is.

Even though Laurel lived in Janet Ling's building, she asked me to return the black book. We divided the money. Laurel insisted I take a third although I hadn't really done anything. Taking out the part we had to pay Janet, Laurel walked me to the hall, pointed downstairs, and told me which door to knock on. I had never met Janet Ling. All I knew was they had made their arrangement in the laundromat. A voice with a slight Brooklyn accent asked who was there. I said I was a friend of Laurel's and I had her book. I was going to say *black* book, but the apartment doors were close together and the walls thin. Anyone could have heard me. *Black book.* It had a sinister sound. She opened the door. Janet was wearing a navy-blue suit with no shirt underneath, and her short hair looked wet. She was barefoot and tall. She wore nothing, it seemed, except that suit and a few jade rings, the kind you can buy on the street in Chinatown. I wanted to poke around her apartment and ask her about the entries in her book. Maybe I wanted her to tell me all those Astors and Napleses were just characters, and she didn't know why an L. Carne had actually answered our call and arrived at the hotel. Behind her I could see boxes full of clothing, dishes, and a lampstand. She was leaving for Los Angeles in a few days. I handed her the book and two hundred dollars. Laurel had told me she would say goodbye to Janet later. (We still referred to her by that name.) Perhaps she wanted to see her alone. Once we were paid up, I don't know if Laurel ever did see her again. For days afterward I would stop to look at navy-blue suits when I saw them in shop windows and jade rings laid out on tables on the street. Janet looked so unbusiness-like with wet hair, a half-empty apartment behind her; she negated what a suit meant. When she opened the door and I handed her the book across the threshold, I had hoped she would ask me in, but she only counted the twenties, thanked me, and shut the door. She didn't ask me whom we had contacted or how it had gone. She moved her lips as she counted twenty, forty, sixty, eighty, one hundred.

I still watched the two or three women down the street, although I didn't actually ever see them soliciting. I only saw them standing alone, one on each side of the block, standing and standing for hours. I only saw them waiting, but they seemed more alert than bored, even then. I asked Laurel if she'd thought what it would have been like to have had no choice but to buy Janet Ling's black book, no choice but to use it for years? Laurel wouldn't talk about it again. Carne became an incident, then an anonymity, a finished and lost hour. We used his money, forgot about him, mostly, and I continued to watch the women on my block as if they knew something I didn't.

So if L. Carne, like Martin, was equally lost and so easily washed off, what will end up mattering? If most of memory is vague, embarrassing detritus, conversations one was ashamed of ever having had, gestures which in retrospect seem clownish (at best), then I think of myself as one of those long, flexible pencils, the ones which erase what they write as they mark along.

I hadn't seen Martin in several months. I couldn't find some of my Electra drawings, and I imagined he had them, although I knew he didn't. Electra standing behind video monitors as if they were part of her spaceship, Electra fanning herself with an orange fly swatter, Electra refusing Lolo's spaghetti with clam sauce. Sometimes I scanned posters which advertised performances and concerts or offered help and solace for all kinds of problems. Brick walls, lampposts, boarded-up buildings are full of these fragments. They read as if fixed newspapers. Martin's name was never on one of them, but I looked for his name there. He might have become an actor, a musician, an apartment painter, a private tutor of algebra or languages. So much about him was incomplete or made up, he could be doing anything.

Martin had once told me he would be disconsolate if he could no longer see me. After he left I looked up "disconsolate" in the dictionary. It meant what I thought it meant. In Martin's absence I couldn't imagine him sitting in his overlit greenish rooms in despair. If he thought "disconsolate" meant something else, what word could he have meant? I'll be delighted if I don't see you again? I'll be spinning in circles if I don't see you again?

The photograph on the cover of *Covert Action* was of Greek women hanging by the neck. At first I thought it was retouched or somehow blurred and not accurate. Their necks were too elongated, like fashion illustrations, like the ones in the *Times*, whose figures have severely turned-up noses; the advertisements Eamonn said always use the word "American." In the photograph, all the women are young; they are all hanging from the same tree, as if they had grown from it. The expression on their faces is so horrible, the registration of terror is absolute. They are dressed as if they've just been taken from their houses. The picture was shot in Greece, presumably by a Nazi photographer. Their necks were so long. I must have seen photographs of hanged men before, but I couldn't get away from this photograph. I was rooted to the spot. It was the kind of picture which returns while you wait for a train, suck at a paper cut at your desk, or are woken up by the telephone.

The magazine was in the window of a bookstore on East Sixteenth Street. The store was between two newly renovated and very expensive restaurants full of flowers, paintings, real and *faux marbre* panels. From the street you can see into one kitchen where young men in white grill marlin flown in from Hawaii, or cut smoked goose into paper-thin slices.

What do I think about Eamonn? What do I remember exactly? What is dimly remembered, and what has been entirely forgotten? There was one postcard, a few letters, and there have been no telephone calls, only messages. There are all his things here which are supposed to jar memory into those rehearsals in which I recall the time when he was . . . or I did . . . Those bits of things really are just a string with clips to hold strips of negatives and a box containing out-of-date rolls of film. They don't suddenly speak with his voice or develop cracks which resemble his profile, although they do smell like him, because he often had a filmy, chemical smell. Like Electra enjoying the solitude of outer space, in spite of her pleasure, there was an irrevocable moment when she headed toward Earth. My situation seemed, to use the language of Loonan's Electra, full of impossible and blinding contradictions. The amnesia began to wear off. Photographs realigned themselves, had meaning again, even hinted at stories.

Here's one possibility. When the Mets won the World Series, we went downtown to watch the parade. We stood on Broadway near Wall Street. The air was full of paper snow. Everything was being thrown out of offices. Floor after floor poured out middle management's memos, director's letters, president's reports, all kinds of documents, pages from telephone directories. The financial district generates so much paper and it was all tumbling out as if the world were about to end. (The Series had been won, after all, and now, if the world was to be finished off, things could proceed.) "What if all this represented the end of capitalism instead?" Eamonn asked. The air was thick with torn pages and crumpled papers; the bits rose to our ankles. Next it would rise to our knees; we would be smothered in ticker tape, pages of law journals, *The Financial Times*, and receipts from yesterday's lunches. The pictures from that afternoon are grainy, full of bits of faces and arms poking out behind the paper storm: an end of a hot dog, a hat without a head underneath it, things isolated by masses of ticker tape. I began to pick up bits of paper, looking for any sort of handwritten message. Eamonn stopped taking pictures and began to do the same. *I love the Mets! I love Keith Hernandez! The thirty-ninth floor of Cadwallader, Wickersham, & Taft loves the Mets! I love Mookie Wilson!* Some of the messages were followed by telephone numbers. Eamonn found a plain *We love you* and he gave it to me, or perhaps I found that message and gave it to him. I no longer remember. I think it's lying crumpled in a desk drawer with a fortune from a fortune cookie that was significant only by chance, and that significance, too, is pretty much forgotten. (The simplest, most inane, useless, yet saved expression. Cheapest, yet sought after. Said somewhere every second. It's almost one word.)

So there are all these reminders, and sometimes they have a life of their own. Sometimes they are animated and raucous. Sometimes they are dry husks, deaf-mutes, relics out of context, and therefore rendered mysterious, at best.

The photograph was labeled August 1981. A newspaper article was clipped to it. The article was about the owner of Quality Meats of El Salvador. One hundred neatly decapitated bodies had been found outside the towns of Santa Ana, Sonsonate, and Izalco. Thirty-three heads which didn't match any of the bodies were found along different roads not far away. Little blood, clean naked bodies, so sharp and methodical, impossible to make positive identification, I read. And there was evidence against Quality Meats, whose owner was both a wealthy industrialist and a formerly institutionalized lunatic. He had a house in Florida. The plant's machinery had been kept running twenty-four hours a day and bodies were found near it. Two workers said they thought the slaughterhouse was being used for nightly executions. Then they disappeared. A few days later, the reporter, who wrote for a Mexican paper, had to seek refuge in the Mexican embassy. I wondered if Eamonn had been the photographer. The black-and-white print was of a brick building with trucks in front, but there were no signs in Spanish or English. The photograph could have been taken almost anywhere. I might have looked for his passport and checked its stamps and dates, or I could have just asked him, but he was far away and so were his identification papers. I didn't want to look through Eamonn's papers anymore, and when he returned I wouldn't want him to know that I had opened this big manila envelope and looked inside. Looking approached the same kind of trespass, almost the same kind of terror as walking into Quality Meats itself.

If I had gone to Quality Meats, if I had been the one with the camera, I would have been afraid to leave my hotel room and doubted I would have had the forethought to locate the Mexican embassy just in case . . . Though I knew, even from the distance of New York, *just in case* . . . would certainly happen. The owner of Quality Meats had been charged with the murders of two land-reform advisors and the head of the Salvadoran agrarian reform institute. The murders had taken place at the Sheraton Hotel. Charges had been dropped.

"Did you photograph the death conveyor belts? How did you get out of the city, out of the country?" I didn't ask.

"How did it feel to be in the factory where all this happened? Were you afraid of being caught, of being next, Nikon knocked from your hands and smashed on the concrete floor?" I went on not asking.

One of the reasons I stayed with Eamonn had to do with

the image of the broken camera. He had always survived, so by the end of each story, by the time he returned from each trip, it was safe to look back and agree that he was invulnerable. During his absences, images of the risks he took, however unconfirmed, seemed important. Obvious practical matters lost their concreteness in comparison. Occasionally, even as a temporary colorist, I have been sloppy and could walk away from a job badly done, knowing I needed the money but not caring all that much about the Loonans, Regozins, or the audience, not caring whether or not I would be hired again. Stop being a colorist, then, Laurel had said. I could easily stop being a colorist on the terms demanded of me. I could come and go and not take the superheroes seriously, but the image of the broken camera still made me anxious, even if I myself was safe in my apartment, and it wasn't Eamonn behind the supposedly splintered lens. There was always the possibility. In theory, almost anyone can take a picture.

A cool red, a hot blue.

Eamonn can behave with Electra-like heroism without ever stepping from the darkroom/bathroom into the strip. Like her, he knows, he just always knows where the escape hatch and the secret buttons are. They seem fearless. I live with both of them; they change places, and it doesn't seem to matter. She can behave with his vision without stepping from the strip to that squinting, winking place behind the lens. If they are brave, the reader might think I'm a coward; a wet noodle cowering behind a paintbrush.

My apartment no longer seemed like my apartment. It was a room of transit. I would watch the clock: four more hours, three more hours, two and a half more to go until it would be time to leave. The familiar will seem unfamiliar and useless. What do you do with these socks, this broom? It's too hot for wool and too late to clean, no reason to. *Occasionally there is a way out*, Laurel had said. *You find yourself with wads of crinkled cash and a stolen credit card that will probably be good for twenty-four hours*. We hadn't used the credit card; I only imagined leaving. Another goodbye, the big one, the real one. Someone will ask me if I have the letters of transit. It's supposed to be a joke, but in a dim way I'll feel that there was some document I might need and don't have. At immigration, officers will demand more than a passport. A document of history, intention, stated purpose. Whom are you going to visit? What does she do? How did you meet him? How long have you known her? It doesn't have to be in writing, you can make the statement orally if you let us record it. Letters of transit no longer exist. All you need is a passport, but that seems too simple. I hang up the telephone and turn the answering machine back to zero.

The airport bar is dark, orange, hard to find. Marco Polo is on the television. Richard Chamberlain meets the King of Shanghai or Ceylon. I can't quite hear the sound. Only a few people in the airport bar look like travelers. If you work in the airport you might go to a bar like this one after work because it's close, because some of the people you work with live on Staten Island or Long Island and the JFK lounge is the closest place you all could get to before everyone goes home. The airport lounge keeps cardboard displays on most tables. The folded photographs show three kinds of drinks. I make dents with my thumbnail in the glossy margaritas, trace pale yellow and pink umbrellas on the other side. I don't want to talk to the man who looks as if he's slept in his black suit and chain-smokes short cigarettes. I'm always behind this kind of man in lines, never behind the ones who look as if they have just gotten out of the shower. There is no one to say to the camera, I saw her just before she got on the plane.

Other versions: I'm not alone yet. A few friends come to see me off, to say goodbye. Edmund Wilson wrote that he and John Bishop were afraid to see Edna St. Vincent Millay off to Europe. They were afraid of whom they might meet, other lovers on the pier. Actually I think I'll say goodbye to everyone separately. I'm not an auburn-haired poet, it isn't 1920, no amount of mental dimness or wishful thinking will turn Kennedy Airport into a midnight waterfront or transform a cheap flight into a lovely boat. I would play all the roles in my 1920 departure, waving to anxious suitors in striped suits twisting bunches of gladiolas on the pier. I would find no flattery in scenes certain to be embarrassing. If I left I wouldn't want anyone to see me off.

Marco Polo learned about gunpowder.

Waiting near the gate, one of the passengers looked like John Huston. I took this as a good sign.

Everyone on the plane would sleep but me. Back in the airport bar, Marco Polo kissed a Chinese girl for the first time.

I read in the paper about the captain of a Staten Island Ferry who was bored at his job, going back and forth across the Upper Bay. One day during evening rush hour, with a boat full of passengers, he headed for Tangiers instead of Battery Park. He got past the Narrows, past Lower Bay, and well into the Atlantic Ocean before the Coast Guard caught up with him.

I didn't go to the airport. I hardly left my apartment except to go a few blocks' distance, and felt extremely uneasy about going any farther than that. I thought about traveling but didn't leave. I had a certain attachment to things as they were and was afraid if I left, whatever flimsy constructs I relied upon would fall apart. I could take Electra with me, could take

Eamonn's absence and my embarrassment about Martin, but could not take Laurel. Some of my life traveled easily, other parts were immobile. I thought about the airport, and thought about it for too long. Someone might have found L. Carne's gold American Express card a few seconds after we deliberately dropped his wallet, and that person might have gone to the airport in a flash, but I had no cards, genuine or stolen, and I stayed where I was.

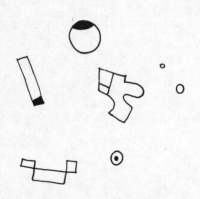

A last letter arrived from Eamonn. He had stayed at Saint Paul's Crescent before, but this time what little money he had left from Driscoll's original payment was quickly running out. When he first arrived, he stuck his camera away in a box, as if it were an ostracized troublemaker. Even those who had known him as a photographer never saw it, and when they asked what he was working on, he would say it had been stolen, he wasn't working at all. He considered selling the Nikon and went so far as to take it to a few shops. Without the sense of purpose which his camera had given him for years, he wandered aimlessly in the city. He had used his Irish passport to enter England and had gone straight to London.

Prince Faisal as a boy lying on the palace floor in the middle of a dark marble gallery. Buster Keaton in a white shirt and black trousers, obviously off the set, looking lonely and deserted. The Cecil Beaton photographs were like flies in amber but assembled carefully, without the fly's accidental fall, and composed with a theatricality which usually escaped Eamonn's eye.

War photographs: A woman mailing a letter. She was perfectly dressed, a fashion photograph, everything around her had been demolished except for an intact letter box. A picture titled *The Hairdresser*, a mannequin head in the middle of acres of rubble. Eamonn looked more closely at these, but at the end of the afternoon, the Beaton pictures only made him feel more paralyzed. It had been cheating to look at them. He tried to sell his camera again. It was used and he couldn't get what he thought it was worth. He waited a few more days.

The tour of Highgate Cemetery was led by a woman with long white hair. She spoke about the preservation of landmarks and asked for donations first. At the gates she described the Victorian attitude toward death, their Sunday outings at Highgate, where they would chat about bad cousins, crazy aunts, or reclusive uncles. It was while watching one of these picnics, the tour guide said, that Bram Stoker got the idea for *Dracula*. Queen Victoria had all her staff buried here, regardless of rank. The head of her stables (horse figure on his stone) was buried near a famous boxer (boxing gloves weathered to lumps). Notice, she went on, Egyptian and Greek sculpture, very few crosses or signs of martyrdom. Eamonn felt he had joined a

Sunday afternoon necrophilia society. The tour guide berated Karl Marx, who was buried in the new part of the cemetery. She referred to Marx's youngest daughter as Eleanor Aveling, although she hadn't ever married the man she lived with. In a loud voice she told the group that Eleanor had committed suicide as if it were an undisputed fact. He wandered away from the crowd. Aveling had been suspected of Eleanor's murder. When family portraits were displayed his own nieces and nephews were not allowed to know which picture was his. Only when they were over twenty-one was the identity of his photograph revealed. Only then were they told the story of wicked Uncle Edward. The rows of more recent stones were covered with roses, gladiolas, lilies, asters, and chrysanthemums in loose bunches, formal bouquets, and wreaths. On a child's grave (d. 1938) lay a headless doll which looked relatively new.

Across the road Eamonn found Karl Marx's grave and noticed that although the stone mentioned other family members, Marx's illegitimate son, Freddy Demuth, was not among them. As he turned to leave, a fat young man in mirrored sunglasses yelled at Marx's guerrilla-like stone head. He screamed about fucked-up Poland and fucked-up Czechoslovakia. Eamonn wondered if the man would have allowed him to take his picture, but he didn't have his camera with him. It was a pointless imaginary request, and he seemed to grow angrier as Eamonn stared at him.

He heard a dosser taunt two policemen, telling them they were the prime minister's personal thugs. He saw graffiti in Brixton which read *Free Winston Pilcock*, and under it a boy wrote, *In every box of corn flakes*. Eamonn could have taken his picture before he ran away, but he didn't have his camera.

He walked through Kentish Town as it grew dark. People were still outside trimming rosebushes and tinkering in their gardens, and it seemed to each of them, and to Eamonn himself, that nothing serious had happened that day.

When he returned to the flat, one of the upstairs residents, having heard he was a photographer, asked if he would do a job, and at first he turned it down. A friend of a friend, a distant relative or a neighbor, he wasn't sure what the connection was, but it was a wedding job. Not the kind of thing I do, he had said, and then he changed his mind.

Women in blue, pale green, and pink veils; the men on one side, the women on the other; parents on one side, children altogether, *that's it*. He borrowed a suit and chatted with the musicians and the caterers. One of the musicians clued him in as to when to take the pictures. Eamonn really had no idea. When they come out of the church, the organist said, then one of the bride and groom alone, the bride alone, the whole family, the flower girl and the ring bearer alone. The bride's name was Fiona, the organist said, and her father was in assurance. The groom was not a young man of good prospects, the organist didn't know what he did exactly, but the family was not happy about the marriage. They all looked happy. They all smiled for Eamonn, except for a grandmother who looked angrily at the mother of the bride. It was easy and didn't take long. One of the bridesmaids invited him to the reception, but he told her he had to return the suit. Eamonn actually returned it the next day and decided he'd never do that kind of work again, when he got another telephone call.

Eamonn was better at wedding portraits than he thought he would be. The jobs increased. People who were getting married always seemed to know other people who were getting married. He arranged members of the wedding according to their relationship to the bride and groom, according to the colors people wore. He arranged them formally and took their pictures informally as they spoke during the service, and as they ate cake afterward. He spoke to people he sensed were uncomfortable and instinctively separated family members who would later argue with one another, although at times he perversely put two antagonists beside each other and asked them to smile, please. As jobs grew he took along a boy from the squat as his assistant. There was always free food. He learned a lot of bad marriage jokes, told by uncles, mostly. Bored bridesmaids flirted with him. Divorced fathers asked him about his business. He didn't have a business, he just took pictures, he would say. He didn't have cards printed up or stationery with his name at the top; he never thought of the wedding photographs as a business. He learned how to avoid rice showers and not to get his camera caught in billowing veils or trains of tulle during close-up shots. He could always tell who took the proceedings seriously and who couldn't wait to leave.

One job took him to Liverpool. It was the first time he'd been out of London in months and he started to take other kinds of pictures again. Boys playing football in the street, election posters peeling from walls, a woman leaving a wedding on a motorbike.

He shot a racehorse for a newspaper and sold photographs of a wildcat strike to a magazine. Editors called him again, and he began to turn down wedding work. He could have moved out of the house on Saint Paul's Crescent, but he stayed. Driscoll showed no signs of looking for him. He still had the film from the Belfast pictures, undeveloped and hidden, wrapped in a paper bag from the fish-and-chips shop on Cliftonville Road.

For some there are a superfluity of photographs, for others a paucity, Eamonn wrote. The last photograph of Myra Hindley had been taken in 1963, at the time of the Lancashire murders. She had a blond beehive, and sinister wings of black makeup flew out from the corners of her eyes. Twenty-five years later, still unphotographed, she returned to the moors to locate the grave of one of the children she helped murder. The area was cordoned off for one hundred square miles because parents of the murdered children threatened to go after her. One father holding a carving knife had to be stopped at the cordon. Photographers boarded heliocopters and tried to take her picture with telephoto lenses from far above the moor. Reprinted in newspapers, Myra Hindley's blurred head was circled. Her face couldn't be seen. She was wearing a scarf around her head, and sunglasses, although it was winter. On television he briefly saw a broadcast of congressional hearings. An American Marine was ringed by lenses, blue-black and blinking. The Marine smiled a smile which would make you never want to smile again in your life. Shutters snapped like a storm of crickets and he went on smiling.

One day Eamonn got a message that Freddy Driscoll had called. He did not return his call, but Freddy was persistent and left several messages during the following week. Eamonn went north to Scotland for a few days to photograph a duke and duchess who had opened their house to the public. He hoped Freddy Driscoll would give up. When he returned to London, the calls continued. There were two other people presently living in the house, and he asked them to tell Driscoll that he no longer lived there, they didn't know where he was, and he shouldn't call again. The woman who usually answered the telephone said it wasn't a man. Freddy Driscoll was a woman. Her number was written out by the telephone. Eamonn called her. She was a Nell Driscoll's Auntie Freddie. Nell was getting married, and she needed a photographer. He must be very busy, she chattered; she was glad he finally called, and would he do the job? It was a wedding portrait, and had nothing to do with Freddy Driscoll of Staten Island. It would have been difficult to trace Eamonn to Saint Paul's Crescent. He could be found through magazine or newspaper photo credits, but Driscoll would have to be in England, and Eamonn doubted he would know where to look or go to quite so much trouble.

He agreed to photograph Nell's wedding. The brides-maids wore yellow. The flower girls dropped fistfuls of rose petals. His assistant got sick from too much champagne. The idea of Driscoll searching for him seemed absurd and stagily paranoid. When he returned to Saint Paul's Crescent, he canceled all his future jobs and made a reservation on a plane back to New York.

I had seen a sixteenth-century print of Joseph and Potiphar's wife. An unmade bed was between them. She had her hand on Joseph's shoulder, but he had his back to her. He was on his way to the door. According to the story, Potiphar's wife falsely accused Joseph, and he was thrown into prison. Adultery, the desire and potential crime, is pinned on her forever. The bed looks slept in; there is evidence Joseph shouldn't have gotten off scot-free in history. What's a few years in jail by comparison? They aren't wearing biblical costumes but the kind of clothing the artist wore and saw around him. I liked the idea of a story told in two or three panels, but Laurel thought the names of the characters, though accurate, sounded ancient and unattractive.

I came home from a job to find Eamonn in the apartment. Had there been a telephone call? Probably, but I don't remember. I saw the back of his head first, as he was sitting on the floor. It seemed as if he'd never left. To appear and disappear without warning—should I have thrown a frying pan? He didn't duck when he saw me so I could easily have made a direct hit. It never occurred to me to try.

His photographs were spread out all over the floor. There were pictures of an estate in northern England and portraits of the duke and duchess who lived there. Acres of green lawns, coats of arms, a neo-Jacobean gallery, twin leopard-skin rugs with their heads facing each other, and every eating utensil was made of solid silver. The duke and duchess had met when the duke was stationed in Northern Ireland, Eamonn said. They recently opened their house to the public. A friend of Eamonn's had gone to interview them, and Eamonn took the photographs. They had been sold to a travel magazine, but on the apartment floor Eamonn laid them out next to photographs of derelict buildings and a mass funeral. The estate covered thousands of acres. The duchess would have preferred denying the public access to it, because she was afraid the presence of strangers would linger even after they'd gone.

Eamonn told me that he had missed me inordinately. After he went out I looked up "inordinately" in the dictionary. It meant what I thought it meant. In Eamonn's absence I couldn't have imagined his staring out a train window feeling personally hopeless and inconsolable. He was too involved with his camera, and that was what was compelling about him. If he thought inordinately meant something else, what word could he have meant? I missed you occasionally? I thought about you at night? I missed you like a hole in the head?

I've been speaking English for a long time. I know that one person doesn't control definitions. Even words that are subject to changing fashion require more than the idiosyncratic redefinition of an isolated individual to make the new meaning stick. Why do a couple of odd misuses seem to represent language upheaval? Because, in this one case, I'm the object of the upheaval, the misuse, the confusion, no one else is even within earshot.

According to Martin, quoting his book in the middle of the office, the meaning of green was appropriated not by jealousy or envy but by hope. Therefore, the color of Hermes' hat made perfect sense.

Color is taken for granted. You look and it's there. But imagine this isn't so and each person begins life completely color-blind, developing the sense as they grow older. Perception of color might begin with essential primitive totalities, those tiny bits, paper-thin lamina, which contain color universes. An oil slick spreading across a puddle, indigo and sea-green. A soap bubble, a pellicle over whose surface colors chase each other; lilac in pursuit of pink, pink trailing mineral green. Glints on a microscopic branch of frost. Breath misting on a pane of glass; I draw my finger across, write my name, look closely at the droplets. Those delicate sudden-color encyclopedias have brief lives. The glossy surface of film negatives, bent and twisted near a light, when you squint, you see the rainbows.

A few of Eamonn's pictures were in color, but most were

black-and-white. I knew the hooded armed men at the funeral were wearing black. I knew the flag was green, white, and orange, although most of Eamonn's earlier pictures of Derry were photographed in black-and-white. Gradually color crept in. The row houses, the cemetery, the murals of soldiers and crosses with writing splashed across.

Black-and-white often does the job, but at Fantômes black-and-white frames were considered empty, unfinished business. It would have been anathema to suggest they were full of meaning in their incomplete state. Each frame was treated separately, painted with fighting colors. If I worked there now, I would like to leave a scene free of color, a scene which would take place in an ordinary sort of room, the kind of room which would be familiar to most readers but one which Electra herself hadn't ever seen. Black-and-white, black-and-white, making everything as simple as possible.

There was still the chance Fantômes would bring back the *Electra* series. The office would call and ask us if we wanted our old jobs back. Mr. Loonan would not be rehired, but Regozin might find Martin's number in the Rolodex and hire him as a permanent letterer, making my life miserable. The new version would begin with Orion's murder, which would leave Electra free to carry on her own adventures without his interfering shadow. There might be a vague subplot about avenging his death, but it could be overlooked in most episodes. Orion, too, could eventually be resurrected, but I hoped he would lie in neglect. There would be a party when the first issue came out. I would tell Martin I didn't care what happened to the twins, the cab driver, or if he accidentally met his half brother. Laurel would notice the sound-effects library was missing.

Eamonn tried to persuade me to give up being a colorist. He wanted me to learn how to be his assistant when he went on shoots. I had trouble with the idea of taking pictures. It was easier to think about a character and draw him or her in a cartoon, muted by a safety net of caricature and distortion. (A fictional, cartoon Eamonn was easy to draw, effortlessly put in one situation and extricated from another. In his cartoon form Eamonn more or less left me alone, refrained from giving advice, and kept to himself.) Framing, focusing, checking the light, snapping the shutter had, it seemed to me, the calculation of an assassin. Eamonn would say, If you think about betrayal or making fun of someone, then you're only thinking of the photographer (yourself) and you miss the point.

He focused more with one eye than the other, but I'm not sure if it was the left or the right which dominated. In the summer, parts of the camera hardware left momentary impressions on Eamonn's face. Where did the blue aperture of his eye end and the black one of the camera begin? One, though at the beck and call of the optic nerve, is considered thinking and reflective; the other, written off as a purely mechanical invention.

When I asked him about the pictures taken in Belfast, and about the potential betrayal in the undeveloped film still in his possession, he wouldn't talk about it. The wedding pictures and the New York pictures taken since his return were entirely composed, contrived, more formal than any others I could remember. His pictures became functional, as utilitarian as windshield wipers. If I didn't know the story of Quality Meats, I might think it was just a truck in front of a factory loading dock. The building could have been in New Jersey or southern Connecticut. If I don't know the story of the duke and duchess, they look like nice people in their sitting room having tea. The bride is in love with another man, not the groom, but unless you're the bride or a knowing member of the wedding, the picture is a sentimental keepsake, as bland and as ordinary as can be. No secret panic is evidenced in the smiles and billowing tulle. Blue iris blinked. He cleaned his lenses with thin white paper, screwed on the lens cap. *You want me to tell you everything, to lay it all out in a single shot, and I can't do that*, he said.

There's a painting in the Metropolitan by Vermeer, *Girl Asleep*. She's sitting at a table, eyes shut, daydreaming more than actually sleeping soundly. Originally, according to radiographs, a man was painted in the doorway behind her, but Vermeer painted him out, thinking there would be more of a feeling of lovesickness or dreaming if the lover was absent. He painted *Girl Asleep* around 1656, it said on the card next to the picture, shortly after the more explicit Dresden *Procuress* was completed. I searched through the negatives from Eamonn's Irish pictures to look at the woman's face before he obliterated her eyes. I turned on the red light in the bathroom/darkroom. I felt as if the place was full of afterimages which only I could see. Eamonn didn't seem to notice the crowd.

Electra was not supposed to be revived, but the idea of cycles was such an integral part of each series that Laurel and I decided to bring her back, even though it gave an imaginary reader much less reason to trust us. We had been so sure of ourselves. No revival, but we gradually became less sure. We didn't want her to end up as a sacrifice to those who tortured and teased her. We weren't sure she ought to have been killed in the first place. It was difficult to know how to approach her unmitigated sense of dislocation and deracination. We didn't know exactly where she belonged, but that was a problem which, once solved, would finally mean the end of Electra.

EPISODE VI
ELECTRA RETURNS

She regained consciousness and tore her way out of
the garbage bag that Roper's actor had placed her in.
Electra again had no money and wandered back to the
part of the city which had been her home when she first
landed. It had changed in a wholly unexpected way. She
saw people in fur coats who, a few months ago, would
not have even known her neighborhood existed. They
walked small dogs and ignored her and the others who
still lived on the street. She met two men who lived in
a movie theater exit. Sometimes it was possible to enter
the theater when the doors were opened and sit inside
for several double shows. If you were lucky, no one
checked the house between screenings. The theater had
a sticky floor; drifts of withered popcorn accumulated near
the chair legs. Electra was not above eating some when
she was hungry. The stage was covered by a torn red
curtain, and Electra planned to look behind it if she could
manage to stay in the theater past closing time. Finally,
after one midnight show, she did. Backstage was full of
interesting and baffling junk: an old projector which resembled her image duplicator, a box of gloves and mittens
which had no mates were among the things Electra
looked through. The lights in the theater didn't match
and were twisted in different directions, as if they'd just
had an argument. She thought of the two men who lived
in the exit as lovers who could meet only in the movies.

Laurel's version of the story drifted from Electra to the
two men who lived in the theater exit. The movie house in
which I had placed them was, in actuality, being gutted and
turned into some sort of urban shopping mall. Laurel didn't
know where the two men would go once construction was

complete. They had no place in the series either, but she couldn't get rid of them. Laurel accused me of imposing new situations on Electra, one after the next, as if she had no will of her own, or whatever bit of will she did possess was nearly useless. So the two homeless men who hoarded cans and bottles in order to turn them in for a refund, who huddled together for warmth although they may or may not have been lovers, who may not have had a clue as to what that word meant anymore, who, if they were told that word, would have been confused or shrugged—they entered the story. To be lovers it helps to have a place to live and you need money, and a job wouldn't hurt, because it keeps you out of the house. Laurel drew them in empty frames. They filled each square with their shopping bags and empty bottles. She wanted them to become rich and lucky overnight. Then the two would have a place or places to live, and if they weren't lovers, each might find someone to be in love with. They wouldn't need jobs, but what would they do with their endless spare time and disposable income? In one frame they met with their account ants. In another frame they had fittings for dress suits. None of these was worth pursuing as a story. In a third, they were on their boat, cruising in the Caribbean. The boat landed in Haiti, on a shore which seemed deserted. They came across an abandoned hut which was occupied by a former member of Baby Doc's Tonton Macoute. He had been reduced to living a tropical version of their lives in the movie exit. They argued as to whether or not to take him aboard. One said yes, he'd had a hard life, he'd no doubt reformed, let's take him on. The other said, "Are you crazy? The Tonton Macoute have been killing and torturing Haitians for decades. He made a choice to earn a living by inflicting pain on innocent people.

"Imagine he goes to your house looking for you, and when he can't find you, he shoots your wife. You run into the jungle and live on mangoes. You are caught and put into a jail cell filled with so many other men that no one can even sit down. You escape, and if you get on a boat, also very crowded, you might make the seven-hundred-mile trip to Florida. It takes seventeen days without compass or maps. You avoid the United States warships in the Windward Passage. It is spring, and you hope the trade winds shift in your favor. If you are lucky, and the boat doesn't capsize, you might make it, or your body might simply be washed up on a beach near Miami."

The second formerly homeless man wondered how and where the first learned all this. Number 2 said, "Think about unemployment. Perhaps that was the only kind of work he could get." Number 1 replied that was no excuse. While they were arguing, Laurel needed something to be going on in the frame visually. The former Tonton Macoute crept behind them as they spoke, ran along the beach, and stole their boat. The two men would be left in Haiti, impoverished again, and unable to speak French. I said that they couldn't be entirely broke. They would have to have credit cards by now, property, and social connections. They could always get back to New York. Laurel asked if I had ever seen a credit card in a comic like *Electra*. Money didn't exist in a graphic way, but it was very important as a concept.

We kept coming back to the two men and Electra stuck with each other in the movie theater. Money was something none of them had. Long voyages were out of the question. The movie changed every week or so, but during any single week they could see the same picture over twenty times. Memorizing various parts, they relinquished their personalities to become those they saw repeated on the screen over and over. They repeated lines to each other they would never have said otherwise and treated each other in a manner completely out of character. Their mimicry stopped short of kissing, slapping, and murdering. When gestures of this sort were called for, they faked it.

Laurel was at a loss as to how to help her characters survive. If any of them ventured out of the movie theater to beg or look for food, he or she would risk not being able to get back inside. In the cold, it was a difficult decision to have to consider: sacrificing food for shelter or relinquishing shelter for food. These were circumstances her original publisher had ignored. There had always been money and food in space. At Fantômes Laurel hadn't ever drawn so much as a sandwich or a dime, but it was understood the characters had access to whatever ensured basic survival under ordinary circumstances. Characters were subject to all kinds of threats in space, but starvation, undramatic and without obvious bad guys, was a rarity. Even now, she had free license to draw all of them as millionaires but couldn't logically get them out of the movie theater.

I drew Electra's street. It was night, it was empty, and then I lightened the sky. I needed daylight. I drew Eamonn walking down the traffic meridian, taking pictures of shells of buildings and the scaffolding of new construction. The cartoon Eamonn had given up taking pictures of anything but the erosion of the city. It was constantly being torn down, erasing itself, and being rebuilt. (I drew examples of some of his photographs: bricked-up windows painted over to look inhabited, exposed sides of buildings in which each floor was painted or papered differently, like a dollhouse blown apart; wrecking ball smashing into a red tenement; *Stephen Spielberg Go Home* written on the side of one building, part of a movie set faked to look like a crumbling squat.) Eamonn left the meridian, crossed Allen Street, and found Electra living in a new refrigerator box. At first he nearly walked by. The homeless don't like having their pictures taken. (In flashback frames, they threatened Eamonn as he focused. Black-and-white represent memory and the past tense. Otherwise, the serial was nearly always in the present and in color.) He assumed she wouldn't want her picture taken, but she was asleep and so he did. For the first time in months, Eamonn took a photograph of something other than ruins or anonymous construction. I drew Eamonn frantically cutting negatives and printing them over and over, holding them up to the light, but the images of Electra hadn't registered. He was certain he had taken her picture. There was film in the camera. Pictures taken before and after hers came out perfectly. The darkroom scenes weren't very interesting as drawings, just as Eamonn's face registering shock, but the point was that this was Electra's talent on earth: she could resist duplication.

If I made Eamonn into a character, should I have put myself into the serial as well? I could draw myself drawing myself, drawing myself into infinity. Eamonn, however, lent himself well to comics because he knew how to behave heroically. In every episode he told me of, he instinctively made those kinds of choices. Eamonn tended to do the right thing, to at least attempt rescue even indirectly, even if he failed. As a comic figure, there was something a little ordinary about him, something pedestrian about his patrolling the streets with his camera. Hardcore realism is only narrowly believable in comics. I'd say almost never. It's undermined by the format, seen as an exaggeration. People aren't really living in burned, crumbling buildings. It's not that bad. These fibs can't truly be the facts. If he saw these drawings, would he be angry at the way he'd been represented? Like me sulking before the camera. Well, that's just too bad for you, we say to each other.

You hear stories about haunted people, objects, or figures in paintings which refused to appear in photographs. There were no explanations. Eamonn didn't believe in these absences any more than he believed in the ghosts of dead people reported to have been seen in photographs taken of living relatives. "How did that woman in a big hat, she's sort of smoky-looking as if translucent and out of focus, how did she get behind you when I know no one was standing there?" This was not a question Eamonn couldn't answer. Old film, accidental double exposure. Eamonn was too pragmatic for cartoon caricature. I rolled the drawings into a tube and put them inside a roll of paper so they wouldn't be found again for a while.

I wouldn't want him to see the drawings. He might laugh at them; then we would both laugh together, but I didn't want Eamonn to make assumptions about how I saw him. Everything he observed contributed to his attitude of superiority. Not the nose-in-the-air kind, but the way he always understood so well and never appeared to need a second explanation. So Electra went down the tube. She had no audience. She resisted duplication.

I dropped all kinds of things down the middle of the long roll of paper: fingernail clippings, failed cartoons which I wasn't certain I wanted to throw away, a postcard from Martin. Although mailed from a few blocks away, it was a depiction of the Resurrection from a church in Padua. Mary Magdelene was on her knees reaching out toward the risen Christ. I hadn't written back.

If Martin were incorporated into the strip, he might be that wrong man, the one met accidentally, the disaster who leaves Electra obsessed with the most trivial memories. Or he might be the one who straightens her out, marries her, teaches her the meaning of money, instructs her in the idiomatic twists and turns of the English language, and this would turn into another kind of domination. The postcard read, *I hope you had a happy New Year*. It was early June. Finally, months later, this shred of evidence came in the mail. It was the only proof I had that Martin ever existed. The postcard was like an alarm which shrieked that I couldn't be entirely rid of him and that if I continued to pretend he had disappeared, there might continue to be surprises in the mail. The gesture of saving anything of his seemed mawkish, but not knowing what to do with the Giotto postcard, and not quite able to toss it, I dropped the card down the tube. If I did suddenly go to the airport and got on a plane, and if Eamonn, Laurel, or anyone else found the detritus stashed in the roll of paper, they might entirely misread these things as secret and precious. What the contents really represented were objects in limbo, a source of confusion, nothing else.

Besides resisting duplication on earth, Electra, as Mr. Regozin had complained, never fell in love with the wrong person. She was never duped in that way. I myself was good at this. I was often duped. When I woke, the object of obsession seemed so spectacularly trivial and insignificant; the person hard to remember, impossible to identify in a crowd. I pulled out the Giotto card. Blue sky peeling from the wall, symmetric stars, soldiers framed off from the rest, sleeping in a corner. I didn't like the way Mary Magdalene's hands reached out, and she looked as if she was being pushed away. I wasn't sure of the story, perhaps Magdalene wasn't being shunned, but I couldn't read the figures any other way. I threw out the post-card, then retrieved it and slid the thing back down the tall roll of drawing paper. The painting was about resurrection and that's what kept happening to Electra. It seemed worth putting in tube purgatory as a future reference.

The wrong man or woman, the misplaced object of de-sire, failed to appear on Allen Street. Like the solitary Loonan, I kept Electra for myself. When I drew compelling ne'er-do-wells and planted them on the traffic meridian, the story broke down. Endings, happy or otehwise, were hinted at by the appearance of potential partners, whether the characters I invented for Electra were satisfactory nice guys, hopeless cases, or dangerous felons. After all, Electra's approach to life on earth was still syncretic. She was not entirely converted to human behavior. Dr. Atlas hadn't genetically coded her for anything remotely resembling excursions into romance. Whether this was due to cynicism, some kind of oversight, or repression was unrecorded. I could have had the code changed when she entered the earth's atmosphere but I didn't. Electra had formed an attachment to Lolo, but Lolo was too dangerous to bring back, and Laurel considered Lolo a stuffed parrot of a character, not an appropriate object of veneration or obsession. Electra was as cautious on Allen Street as she had been in space. She applied the same rules to chance collisions with doormen as she had to meteors or random messages from Orion. She ignored them. She slept through Eamonn's stymied photography session.

There were some basic problems with the serial. It moved laterally, just as it had at Fantômes. Electra wasn't getting anywhere. Earth, for her, was a mistake. We kept going back to her landing beside Cleopatra's Needle in the park and tried to rewrite her fate. We found that once she had abandoned the package of money, her choices narrowed considerably.

Electra discovered a book in the garbage on the morphology of the English language, and it suddenly occurred to her that every creature she had ever encountered in space (her memory was returning) had spoken English. The book didn't explain how this had happened. The same garbage can contained a book on Esperanto, which she learned quickly and often tried to speak to the odd policeman or shopper. Knowledge of the internal structure of the forms of words was useful, but Electra got carried away. Frames became filled by speech and thought balloons. Image retreated until it wasn't even a sliver at the bottom of the page. In comic terms, it was a disaster. We made rules about limiting thought balloons and establishing dialogue quotas. Every fourth frame had to contain a holophrase or no language at all.

As previously noted, Allen Street had changed during Electra's imprisonment in Lenny's warehouse. As she learned more about human behavior and language, she began to steal. At first she stole only for personal survival, but eventually Electra stole altruistically. Her victims were always those who could well afford the loss, and she never hurt them. The beneficiaries of her crimes were people who lived on the street. It was a facile story with a ready-made morality that didn't even begin with any ambiguities. We succeeded in bringing action back into the serial, but we did so at the risk of reducing the story to the simplest possible series of causes and effects. We had enough situations for several episodes and each frame seemed to draw itself predictably. Language could have been dispensed with altogether. It was what Electra had always meant to do: heroics. Realism (long shot of a tense meridian; close-up of each wallet, each gold cigarette case, each diamond, each Rolex) battled science fiction (some man's exercise of an imaginary world which was chock-full of received ideas about life beyond Mars. It was nothing but Earth all over again with different props). There was a vicarious satisfaction to be had from stealing diamonds. If realism had been a consideration, Electra would be caught red-handed once in a while, perhaps often, and speaking Esperanto to a police officer would do nothing to prevent her from landing in jail.

There were so many pieces missing. *Why did you save all the negatives from the wedding pictures, pictures of people whose*

names you no longer remember, people you were never intro-
duced to in the first place, and you carried all of it back from
London? The old wedding negatives were left around, as if
Eamonn expected someone to visit who might want to look
at them. In negatives, the bride wears black. If I cared about
a neat and tidy apartment, I would have had a fit, but this
gave me license to leave cartoons tacked haphazardly on the
walls. The pictures of the *Grace O'Malley* were nowhere to
be found, and again, in asking Eamonn, I got something less
than a straight answer.

Grace O'Malley spoke English and so did her prey. The
Spanish galleon, Dutch or French ships didn't interest her
very much. She got tired of robbing colonialists, tired of being
a pirate on what was, for the Elizabethans, a global scale. One
evening Grace O'Malley knocked on the door of Howth Castle.
Whoever answered the door thought she was a wild animal
and wouldn't let her in, so she kidnapped their smallest boy
playing in the drive. She would return him only if they promised to lay a place at their table for a stranger every night. The
family agreed, and the boy did not grow up to be a pirate.
Eamonn, I said, I ask a simple question, and I get a bedtime
story for an answer. Did he mean the business about the boat
off the coast of Maine was a red herring or a dead end? It
seemed to be over, finished, and the bathroom was festooned
with the evidence of distant, unnamed marriages.

A friend of a friend, a telephone call out of nowhere led Laurel to a man who made reproductions for the Metropolitan Museum. His name was Jack Ladder, and when she called he said he wanted to see her immediately. As Laurel assembled storyboards and books from Fantômes as examples of her work, she began to feel the interview would be useless. She zippered her black portfolio shut, then sat in a chair and watched sunlight hit a plant. A family of five now lived in Janet Ling's old apartment. They left their front door open and often spilled out into the hall.

She walked slowly to Ladder's studio off the Bowery, looking at deep metal sinks and secondhand vats displayed in front of restaurant-equipment shops which she had always ignored before. She was late for her interview.

On Second Street she found his building and pressed a bell labeled Ladder's Repro. Jack answered the door himself. She expected a middle-aged man who spoke terse, rapid sentences, but the entrepreneur of reproduction was only a few years older than Laurel herself. Though balding, he pulled his hair back into a stubby ponytail and had a small clay-colored hand stuck in his left rolled-up shirtsleeve. He explained that it had broken off during a faulty casting.

He had converted an old garage into a studio and lived in the back, in a separate, walled-off section. Drawings hung haphazardly wherever there was a clear bit of wall space. From tiny medieval manuscript illuminations to unmounted fragments of Russian Constructivist jewelry, most periods of art history were represented somewhere in the studio. Pietàs and Holy Families leaned against one wall, alongside an old Mobil Oil sign with a horse flying across it from the original garage. Small ivories of Eros and Mars were laid out in lots of twenty each. "Cast from a direct mold of the original in Hadrian's villa, as identical as possible," Jack Ladder said. Laurel didn't ask him how ivory was cast. The Mars and Eros figures would be fastened onto letter openers and magnifying glasses. A woman wearing goggles, introduced as Ladder's assistant, chipped noses off rows of Tutankhamen heads. Noses and other body parts were piled in the garbage. Ladder selected a gray nose, ran his hand along the chip marks. "All these noses, ears, and such, all useless. We have to be painfully authentic." He held up body parts from the trash. "Composite stone, cast marble polymer. A very authentic look."

The woman in goggles lined up busts of Amenhotep III, studied a prototype, and proceeded to lop off the right ear of each. "Van Gogh in Alexandria," she said to Laurel.

Laurel followed him to the back of the studio. He was reading Cellini's autobiography, which he called a lie-ography, because Cellini constantly lied about himself. He flipped through the book and described Cellini fighting against fantastic odds and always winning, behaving too courageously to be believed, dropping names of cardinals and dukes whose titles meant nothing anymore. The lies seemed transparent. In this kind of work, he explained, you shouldn't exaggerate, everything should be the same. He spoke contemptuously only because he was a better liar. His lying was concentrated in product, not personality, and actually he would balk at the idea his work could be interpreted as a kind of lying. He removed the hand from his rolled-up sleeve and drew shapes in fake marble dust. Cellini's golden saltcellars and duels were transformed into another kind of bragging—large fees commanded for rows of Degas dancers of bonded bronze and one hundred little statues of a queen from the Ptolemaic period, all waiting for bases of Honduran mahogany. Laurel picked up the hand and raked the marble dust into ridges.

Ladder moved to another table, cleared order forms and invoices away and looked at the cartoons in Laurel's portfolio. He held Electra up to the light and followed her story without smiling. As he looked through Laurel's portfolio, he told her how he had started his business. Jack began fabricating museum reproductions soon after he finished art school. He ran out of original ideas, so he copied other artists' work, as a depressing sort of joke, he said, but he was very good at it. From works of German Expressionists or Cubists to whatever was in the gallery around the corner, regardless of the style, he could produce copies of older works as if he had no knowledge of the intervening years, and Jack could copy recent works as if he had no style of his own. His business began small, on money borrowed from his family. His first pieces were medieval manuscript illuminations. These were simple, just large letters formed from gargoyle-like figures. Done by hand, they sold well, especially around Christmas, but he grew bored with the redundant nature of the work. The museum said it would pay to have them specially printed up, so each card would look as if it had been individually painted. Soon he developed copies of other paintings, casting sculpture, hiring more assistants and allocating projects to other artists. He traveled to museums in other cities and studied their collections to determine what he could copy that the particular museum might be interested in selling. He had no acquaintances who weren't directly involved with his business, and spent most of his time looking at originals and pushing his copies.

In the back a woman was doing research while another outlined a Mayan codex on a roll of paper. They painted and read while Ladder spoke to Laurel. He introduced her to them, but explained that he preferred to have his artists work at home and return pieces to him for inspection, payment, and shipping.

Forgery as mirror, not forgery as crime. Jack showed Laurel the process of copying Egyptian hieroglyphics. She did exactly as he did. Although Ladder made her nervous, outlines of profiles, arms, legs followed one after another nearly perfectly. He was an audience who stood too close, but she tried to ignore him. Her hand and eye were as if one piece, directly connected. Her control of the pen was so steady, figures of Horus, Anubis, and each unknown symbol appeared automatically, with little hesitation and few mistakes. There was no need to watch her any longer. Jack was dismissive. She could take assigned materials from the storage closet and start working at home right away. He didn't ask her about Fantômes, why she had left, what she had done since, or where she had gone to school. She was part of his system of production, which didn't include office parties or talking over personal problems. Once he had looked at her work and hired her, that was all he needed to know.

Her skill was not as mirror-like as Ladder's, but she was very good. In her apartment, working near a window for natural light, Laurel would try, for a few hours, not to answer the telephone or turn on the radio. It was a Halloween trick in the sense that she pretended everyone else was participating in the ruse. She would try not to look out the window, avoiding the sight of non-participants who wore modern clothes and carried radios. She would imagine she was an Egyptian scribe concentrating on real papyrus, relieved she wasn't aligning blocks of stone on a hot pyramid. She didn't know what class artists had belonged to in Egypt, but it didn't seem a bad status to have; not a drudge but not a Pharaoh either. In one papyrus she'd copied, the scribe Ani appeared as a god and this was encouraging. To be represented as immortal in a painting done thousands of years ago was preferable to thinking of herself as a forger who lived in a walk-up with a view of a bus stop. The heat, the drought, the subsequent water shortage; during the summer it was easy to pretend she was in Egypt, if not the Nile, but she eventually had to turn on the radio, plug in the fan, and answer the telephone.

Once a week Laurel picked up new assignments and materials from Ladder's studio off the Bowery. She tried to prolong her third visit by talking to Jack. Ordinarily he was brusque, but he did like to discuss his work. As he smoked a cigarette, taking up one of the Ptolemaic queens in the other hand, he said he was a great populist, bringing art to people just as movable type had brought literacy. A truck arrived with plates of bonded bronze and cast marble; then the telephone rang and that was the end of their conversation. Laurel watched him disappear into the back of the studio. From the little evidence Laurel had, it didn't seem as though he enjoyed his money very much. He worked constantly, and when he wasn't working, he hatched new schemes to earn more. One of his assistants told her that Jack's idea of a good time was ordering out from Buster's Crabhouse down the street. He was more distant than the managers at Fantômes, who had always wanted to know a great deal about their employees. Jack had no concerns with narrative to slow him down. Storyline wasn't his province.

On her fourth trip to the studio, Jack was visiting a museum in Chicago. As she separated layers of gold leaf, the woman who made Incan figures in silver and gold told Laurel that she suspected she was producing far more figures than that museum had probably ordered. Some reproductions, the women said while twisting her hair up with a black chopstick, were separated from the lot and never shipped uptown. Ladder, through his own channels, tried to pass these off as originals. If there were people who could be fooled, Ladder would find them, she said, and this made Laurel anxious. She wasn't afraid of Ladder going to jail. She told herself he was little more than a voice at the end of the telephone, the man who signed her paychecks. As she worked alone in her apartment, Laurel was afraid Ladder had hired her because somehow he knew just how easily she could fool herself. As if by reading *Electra* he had been given a clue.

Jack began to make up reasons for keeping Laurel at the studio. He watched her draw from across a table, or from the other side of the room. (She wasn't that complacent, didn't forget that finally or that stupidly the hints of the woman with the black chopstick in her hair: *Ladder spells trouble.*) Either there were many women who entered when all the assistants quit for the night, and those same women left before Laurel and the others arrived, or there were none at all. Laurel heard a rumor about a divorce or a green card marriage. Even when they were alone in the studio, she didn't ask.

She imagined bringing Jack to Queens to meet her mother. He might examine small Chinese paintings, bronze horses or even the ceramic jars with good luck characters painted on them kept in the kitchen, and he would talk about his business. Or he might describe the live turtles he'd seen in a tub in front of a shop in Chinatown, they were large and blunt-nosed. He had also seen live crabs put in paper bags. The bags marched down Canal Street, not far, but it had been funny to watch. He had told Laurel this story at an awkward moment, and there was a good chance he would repeat it if he felt ill at ease. Her mother would pretend everything was all right, then she would begin to chop ginger root so quickly, fingers would fly. Later she would accuse Laurel of being like an angry stupid crab crawling away in a paper bag, only to be cooked and eaten anyway.

She wanted to work at home again. She wanted to continue working in his converted garage. There was a great demand for Egyptian hieroglyphics; he might need someone else. Laurel decided to suggest that he look at my portfolio. He explained in a grandiose tone that there was no room for hacks in his business, but Laurel told him my sense of color, my eye for matching each hue, each different tint, would dazzle him.

He finally agreed to see my portfolio. Laurel didn't know if Jack's faltering stemmed from a reluctance to have a third person enter their intrigue, or was just managerial cheapness when it came to hiring more workers in a crunch. But he did call and I brought in my portfolio full of brilliantly colored *Electra* storyboards. As he looked through it, he told me the same story he had told Laurel, about how he had begun making copies out of despair, although it seemed partly a joke now. I was eventually hired to work on the Egyptian reproductions with Laurel.

We would pick up the papyrus we were to work on at

the beginning of the week. Each set contained a picture of the hieroglyphics to be copied, boxes in which to pack the finished pieces, and printed notes which explained the symbols or situations depicted in each reproduction. Most of the paintings were from the Pyramid Texts. The examples indicated correct colors, and paint was included: copper, reddish orange, peacock green, a turquoise with gold flecks named green oxide, a color called Nile blue, and another simply labeled sand. The papyrus was actually a heavy paper, and Ladder gave us a large package containing hundreds of sheets of deckle-edged phony parchment, as well as free ink.

The most popular subject was Osiris, god of the underworld. He was often placed standing between his wife, Isis (who was also his sister), and her sister, Nephthys. Both sisters were in love with him. According to the explanatory notes, Nephthys was associated with Aphrodite later on. The three of them were frequently painted together: Isis and Nephthys mourning the death of Osiris; the three bound together by Horus, who had the head of a parrot. In the traditional version, each woman had one wing, and Osiris stood between them, as if they were some kind of moth. None of the eschatological explanations discussed how Isis felt about Nephthys's intrusion. There was an allusion to a child hidden from Isis, but there was no picture of this in Ladder's series of reproductions.

To smell, to give breath, to kiss, it's all the same word; in Egyptian, the three meanings are connected. You kiss someone to life. Remember the story of Sleeping Beauty awakened by a kiss: a dark-haired Disney prince bending over a blonde narcophile. There's another myth about being kissed into life, the story of the dormant beauty inside the living beast. I placed the prototype and its replica on a table; books, papers, and paints cleared off. Here is the bad, and inside this ugly thing is its good twin. In which lies the "good double" which only a kiss will release? One was a photograph of an authentic

Egyptian painting; the other was my copy, which I breathed or painted into life.

Isis and Nephthys, doubles, two halves of a moth, each wing in love with Osiris. The figures were colored in, nearly identical to the original. The explanatory notes only went so far. The little printed bits discussed mythology, not personality or the origins of individual psyches. Isis and Nephthys, if Ladder's texts were to be trusted, accepted their fate. If a papyrus had existed which depicted them scheming against each other, it wasn't sold in the museum shop. In searching for an explanation, I came up with some reasonable falsehoods: the notion of the difficult triangle was a relatively modern invention. In ancient cultures, marriage was a vague thing, everyone led industrious lives, happy and inquisitive, inventing myths, water clocks, leavened bread, and beer. The myth of Nephthys's hidden child put the nuclear family on a slippery footing, but it was only a hint. At first, as at Fantômes, I kept wanting to learn what would happen next. Would the child return, grown up and demanding? Would Nephthys go into exile in Thebes or Cyprus? Would Osiris, under some pretext, look for her? Each week, in Ladder's converted garage off the Bowery, I picked up a new episode, outlined or inked by Laurel, but images were selected for pictorial or decorative value, not for their sequence in a story. There were too many missing frames between the odd episodes the museum requested for its reproduction shop. As an ancient colorist I coughed on the sand and brick dust. The pictures seemed devoid of any kind of meaning unless I made a meaning up. Laurel was more seduced by mimesis. She would think about the pyramids, turn off the fan, and pretend she was in Egypt, but I was looking for the sentences, the frames that Ladder had left out.

In every picture we copied, they appeared, the three of them, bound together with no hint of tension. They were symbolic, all tied together, but of what I didn't know. The picture hadn't yet arrived which showed Isis beaning Osiris with a frying pan or a brick. If I were Isis, I'd find it difficult not ever being able to get away from the other two. There was a preponderance of serenity in the pictures. I was instructed to take a heavy hand with the green oxide and Nile blue. Remember, it's the underworld, Laurel said. The greens and blues you think symbolized serenity might have actually implied passivity, boredom, or sleep. No one is supposed to have a good time, and the three of them are stuck with each other. Blues and greens can be deceiving.

Another picture: The weighing of the heart at the hour of judgment for a soul unnamed in the explanatory notes. There isn't any spatial perspective. Large and small figures are scattered all over. The jackal, Anubis, guards the scales. Maat, who represents law and order, stands nearby with an ostrich feather in her hair. The soul is represented by a bird with a human head. The Devourer, a chimera, not a devil, will consume the soul if the scale indicates guilt. I can't paint the judgment scene without putting myself in the place of the bird with the human head. Somehow I think Maat will understand me and not turn me over to the Devourer. She will understand that, of course, L. Carne deserved to be robbed. She won't say a word about Laurel and I pretending to dispense justice, attempting to mete out humbling experience, and there won't be a word said about the possibility that in doing so we stepped on immortal toes. She'll look indifferent when I come to the part about Martin. "Of course," Maat will nod in agreement. "He was an insignificant episode, not worth a feather." The scale is motionless. Martin gets the divine brush-off. My contempt for the lonely Loonan might send me into the jaws of the Devourer. I tell Maat that I'm very sorry, I didn't intend to be contemptuous of him, but Loonan was paid more and had a better job, after all. I mean, I think he'll live.

Here's a third picture: The daughter of Re, also known

as the Eye of Re, was turned into a lion and lived in the Nubian desert until she was persuaded to return to Egypt. Neith, another god, is in the picture and threatens to cause the sky to collapse. Ladder's brief notes skirted the issue of what the source of Neith's anger might have been and left the impending disaster hanging. If Neith wished the daughter of Re to remain in the desert, there was no explanation of Neith's attachment. Whether for reasons of love or complications of immortal power struggles, I can only guess. The sky is about to collapse, but perhaps it won't. The gods were anthropomorphic and the borders were full of hieroglyphics which Laurel inked: birds and eyes for the most part, a few snakes and triangles thrown in, as well. Laurel could have made up any number of symbols as long as they looked Egyptian. Instead of copying hieroglyphics which meant the lioness preyed on Nubian monkeys, she may have inadvertently drawn figures which translated as *How could Janet Ling stand it?* or simply: *This is fraud, but it doesn't matter.* I stuck to the rules laid out for coloring. There wasn't much choice when the paints themselves were limited. Neith's skin was sand-colored and her clothing was painted white, peacock green, and orange-red. The Egyptian word for sky was feminine, while the word for earth was masculine. This fact was contained in the first sentence of the explanatory notes.

The FBI put on an exhibit made up of known forgeries which they had confiscated over a period of five years. Léger, Miró, and Georgia O'Keeffe were very popular. These three had been the specialty of one forger/painter in particular. (One day he might wake up as Klee, another day he might feel unhappy and find himself painting like Rothko. It was naïve to think a forger actually took on the personality of any individual, but an agent with romantic ideas, if there were such a person, might imagine it would help.) Dealers and curators wondered if they were serious about the show, or was it the FBI's idea of a joke? Who in the FBI could tell the difference between a real Léger and a fake? Federal experts would have to be trained. An officer previously assigned to infiltrate church groups who gave sanctuary to Salvadoran exiles might be selected to take art-history classes. He would travel from Arizona to New York, where he would learn how to look closely at canvases. He would learn when brushstrokes should be continuous and when they should be broken. He would tell crooks that he spoke French and Italian. He would try to pass as a connoisseur. The agency's concern with the forgeries was in the interest of devalued property and trickery, but there was something comic about the exhibition. An organization associated with secrecy, now given to display, to showing mistakes, seemed a contradiction. It was as if they were exhibiting gadgets which looked promising but which didn't work; like footage of early airplanes which crumble and never get far off the ground. Either the FBI recruited from ranks of ordinary dealers and collectors or they became poseurs themselves, learning the signs of a certain class and education.

As we inked and colored Isis and Osiris, I proposed to Laurel that we could paint copies, say they were duplicates but not fakes. We would sell Stellas, Salles, Lichtensteins for a few thousand dollars each. The pictures wouldn't be cloaked in criminality. We wouldn't claim any of those men had actually painted the canvases themselves; we would sign our own names to them. I had a few nosy neighbors who might be curious about the canvases, but most were indifferent. The suspicious ones might complain about the racket of crates maneuvered down narrow tenement stairways. The paintings would have to be small. Hands numb, frozen around brushes, looking and drawing, looking and drawing; the repetitive action would get boring. Painting the same few pictures day after day, we would begin to see double.

I waited in Jack's studio to pick up more sheets of phony papyrus. The forger's garbage was full of bits of body parts, a parody of Eamonn's Central American photographs, if they could ever be said to be parodied. Polymer ears and hands freshly hacked off lay in a heap. I was bored as I waited; there was little to really look at if you'd been in the studio before; everything repeated. I didn't handle the bits as I'd seen Jack do. He had just come back from a foundry which could cast surmoulage sculpture and was taking off his jacket. Surmoulage, he explained, was a technique in which casts were made from molds taken from an original. Because the technique created an object several generations removed from the source, the results tended to be a little blunted. Edges and lines were markedly less sharp and the copy was a little smaller, too. Jack thought the technique had a lot of potential, because the original was at the core, mechanically speaking. An object made this way was cheap and less fallible. The usual process of looking and copying by hand seemed primitive by comparison, subject to the vagaries of human skill and accident. He wanted to try to iron out the bugs. Then the telephone rang, and he sounded as if he was speaking to a woman he was meeting later that night. He was sort of familiar, only a little nervous. I thought of how I would tell Laurel, how I would imitate the way his voice and manner changed, then I decided not to. When I described his new copying technique, my explanations faltered. If Jack explained something to Laurel, or if she was nearby when he was on the telephone, he put his arm around her. He hadn't done this to me. Laurel said I made the process sound as though he were constructing a series of Russian nesting dolls.

When I became impatient with coloring panels I barely understood, Laurel gave me a book on ancient Egyptian mythology. I became intrigued by the bad girl Isis. She was notorious for her knowledge of a catalogue of spells. Her notoriety began when Osiris was murdered, and she brought him back to life. The explanatory notes said spells bearing her name survived into the Christian period in Egypt; parts of Osiris's story easily adapted to early Christian theology. The picture I was to paint contained a spell preserved from 1300 B.C. which would "kill the poison—really successful a million times," according to a translation by an authority from the University of Pennsylvania. It sounded like an advertisement for aspirin. The object of the spell was to trick Re into telling Isis his secret name. He had been bitten by a snake (an event Isis had arranged), and so she offered to cure him. She could neutralize the venom in a snap if he would tell her his real name. They bargained. There was no other remedy. The poison began to take effect, paralyzing his feet. With the exception of Re's calling, Isis knew all there was to know in the world. She claimed his name was necessary for her spell or the cure would be useless. Re offered her a few other titles in place of the unknown, secret one. She wasn't interested, and he eventually relented. In the end, the spell that cured him didn't contain his name at all.

I colored a panel that corresponded to this tale. Besides the glyphs which told the story around the edge of the papyrus, the picture contained only Re sitting in a chair and Isis standing before him, holding a snake. This was the first time I had painted Isis without the other two. If she could threaten Re, god of the sun, among other things, why did she tolerate the attachment of Nephthys and Osiris (to her as well as to each other). How did she get them out of the picture for the affair of the poison? Isis's role as a magician whose knowledge was limitless, her capacity for guile and possessiveness, composed an identity I knew nothing of until now, and it was a disturbing twist. If she could do anything or have anything, why did she settle for the position of excrescence, tied to her husband and his lover? A few new colors had been added to the usual lot, and I privately questioned their authenticity, hoping Ladder knew what he was doing. Brick red, the color of an imaginary New England schoolhouse. Black with a touch of aubergine in it, the color of patent-leather tap shoes. The third bottle was labeled gold leaf.

Sometimes the books didn't help me. The instructions which came with Ladder's Metropolitan reproductions described writing that had been worn away and coloring which had faded. Fragments composed of broken-up symbols and pictures were rendered meaningless, even to those able to decipher the hieroglyphics. Documents which originally appeared in scrolls or codexes were now as senseless as torn bits of newspaper columns. Christian defacement and editorial changes, damage due to fire or flood posed aesthetic problems when reproduced. Jack didn't care if the meanings of the Egyptian texts were entirely obfuscated as long as they looked accurate.

When they were alone one night, Jack told Laurel a story. He turned off the lights in the rest of the studio, and they sat at his desk in the back. It was an Italian fable about a king who had three sons. He drew Corinthian columns and a fountain, the water pouring out of a face which resembled his own. Royal succession, he said, was based on a ring which the king would pass on to the child he intended to inherit his kingdom. When he was dying, he couldn't decide among his children, and so had two additional rings made. They were identical to the original, and he gave one to each son. After his death, no one knew who was meant to be the true king. Jack gave Laurel a ring which had been the result of a latex mistake. He had colored over the curl of plastic with red and gold acrylic paint so it looked gaudy and primitive. She wore the ring until she got home. It flaked and dissolved when she washed her hands, so she left the remains on a windowsill.

Jack had a plan that was illicit but profitable and offered Laurel a percentage if she was interested. Through the museum Jack had access to some original plaster molds, and along with his foundry friends, he planned to have bronze and terracotta sculptures recast from these molds, although it was decades after the deaths of the artists who had originally made them. Some bronzes from the first castings might date from 1907, others might be circa 1977. If discovered, the original sculptures might lose their value, certainly they would no longer be rare, yet in all respects each sculpture would be identical to the other. Thousands might be produced. The only difference between various castings would be the knowledge of particular dates, a sometimes secret and easily concealed fact. The passage of a few decades left minimal evidence on the bronze, so the problem was only of conceptual importance. Ladder didn't concern himself with clues of aging, marks added only for the sake of authenticity. *All castings are original*, he said. If the original is a plaster mold, then there are no originals. Bronzes, like prints or photographs, are intended as multiples, but editions might be limited.

It was to be a posthumous business, he explained on another evening. Laurel wondered if this were a reference to

a suicide, but he brought out a folder of black-and-white photographs, each wrapped in glassine and confessed to her that
he felt like an extension of the various artists whose molds
were found in the museum warehouse. He sweated over the
castings, not because they were illegal (he didn't believe his
business was illegal), but because he had convinced himself
he was acting for the artist. His wishes were the same as the
deceased's: the more works the merrier. He asked Laurel how
anyone could object to that. Widows and wills, heirs who
knew better, these could be easily brushed aside. It could go
on forever. Unauthorized castings could be made during an
artist's lifetime as well. Buyers would be collecting *Ladders*
whether they knew it or not. What harm was there in multiples, he'd ask again. None of the castings could be hurled
across a room in a rage or used as a lethal weapon by an
intruder, visitor, or family member. They were too heavy.
Solid objects could not be used for the purpose of drug smuggling, and if one of his hollow sculptures was fitted with an
artificial base and used for such purposes, it was entirely out
of his hands. Laurel told him she had nothing to contribute,
she was an inker, she couldn't help out with this project.
Nothing lasts forever, he said.

Jack was concerned with contingency plans in case his
contracts failed to be renewed. The museum business seemed
secure, but there were elements of certain technical processes
which could go out of his control. The arabesque legs of a
series of Degas ballerinas might fall off, the ivories of Mars
and Eros might turn unnaturally yellow, the Mayan codexes
might crumble in their boxes. He would be wiped out. The
museum buyer, left with no choice but to suffer a loss of trust,
would leave Jack alone in his converted garage with piles of
useless, unsellable reproductions. At times his vigilance over
the work waned and his allegiance to the word "exact" faltered.
Laurel overheard him whispering "circumstances beyond my

control." She insisted that circumstances were very much in his control; he anticipated the accident by occasional laxity. Jack seemed to be getting lost in his explanations. Even his outline in the darkening room seemed blurred and dim. Laurel wondered how she might get him to show her his rooms in the back, thinking that if she could get him over that threshold, a slice of marble from the garage's bathroom, gray and warped, if she could get him into those rooms, he might be himself again, whatever that self might be.

Laurel didn't spend the night at Ladder Repro, but she imagined what it might be like. When he was alone in his studio, after all his assistants had gone home, and the telephone had stopped ringing, the only sound in the studio was the buzz of the industrial fan which Jack kept going to sweep out fumes. The Mobil Oil flying horse glowed in the dark, or seemed to, because of indirectly reflected light from outside. At the far end of the studio, rows of Degas dancers balanced in arabesque looked like unspooled barbed wire, their little legs sticking up, a series of spikes. He thought them too precious and senti-mental, but he often had to reproduce pieces which he didn't like. He locked the Russian Constructivist jewelry in the safe before going to the back part of the studio, which was where he lived. The back room was little more than a bedroom with a small refrigerator and a hot plate. Few people had ever been in it, certainly no one who worked for him. The two sections of the former garage had separate bathrooms. A curious as-sistant once claimed the studio bathroom was broken and asked if she could use his. Jack told her to go over to Buster's Crab-house, say she worked for Ladder's, and certainly they would let her use the bathroom. He handed her twenty dollars and told her to bring back a few orders of soft shell crabs.

Jack liked to sleep with the door between the two rooms ajar. His rooms were so small and the studio expansive, but being a glutton for privacy, he was also afraid an assistant with keys might come in early. There were lingering fumes which he might not want to inhale while sleeping, and although he didn't mind answering the telephone, the very early callers were often the annoying ones. He preferred to let one of his assistants handle the pills. Laurel never came in early.

She looked at a photograph of an attractive young man, not an advertisement, but almost. It was something passed by quickly, flipping through the pages of a book or a magazine. Laurel was drawn to the picture, although she didn't turn back to it. She put the volume down and left the store. Even if the man himself stood near her in the store, she would have left. That kind of pursuit, whether she was its object or the pursuer, seemed unfathomable to her. It was something she was no longer capable of, she'd lost the language. As engaging or as easy as he or any random person looked, she knew she'd only feel embarrassed about it later.

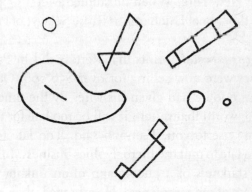

Eamonn didn't make many prints of any single negative. Weston, Brassaï, Evans, Modotti, Smith, sometimes he thought about them when he was in the darkroom, but he did not take photographs like theirs. Decades after his death, when he had no control over the fate of his work, out might march white matte boards, pieces of glass, frames; and a monograph on the work of Eamonn Archer. Dealers would rummage through his "estate," which would consist of the contents of his rent-controlled apartment packed in cardboard boxes and stored in what had been his mother's house. They would search for vintage prints, those made within a year or two of the date the original picture was taken. Those would be the most valuable and there would be so few of them. He was not the sort to burn negatives. They could print as many copies of his photographs as they liked. The negatives might be wrapped in glassine, kept in a vault, and over an infinite number of years, the print value would grow or decline accordingly.

Reproductions in a book I had given him: vintage silver gelatin prints like Man Ray's protrait of Meret Oppenheim printed in 1933 or Mondrian's *Pipe and Glasses* (1926) by André Kertész were worth a great deal. Pipe and glasses, a woman's face, no violence, no agony, as minimal as the images were, they were as much about their moment in Paris as his were about New York. When he studied Meret Oppenheim's profile, he thought of Duchamp as Rrose Sélavy, of Paris before Laval.

The *carte postale* prints that Kertész did in Paris in the late twenties were now selling for over $50,000. One had, at least. It was one he had given his wife. By the time my photographs are worth that much, it will be too late for the money to be of any use to you, Eamonn said. Too late to quit the comics, too late to quit the hieroglyphics business. In the black-and-white starkness of a photograph of an unknown woman he read traces of my remoteness. He arranged, then rearranged my pens as if they were Mondrian's glasses, but he was no Man Ray. Eamonn partly wanted to be thought of as that kind of photographer, yet at the moment he prepared for a shot, if only conceptually, he resisted making the kinds of decisions which might make him one.

I once told him I thought his pictures were beautiful and I did mean it, although I thought he'd snap my head off. *How can you say they're beautiful?* He had been showing me a series of black-and-white pictures. One was of a row of mostly empty Coke bottles, some filled with petrol; a couple had twisted rags which served as wicks sticking out of them. A bottle of dish detergent lay on its side nearby. This was used as a sort of glue to hold wicks in place. I knew these were

Molotov cocktails which would be thrown by boys and girls, probably in Derry, but Eamonn didn't say exactly where he had been at the time. I knew there was really nothing beautiful about the glint of glass and the dull gray-white of the over-turned bottle of liquid soap. I was just looking at the sharp blacks, none softened by aubergine, and chalk whites. Eamonn set the bottles up; he, not the children, had set up those bottles so symmetrically, a geometric pattern of small oily reflections. I turned to one he had shot in color, set apart in a different stack. He had taken it among the tinkers or travelers. They're like gypsies, he said. A girl with wet red hair leaned against the aluminum side of her family's caravan. Everything glinted in the sun. He might have taken it in Florida, but the other photographs of the tinkers said certainly he had not.

He told me about pictures he couldn't take. The armed honor guard at a northern funeral who are not allowed to perform the ritual of firing guns, for example. It was known that they would fire them, and that he mustn't photograph guns, gunners, or mourners.

There had also been meaningless, unprintable pictures. It wasn't even fair to say they were over- or underexposed, or that they hadn't come out. An occasion when he snapped the shutter just to break up an argument in a playground filled with rubble, that was one. The picture didn't matter, he'd barely focused, it was just the sound of the shutter being snapped that drew the children away from their fight and made them aware that they were being watched. A blur of a face smeared across the frame, car parts and an empty vending machine stacked in a corner; Eamonn printed it anyway.

Laurel had used the word "beautiful," as well. I trusted her impressions almost before I had any faith in my own. She never seemed to hesitate or back down, so it was easier to trust her opinions than to form my own, but I did want to say the picture of the empty bottles was beautiful, in the same way

that the Man Ray picture was. That's wrong, too, Eamonn
said.

Eamonn had telephoned two weeks before. We had an appointment, but the guard at the front desk stopped us. We
needed a special pass. The photography archives were rung
up. Someone on the other end confirmed Eamonn's appointment. The guard wrote out a pass and directed us to the
elevator. Eamonn had his camera with him, thinking the
Nikon gave him the aura of professional legitimacy, but it
meant little or nothing to the guard at the front desk, and to
the assistant curator who led us into the archives it was something that had to be left outside the study room. The assistant
would lock the camera in his desk. Photographs had been taken
of photographs. Cameras were no longer allowed.

The assistant curator told us to wash our hands, take out
any pens we might have in our pockets and leave them by the
sink. "Take a chair," the man said, and we did. He returned
a few minutes later with two long black boxes labeled *Arthur
Felig*. The boxes and the somberness with which they were
delivered reminded Eamonn of boxes of possessions delivered
to the family after an accident, or boxes given to prison inmates
upon release, a scene Weegee himself had probably been familiar with. The larger box was full of unmatted prints. We
began to go through them, whispering to each other.

Under a photograph of Weegee getting a shoeshine at
his desk he had written: *Removing BLOOD after a murder story*.
At first glance Eamonn believed the caption, and then he
realized it was probably a gag. The photographer would have
to have been at the scene of the murder before it happened,
and he would have had to stand very close in order to get
blood on his shoe. Weegee had a police radio, Eamonn knew

that, but guessed he got there just when the police did. Could he really have blood on his shoe? Weegee sometimes called himself a Psychic Photographer but Eamonn hadn't taken his ability to predict crimes seriously. To claim to have been a psychic regarding pictures was a joke, that was all. Eamonn himself had taken ridiculous pictures, but not ones involving the phony blood of his victims. His Irish pictures suggested an aftermath, but he never rendered it comic or pointed to the mundane aspects of the inevitable cleaning up. He felt set up and taken in.

Macy's Thanksgiving Day Parade. The night before the parade, and it had just rained, so the street was slick. No date; it looked as if it had been taken in the early forties. There was a woman in a Sky View cab, so Eamonn guessed the photograph had been taken during World War II. Above her and to the right floated a huge four-fingered hand. Four men held strings attached to the inflated digits. I didn't know who the character might be. It was too early for Bullwinkle, and Mickey Mouse wore gloves. The float remained unidentified. The quality of city blackness, melted by streetlights and reflecting metal surfaces, was so different from rural nights without metal or electricity. A piece of paper lay near the cab, but the street was surprisingly clean. No tall buildings, almost a European city, except the state of many European cities at that moment did not allow for long parades of happy people and inflated cartoon characters. Inky city fog in the distance and those straight streets; it was certainly New York, even if Eamonn was unsure of the date.

A photograph under which Weegee had written: *My studio*, and on the back in pencil, *Weegee's room near police headquarters*. Half a bed could be seen through the door. The room looked like a closet. The pictures tacked above Weegee's bed fell into three categories: photographs of guns, self-portraits with his camera, pin-ups, and there was a sign which read,

MURDER IS MY BUSINESS. The partial view of the room said one thing to Eamonn: You must be ready to leave as soon as you're called. Weegee was Johnny-on-the-spot. Eamonn, too, felt he could leave as soon as the telephone rang, but if he found they had readiness in common, it didn't account for much. The pictures tacked above his bed were disturbing, as if he was peeping into a corner Weegee had exposed as another one of his jokes.

Eamonn sorted through the box and put all the self-portraits in a pile. Weegee dressed as a king holding a large camera; on it he had written *To All My Subjects*. Weegee as an ice-cream salesman in a movie theater, holding a tray in one hand and his press camera before his face with the other. Flashbulb and mirror were attached to the camera, his eye was as round as a lens. To Eamonn, it wasn't just that the eye had a predatory look, but everything in the box appeared predatory. Weegee whispering a secret in the ear of a female mannequin, Weegee buried under a pile of curled photographs. Weegee asleep on the floor, flashbulbs scattered at his feet, as if they were responsible for his collapse.

I picked out a picture which I thought was serious, but Eamonn got the joke right away. It was a photograph of Weegee looking into an empty trunk in a field. Underneath he had written CENSORED BY, followed by a blank space; then he had added THE PAPERS. I assumed the murder victim was inside the trunk, but no, the victim was as phantomlike as Electra. Usually the gags were blatant: Weegee posing as a playing card, king of an identified suit; crown, robe, and throne, holding his large press camera, and then the image was reversed. Like a card, there was no right or wrong side to the picture. The censorship gag was different. The picture and caption suggested a crime so horrendous that it couldn't be photographed; but the joke was on the audience in the end, hinting that the nasty, unprintable crime existed only in the observer's imagination.

Eamonn had taken very few self-portraits and rarely asked me to photograph him. His conception of his role as a photographer was one of anonymity. The one in Belfast that marked him looking into a mirror in the flat on Cliftonville Road was still his private nightmare. What if he hadn't photographed an informer, what if he was the informer? He didn't know, couldn't find out, and didn't destroy the undeveloped rolls of film. Nothing in all the museum archives seemed as dangerous as that self-portrait, and it even crept into our afternoon in the white-walled archive.

I turned to Weegee's photographs of strippers, naked, limbless female mannequins, and women in jail. A circus performer, *Woman Shot from a Cannon* (New York, 1943). Blurred motion, what happened next? Did she survive? Of course. If she had died there would have been a photograph of the crowd's reaction, if not of the woman herself. Predecessor of Electra, human or cartoon, the risks they take cause the audience to forget about their troubles and enjoy vicarious voyeuristic thrills. The moment of potential physical trauma intercepts hysteria, anxiety. Danger, death defying; if she doesn't make it, I will witness . . . Eamonn said, Try to think like a member of the Depression audience. What if X, a wealthy relative or a miserly boss, was shot from a cannon and didn't bounce back but lay squashed on the sawdust? Y assumes that his or her worries would be over. Maybe.

A photograph of a prostitute being put into a police wagon. She held her bag to the side of her face, but she was unprepared for the camera in the van, which took a picture of her face straight on, unfairly. She didn't look surprised. Perhaps she couldn't be surprised anymore, even by a hidden camera aimed in a damaging way. Then another gag picture;

on the back he had written in pencil (*surprised three-eyed man*). Part of the photograph had been double-exposed, so Weegee appeared as a man with three eyes. He was looking at a high-heeled shoe, a woman's foot inside it. From the angle of the leg, he might have been looking up her dress. It was similar to a photograph of a man grinning a lascivious smile as he attached a Christmas angel to a float. I handed these to Eamonn, who barely looked at them. Another with the caption STRIPPER IN TANK—MINNEOPOLIS. (No one had corrected his spelling.) The performer was a woman named *divena*, small *d*. She swam underwater, eyes shut, close to the glass. Weegee aimed his camera straight at her. Like divena, the women in their jail bunks ignored him as he kneeled before their beds. They must have been told to pretend he wasn't there.

Girl Watching Lovers at Night; She sat in a lifeguard's chair at Coney Island. Eamonn had read that, for the rest of his life, Weegee wished he had spoken to the girl, instead of just walking by and taking her picture. He believed she committed suicide later that night.

Eamonn's favorite pictures were the ones taken with an infrared flash, of audiences in movie theaters. It was impossible to know what kind of movie was on the screen by looking at their faces. Some clutched armrests with suspense or horror, while others laughed. A couple isolated by rows of empty seats kissed.

Pictures of violence and pictures of the hoi polloi all mixed together. The corner of Mott and Pell streets entirely torn up, as if it had just endured a fire and an earthquake combined. Mon Fong Won Company, a Chinese grocery, stood on the corner in front of the abyss. Uptown in the same city, a woman walked three French poodles on Fifth Avenue. The dogs had bows in their hair. Back downtown, eight children crowded into one bed. I came across the small three-by-four version first. It was only when I saw the larger print that

I realized the children were sleeping on a fire escape. The picture had been taken from the fire escape directly above while a boy held a flashlight from a window. A disheveled man on what looked like a shabby corner; on the reverse Weegee had written SOCIETY PLAYBOY *in a hotel room after an all night party*. Eamonn turned the picture over again. If those penciled lines had been erased, there would be no clues to suggest this was a society playboy. The man and the room looked entirely crummy. What was it he had done to look this way? There was no answer. The playboy was followed by two bloodied men in front of a restaurant, the result of a stabbing. A large sign behind them read FOODS. Men looked at the bodies and looked at the photographer looking at the bodies.

We hadn't gone through the entire collection, but picked up one last photograph. A typed note on the back read *Weegee's Subconcious Movie Camera which he used to photograph a dream sequence in which he acted*. Without turning the picture over, we knew it was one of the gags. Eamonn was afraid that when the only remaining evidence of his life was contained in a black box in the Museum of Modern Art archives, people might produce theories about the subconscious content of his work. The Nikon was an arm of what he didn't talk about, what he kept hidden. He said his box in the museum would be incoherent and disordered. Quality Meats, the Mets parade, wedding pictures, the self-portrait in Belfast, the prisoners in Long Kesh, a picture of me holding a bottle of titanium white; the contents of Eamonn Archer's box, the curators would say, look like the work of six or seven different photographers. Eventually his inclusion in the museum would seem like a mistake and they'd carefully lower his black box into a dumpster on Fifty-fourth Street, he said. No, I answered, don't be silly.

He closed the box, collected his pens from beside the sink, and we left the museum. How was his New York like

Weegee's *Naked City?* Not all but many of the people he photographed pretended he wasn't there. Just as many of Weegee's subjects seemed to ignore his presence; flash, shutter, snap, cigar, and all. Depression voyeurism led spectators to the discovery that someone was worse off than themselves. Even the society figures looked as if collapse was right around the corner. Eamonn's viewer was less of an innocent. His pictures occasionally demanded an audience of converted spectators who looked because they often already had some idea about what lay behind those windows, behind the doors of Quality Meats, or guessed something about the identity of the hands which had filled glass bottles with petrol. Eamonn retreated from Weegee's sense of carnival showman, although he often participated in the same circus on exactly the same streets. On the corner of Mott and Pell he had taken a picture of me. It was an ordinary picture. We were just walking somewhere, he had stopped on impulse and taken my picture. There were no remnants of any disaster on that corner. It was not a picture Weegee the Psychic would have taken, because it had the quality of a memento about it. It was a small picture, the kind which one of us might find at the bottom of a drawer or stuck in a book.

Every object in the frame was a shade of blue, including Electra herself hiding from the police. I intended she should survive, and a new trick was needed. When necessary, Electra began to copy her surroundings as a means of escape. Laurel suggested temporarily turning Electra, not into a man exactly, but into Electra's idea of what a man was like. Travesty, another kind of mimicry, presented itself as a parody of seduction. I wanted to know whom Electra might seduce. It was a problem that would not go away, at Fantômes or at home. Objects of seduction didn't exist in this story; no matter what we did, they remained scotomas, yawning blind spots. It wasn't that objects of desire were invisible but when they did appear, they appeared as distortions, El Greco figures, featureless shadows with slanted stance. Anamorphosis: a distorted image which looks normal when viewed through a special device, Laurel said. She can be helped, Laurel added, to live a normal life.

Following her line of reasoning, bad characters could be treated like optical flaws, and even the long-gone Orion could be remembered as a trivial incident, nothing more. But other characters, good or bad, loved or loveless, were becoming increasingly marginal. Electra's world had turned into a house of mirrors. She reflected or mimicked every situation she found herself in. I considered this condition a kind of disease, one which had lain dormant for years: she'd probably caught it in space. The first symptoms were awkward polyphonic parrotings of other people. Residents of Allen Street avoided Electra because she copied them involuntarily. She would instantly look and sound like each random passerby in turn. Her reflexivity reached such proportions that Electra was, for all intents and purposes, invisible. She had no control over herself. People saw themselves in her, which was confusing to both parties, or she blended in with buildings. It was an anti-solipsistic condition, and it explained why Eamonn's photographs of her were blank. In the early stages of the disease, the camera was more sensitive to invisibility and mimicry than the naked eye.

A cochineal sky, a cinnabar sun. When Electra first arrived on earth she dimly remembered a childhood desert. The green of Central Park and the gray of the rest of the city were not barren in the same quiet way. Her memory began with a dream, but when she woke, she clearly remembered how densely black it could be in the laboratory under Sierra Madre del Sur. She would grow accustomed to the dark; black would be diminished by gray forms and blue areas. Her eyes wanted more definition, more colors, but it was just night on Allen Street. The streetlights, car lights, and lit apartments spilled illumination onto the meridian. Electra couldn't sleep.

Mimicry in the service of parody and travesty but not in the service of survival or seduction. Here's an example. Martin once imitated Mr. Loonan when he was out of the office. He punched holes in a Styrofoam cup, rubbed his nose, and hunched over a drawing table in just the same way. He spoke with Loonan's intonation as he described how lovely Electra was, how she should come into his apartment, make herself at home, while he put on a sound-effects tape. Martin as Loonan couldn't find an appropriate tape. Office sounds, factory sounds, war or period effects, but would Electra know what a water wheel or a steamship was? It was not a romantic solution. Laurel and I laughed. Martin was very funny. Then we saw Loonan standing in the office door. I don't know how much of Martin's mimicry he overheard. He might not have had many illusions about our respect for him, but when we made fun of him, his eyes grew red. This is what I'll have to confess to Maat when my heart is weighed. Mr. Loonan's face in the doorway. Rather than confess, I say to myself that Martin was despicable. He showed no remorse. Maat would ask me, Why, then, did you laugh, and why did you find him so interesting after work? Admit it, she'll demand, he mimicked Mr. Loonan partly to please you, and he went on to mimic your feelings for himself. You never knew the difference between the genuine and the imitation. The bird with the human head tries to escape the jaws of the Devourer by flying away. Maat yells after the representation of my soul, "You thought I could identify with your problems. Forget it. Every soul, every human-headed bird, thinks I identify with his or her side of the story, but how can I? I have to be impartial, after all."

An apricot sun, a mint-green sky, sweet colors, but in this assignment they hint doom of a chemical disaster, toxic spill, hazardous fumes leaked into the atmosphere.

Martin said that green was not symbolic of jealousy, but I find it impossible to dismiss connotations of envy when I paint a character green. The implication is inseparable from the color; the two are unalterably attached. Fire isn't red, water isn't always blue, but red is for the hot-water tap and blue for the cold. In spite of Jack Ladder's instructions, I painted Isis green from head to toe, not for hope, but because there must have been times when she wanted to push Nephthys into the Nile. Color isn't stored in any arsenal, it's an elusive sort of weapon.

If I find myself reducing the names of my paints to the simplest primaries, I go to the drugstore. Here I find a warehouse of names like Jamaica Peach, Oyster Blush, Rose Twist. The names are subject to copyright laws, so one company can't call a color Mood Indigo if a color named Mood Indigo, regardless of what it looks like, has already been produced. The colors themselves can't be copyrighted, just the names. I have never seen a pink oyster; the woman behind the counter said it was a new color for eyes. I find the idea of newness in a color to be a little jarring. Haven't all the colors already been mixed or invented and seen somewhere? I bought a tube labeled Venetian Coral. It's not a color I like, but the container looked Egyptian and so reminded me of my forgeries. It's necessary to appropriate names and colors from the world of Borghese and Revlon when Dr. Barton's has its limitations. I admit I'm easily seduced by all those names. It's not just the references to travel and romance, but the suggestion that these colors have the potential to act as verbs; they resist being reduced to the servant's role of adjective. Electra doesn't wear Mood Indigo. She induces that state in others.

The bull knows this lesson well. I know it too, but I still find it a sign of inarticulateness when Jack Ladder says, "I saw red." He sees red when materials arrive at the studio damaged, when he has trouble with the museum or the landlord. Jack sees red often.

Ladder began to expand his business. Orders came in from the Louvre and from the Borély Musée d'Archéologie Méditerranée in Marseilles. The papyri sent to France varied from these reproductions made for the Metropolitan. They were more detailed, and the first series Ladder assigned to us was about the voyage to the afterlife.

Nageuse tenant au canard. Allegorie du cosmos: le dieu Gueb (la terre) est separe de son epouse, la diseuse Nout (le ciel), entre eux navique la barque du Soleil Re.

I pressed my fingers against my eyes and saw the shape of the window frame opposite; then it dissolved into yellow, red, points of green. The only afterlife I believed in was the brief one of the afterimage. Laurel had drawn a barge full of people playing musical instruments, baskets of food, and animals, especially baboons; there were a lot of those in the French copies. Besides domestic and game animals, there were fish in the river and birds in the sky. The details required more work and took more time, perhaps more time than Ladder was willing to pay for. Isolated figures of women with heads of cats in place of their own made up the next series. No narrative explanations accompanied these solitary feminized versions of Felix and Fritz, Krazy Kat without Ignatz. Laurel complained the reproductions were becoming too repetitious, even the colors had been reduced to the simplest variations of *terre rouge* and a chalky white called *calcaire*.

Then a series began which required no colors and I was laid off for a few weeks. Laurel received large heavy sheets of fake parchment for a single project, paper copies of *Pierre de*

Rosette. Not an exact copy of the Rosetta Stone, but a paper facsimile. It was work for a letterer, not a former inker, but Laurel's rent was overdue so she accepted the job. We looked blankly at the lines of hieroglyphics. I could make out the word "toy." It seemed to be formed across one line, although certainly the formation of t-o-y was not a word and didn't mean an object of play. An explanation was included about the two types of writing found in hieroglyphics. The earlier cursive, hieratic was later replaced by the demotic. When Laurel was tired of looking and copying, she would make up a few of the Egyptian pictographs. One invented hieroglyphic followed the next, ten whole lines began to form. She knew if a sign resembled a man it meant "man." The pictograph of a man holding a feather might refer to the act of judging, since the feather was associated with Maat. Laurel made up ideograms as she went along. According to her system, a figure with wings referred to flying, a figure lying down signified sleep. It was a simple method of interpretation, although the order of the pictographs, whether she read the sequence up and down, left to right, or right to left, rarely conformed to a narrative Laurel could make sense of. She knew some of the pictographs functioned as phonograms, and some acted as a means of making ambiguous signs more precise. She had always assumed the pictograph of an eye indicated looking or stealing. If the eye preceded a feather or a snake, it signified the act of looking at or stealing that particular thing. She stopped short of assigning any personality to the eye. It didn't so much belong to Maat or Osiris as it did to Jack Ladder.

Laurel, like Electra, tried not to fall in love with the wrong person. The cryptic eye symbol belonged to Jack because he checked her work carefully but blindly. Although he had a copy of the original, he pretended not to notice when she made up pictographs. The possibility that he might have caught the discrepancy but said nothing made Laurel nervous.

As he looked through our work she counted the rows of identical queens from the Ptolemaic period, looked through stacks of Munch drawings, Klimt collages, piles of Constructivist jewelry: black, white, and red jumbled into an unfinished pile. Sometimes he seemed to avoid her, and when Laurel returned to my apartment she would parrot the way he smoked and spoke on the telephone to a curator who couldn't speak English. He was like a wire with animated electrical impulses passing through it which Laurel had seen in an old cartoon. He might even dream of his reproductions, but he was far more self-possessed than Mr. Loonan. When he pulled the rubber band from his ponytail a lot of straight brown hair came out with it, but he laughed at men (invariably they were clients) who combed their hair over their heads to hide their bald spots. When he drew her aside she felt his confidence—a position of privilege—but the warning of the woman with the chopstick in her hair kept at her.

To call his reproductions get-rich-quick schemes was to label a straw dog. His ideas took time to execute and required too much capital expenditure. Jack was entirely motivated by the suggestion of pulling the wool over the spectator's eyes, even if it meant losing money.

Admiration, snicker, and routine glance would become all muddled, Laurel had no doubt about it. He continued to miss her alterations and accidental mistakes. He told her she looked nice in red. He could be cursory if he wanted her to leave in a hurry, and she felt ridiculous for hanging around, although probably no one had noticed. Sometimes it was a relief to close the door and leave the smell of plaster dust to Jack by himself.

One evening Laurel stayed late with the excuse that she needed to read about the pyramid texts in the Louvre. The book was large and expensive, and she knew Jack wouldn't lend it to her. He would be gone for an hour, he said. He had to pay for some marble polymer compound and left in his pick-up truck. Apparently the foreman would be at the warehouse late, and Laurel wondered if the marble polymer compound was faintly hot. The telephone rang. Laurel didn't answer it. She absently looked up from her book and out the window. A woman was standing in the telephone booth across the street. She seemed irate and glanced nervously at the Men's Shelter and the people in front of it. Even from the window Laurel could see the woman was wearing a fur-lined jacket, but she thought little of her and went back to her book. The telephone rang again, and this time she answered it.

A woman sounded surprised to hear Laurel's voice and asked for Jack. His buzzer was broken. She'd been trying to ring for a half hour. "I'm across the street," she said. "I'll be right over."

Laurel let her in. The woman seemed to know her way around. She threw her jacket on a chair so the fur showed and plugged in the Mr. Coffee machine. She said nothing to Laurel, as if Laurel were one of the elves who came in the middle of the night and painted Cezanne's shoes. Laurel packed up her things, including the French book which wasn't supposed to leave Ladder Repro., and walked out without locking the door.

For two weeks I called Jack Ladder, but he had nothing for me. I was working freelance, could not claim Unemployment, and so decided to call Fantômes again. Even if I could have gotten Unemployment, I was certain Mr. Belvilacqua in Section C wouldn't let me in the front door. The thought of walking downtown to those offices seemed a fool's errand. Inevitably, he would still be working there, I would be assigned to him, and he would remember me. Mr. Regozin at Fantômes said I should drop by any time for a chat, although they would not be resurrecting *Electra* for the time being and had no new openings for a colorist at the moment.

Electra lay neglected, photography-resistant, as she made her way up and down the traffic meridian. Beside her on the table lay the characters from Ladder's Egyptian triangle. They were standing in a line, holding their appropriate symbols in their hands, Nile blue, orange-red, and green oxide. Electra occupied the future, so far into the future that in her Fantômes context she presented a manner of survival that would have been unfathomable to them. I drew Electra as a simple pictograph. She was Isis, the mercurial Lolo was Nephthys; they were two halves of the same moth. Roper, the poseur photographer, couldn't replace Osiris. The triangle had collapsed. The pictographs limited the story, I needed words. Laurel said, Well, there's no triangle anymore. They're attached to each other. I protested it was dull that they should be bound together, movement limited to awkward twists and hops. Their tie to each other isn't the bond of siblings, for example, Laurel said, you've forgotten Electra was designed under a microscope. Lolo had a mother and father somewhere, just like the rest of us.

The restaurant must have been closed or near to closing. A back door which opened onto Sixth Street was latched to the wall and Laurel could see a man in white pouring oil into a tin as she walked by. Three enormous battered woks still lay on the stove, blue flames underneath. One by one he turned off the burners and poured food out of the woks onto a few plates and then stacked the woks in the sink, one clanging on top of the other. They shone in spite of their dents. Shreds of green pepper, shrimp shells, and orange peel lay on the floor.

A second man in white appeared and took the plates away. The first leaned against the sink and threw an empty box of coconut flakes out into the street, aiming for a garbage can. He just missed Laurel. It was an accident, but the near miss seemed to be a way of asking Laurel why she was staring at them in the first place. She ran on.

Laurel saw a picture of her mother when she was twenty years old in China. She looked so innocent and vulnerable that Laurel said, without meaning to sound harsh, *you look like a nice person*. What was more shocking than the discovery of this picture was one of herself taken when she was sixteen. Laurel had always thought of herself as alert and cynical, an early smoker, street-smart, early at everything, rarely fooled. The face in the photograph, smiling sweetly, looked exactly like the one of her mother in China. She asked if there were any more photographs of her mother when she was young; perhaps that particular picture had been an exception, a moment caught unawares. Her mother had always been as she was now, bitter, often scowling. Other pictures of Mrs. Liu would prove she had always been as she was now, and disprove the evidence of the photograph of Laurel at sixteen. These were flukes. Laurel had always been as she presently was. If Laurel had looked so innocent when young, just as her mother had, she feared that meant she might risk growing older as her mother did, becoming bitter and scowling. They had left China in a hurry. The photograph was the only one saved, or perhaps ever taken.

Compared to the picture taken when she was sixteen, Laurel's face had grown more angular. She didn't trust her judgment of facial expressions. What she remembered, and had been sure of until she found the photograph, was a look of studied sullen indifference. That was the expression she had worked on when she was sixteen, but in the picture she looked exactly like her mother's daughter, a good girl who did well in school. Even if the bitterness had been her fault, she refused to be that good girl again. As if a cure were that simple and all in her hands, she'd say.

It was summer. The city was full of visitors. At night in midtown Laurel saw a group of blond tourists wearing T-shirts with names of colleges written on them. They'd found a homeless man speaking garbled English. One of the boyfriends composed the shot. The man, a ragged amber turban around his head and sheets of colored plastic stapled to his coat, as though it were a waterproof cape, put his arm around one of the girls. The blue and green acetate made a crinkling sound. Her arms were thin and bare. She giggled. He smiled. They all laughed together. Then the boyfriend snapped the picture, and they all walked away quickly, leaving him standing alone. They left him abruptly and without a word, before he realized what it had all been about. This wasn't the scene from *My Man Godfrey*, where Carole Lombard looks for a forgotten man on an ash heap. Laurel followed them a few yards and heard one of the girls say that, after all, they had no address to send him a copy of the print. How will they describe that picture twenty yeas from now? Someone will ask if that's really their mother standing there, Eamonn said. Something like that.

While he had been in England, Eamonn had gone to Paris for a few days. He had brought back a photography magazine that was unlike any I had seen him read before. It was called *Chasseurs d'Image*. On the cover was a woman in a yellow bathing suit splashing out of what might have been the Mediterranean. The magazine contained technical information, but Eamonn said he bought it neither for that nor for the pictures, but for the title. The idea that photographers are hunters and subjects are prey presented a definition of looking which might be useful, but just sat there, overwhelming yet inoperative, most of the time. Cameras might be banned from some courts, museums, and subways, but they could be taken most places. Eamonn believed they ought to be taken everywhere. It all came back to his question: How is a camera like a gun? Weegee posed with his camera, smoking a cigar, above a gun-shaped sign for police equipment. If the magazine was like its American counterparts, images of women were used to demonstrate the use of colored filters, the function of different lenses, or types of printing. Women getting out of water were often used as models; whether from a shower or an ocean, that seemed to be the rule. People didn't want to see pictures of a man who had sheets of acetate stapled to his coat, Laurel at sixteen, or her mother in Beijing, as examples of different styles of lighting. The women in *Chasseurs d'Image* were dressed like characters from Fantômes, without that cast's recourse to superpower retaliation when provoked, but there was something set up and prey-like about these figures, however posed or fictional they might have been.

You no doubt eat oysters, innocently enough, without knowing that at this stage in the animal kingdom, the eye has already developed.—Jacques Lacan

    Now you will see like the women you want to look at.— Paris Métro advertisement for Lissac Frères Opticians

    Oysters: *Nobody eats them anymore: they are really far too dear!*—Gustave Flaubert, *Dictionary of Received Ideas*

A piece of paper with these three quotes fell out of the magazine. The handwriting was small, angular—not Eamonn's. I asked him where the quotes came from, and he denied any knowledge of the bit of paper. It was blue and had been folded into thirds. He said he did remember the Métro posters, the advertisements for the optician. Just glasses, he said, each picture was different. Some contained tortoiseshell frames, in another he remembered the glasses were bright red. He had bought the magazine at the same kiosk he went to each morning. There had been only three mornings, but he had gone to the same stand because the woman who worked there looked like Jean Seberg, and she spoke English. On the third morning he bought *Chasseurs d'Image*. He didn't think the note had been addressed to him. I wasn't sure I believed him, but I pinned the blue paper to the refrigerator and offered to buy oysters for dinner.

There were nearly twenty photographs laid out before Eamonn, some of which he had taken. Some were movie stills, some were news photographs, some he had taken by placing his camera in front of a television screen and shooting almost at random. The last were grainy and ghostly. All were black-and-white. He cut them up and glued different bits together, then rephotographed the revised compositions. The rephotography represented a cementing of the images, scaling the cracks, hiding his handiwork and the clues to the identity of the original image.

1. In the foreground Secret Service agents who were guarding the President stood beside the Villa Condulmer Mogilano Veneto. To the left of one was a heap of Imelda Marcos' shoes. This fragment was cut from one of the television photographs, so the shoes appeared vague; an individual shoe was larger than the head of any one of the Secret Service men. The heap loomed monster-like behind them. A man wearing a *Ghostbuster* T-shirt, cut from another news photograph, had his arm around an agent in sunglasses.

2. Dwight Gooden winding up on the pitcher's mound. Eamonn wasn't certain whom to place under his foot—Klaus Barbie or General Singlaub whispering to his lawyer. The two

looked a little alike, so perhaps it didn't matter which he chose. The perspective was off in either case. He then rephotographed the picture so it would appear more natural than surrealistic. Singlaub, Barbie, and the President, mouth open, caught telling an Irish joke, were thrown into the garbage. He chose a movie still of Walter Matthau putting one of his hands over Jack Lemmon's mouth, a scene from *The Fortune Cookie*. Eamonn cut out Jack Lemmon and replaced him with Singlaub fished from the trash. He had a still of Paul Newman from *Hud*, looking earnest, as if he were giving advice. Eamonn tried pairing him with Matthau and Singlaub, but the final rephotograph looked too artificial, too much like a collage.

3. A family portrait appeared to be floating above a semi-aerial view of Disneyland. The amusement-park image had the blurred quality of a photograph taken from television. Eamonn made an enlargement of the composite print, then added elements previously unknown to Disneyland. The new fragments came from newspaper photographs, also overly reproduced, slightly blown up and difficult to read. Cinderella's pumpkin coach adapted to the shape of the Attorney General's head, pumpkin ribs blending in with his features; South Korean police aimed at the Seven Dwarfs; Nicaraguan Contras perched in Peter Pan's treehouse. The nuclear family, no longer recognizable as part of the wedding portrait from *The Godfather, Part II*, looked down from the clouds.

Eamonn had a still of Ruth Gordon and Mia Farrow from *Rosemary's Baby* which he didn't know what to do with, but otherwise all the initial photographs had been used up.

Over the next week Eamonn reshot the three composite pictures several times over, and with each succeeding generation, the specific personalities grew murkier, and then they were lost altogether. Only a suggestion remained of the action: being muzzled, shot at, pitching, or being eaten by a shoe.

The sky is a hard blue with a great bright sun, which has melted almost the whole bulk of the snow, but the wind is cold and so dry that it gives you goose flesh, he wrote to his brother, Theo, in March 1888. In his letters from Arles, Van Gogh described sunlight that was everywhere and always sulfur yellow, not a pleasant or warm yellow, but one he couldn't get away from. He requested colors he believed absent from the Dutch palette: geranium and crimson lake, chrome orange, emerald, orange lead. My eyes hurt when I read the list. Did he actually see these colors in Arles, or did he visualize the painting before he saw what he would paint? In New York I've seen crimson lake and orange lead, but only in an artificial state, only as paint and dye.

Delacroix had a passion for two colors which are the most condemned, lemon yellow and Prussian blue. I bought tubes of lemon yellow and Prussian blue from a man Van Gogh would have called a color merchant but whom I've known long enough to call by his first name. (He used to offer suggestions about colors in *Electra* and still asks when she's going to be revived.) Oil paint is useless for cartoons or Egyptian forgeries; I bought colors to lay out side by side, looking for clues to a passion or an obsession generated by this impossible combination. I anticipated a hostile reaction between the two which would have been spontaneous, like the splitting of an atom. Perhaps he hadn't meant they were condemned in whatever separate state they might be found. I rarely did see them together. Like paint itself, color experiments seem to lose their stability over time. A lemon-yellow plastic raincoat, a doorman in a Prussian-blue uniform, I don't think that's what Van Gogh had been thinking when writing about Delacroix.

Eamonn stepped in gobs of blue and yellow paint drying on a piece of fake papyrus laid on the floor.

Van Gogh said you can't be at the pole and the Equator at the same time, I told him.

Eamonn wiped the green paint from the bottom of his shoe and muttered about being driven loopy when he'd done nothing to deserve it.

I noticed he had begun to buy more color film.

Paint is innocent. I can assign it any number of tasks, and all those bottles, cans, and tubes will never be arrested. I can send sand up the Empire State Building or launch parrot green down the Nile. I can do what I like with color. It doesn't spread rumors, talk back, or generally behave in a contrary fashion. There are days when I have trouble finding the right color, afternoons when I continually fail to mix it properly. I may spend hours adding more and more paint or ink, finally having to throw out every sodden experiment. Nothing I've mixed comes close to the color I see very clearly when I shut my eyes. When I daydream over the heads of Electra and Nephthys, unfocused, looking out the window at the green of the park, it's blurred into one expanse, moving dots of people erased to drifting smudges, as if the color cones in my retina were taking a nap.

Eamonn also had a passion for the condemned, but his passion became crippled. Somewhere in Ireland he stopped taking pictures. The English photographs and those that followed couldn't have been genuine. He may have snapped the shutter, but they had an aura of fakery. He used words like "consuming," "devouring," even "appropriating," as if eyes were mouths, as cruel as the man who owned Quality Meats. Playing with fragments of cut-up pictures, worrying constantly as if the eight-by-tens were things of danger; he rephotographed collaged pictures until there was nothing left. See, I wanted to tell him, it's only grain, after all, so what did you prove?

When the impulses for vision pass through the photore-

ceptor neurons, they are conducted across synapses to the bipolar neurons in the intermediate zone of the nervous layer of the retina.

Blindness, blinkered, exclusionary seeing, repressed sight; refusing to see; redetermined sight; a picture taken for granted; seeing only sulfur yellow. I closed the medical textbook and left Eamonn to himself.

Jack called; there was more coloring of Egyptian cartoons to be done. As I walked to his studio, I was stopped by a man with a walkie-talkie. He was part of a film crew, and from the east side of the avenue I watched a movie being shot. I had no idea what the story was about. Production assistants would tell you where to stand but would say nothing about the script. You could spot the actors from a mile away almost. As I walked back and forth during the course of the day, buying paint, picking up more fake papyrus from Jack Ladder, I walked in and out of what the movie version of my life might look like. Here was a one-minute scene, this year. The cinema hat had grown life-size and come home to roost. The movie was full of clean strangers wearing the wrong clothes and too much orange make-up. Extras playing homeless men and women were covered in paint that was supposed to look like dirt. A pair of actors in black chain-smoked and walked with an exaggerated sense of purpose. An actress ran down Second Avenue, turning her head to see if anyone was following her, but from where I stood, the gesture was too histrionic to be believable. I stepped in and out of the movie: cameraman on a crane, Camera Mart trucks, enormous generator, artificial rain, assistant directors speaking into radios. I prefer the cinema hat.

I went to the Metropolitan Museum to look for an original depiction of the characters I'd been coloring for Ladder. I wandered past stone statues and sarcophagi, past knots of tour groups and schoolchildren being lectured about history and style. This one is Hellenic; this one is the story of a Greek myth; that one looks Etruscan but is earlier or later or was found in the wrong place. The groups hadn't yet reached the Egyptian rooms in the back, which were quiet and almost deserted. Except for a pair of Indian men and a woman who stood before a worn, faded panel, furiously taking notes, I might have stepped into a private museum; viewing by appointment only. No startling colors, no large paintings or noisy crowds dropping ticket stubs and headphones, only sand-colored walls and an air of serious study. The rooms tried to be closer to Cairo than New York.

Most of the displays contained drawings which represented what one would need in the afterlife. Scrolls placed in tombs were considered to be the equivalent of what they represented. A picture of slaves catching fish or slaughtering cows and cooking them was the same as having and eating and enslaving. I tried to look at the friezes as serial cartoons, like *Electra*, but since the characters were unknown to me, the narrative could only be implied. Unable to find pictures of Isis, Nephthys, and Osiris together, I could allow for exhibitions to be on loan or temporarily removed for restoration. Even if not on loan or in the process of being restored, the museums's entire collection couldn't be exhibited at once. They hadn't enough space. I could assume I was chasing shadows, and Ladder made the whole thing up, but for the fact that his business depended on authenticity. So in the short run he can be considered relatively honest. He can be let off the hook which accuses him of rewriting history. Laurel might tinker with hieroglyphics a little, but as a colorist I was bound to certain margins of accuracy. Ladder couldn't have made up the triangle for his own amusement and profit. One shred, one shadow, one label which read *The arm to the left belongs to a figure of Osiris and the wings to Isis and Nephthys.* That's all I needed to see but couldn't find.

Lolo found Electra talking to herself on a park bench near the basketball court. She had left Roper shortly after Electra had been taken out in a trash bag. When Lolo needed a job she worked in a department store, spraying perfume on everyone who passed her, regardless of whether they were men or women. She quit in a fight with the manager. The argument had been about her dress and her indiscriminate spraying of even little girls and old men. Lolo yelled at him in the middle of the store, and her accusations drew a large crowd. She had enjoyed spinning through the revolving doors and walking all the way home. Now nearly destitute, she would buy the paper and occasionally apply for odd jobs. To Lolo, Electra had been just another nuisance who probably wanted a handout. Then she looked more closely. The woman in a shapeless plastic raincoat could have been a ghost. She thought Electra was long dead, carted off to a landfill in New Jersey. The plastic was torn in some places and mended by bits of colored tape. She couldn't understand much of Electra's speech, until the Esperanto gave way to English. She described watches, diamonds, and wads of cash she'd acquired since she landed in New York, trophies from robberies which she gave away. Lolo didn't believe her. Electra had always been passive and incapable of exhibiting any kind of will. If Electra housed desires contrary to the situation in which she found herself, they were kept secret. To Lolo's astonishment, Electra now seemed content. Lolo believed Electra's will had been steadily dissipated, perhaps since birth, because Electra seemed so easy to control. She did everything she was asked. If Electra's stories were true, Lolo could have asked her to find a few wallets, but it was unimaginable that Lolo would be the one taken care of instead of the other way around. She had only known Electra during her stay at Roper's loft, and she had heard about how he had found her in the West Side Coffee Shop on Canal Street. Lolo believed living on the street was a sign of surrender, and served as further proof that Electra had been well-meaning but spineless. When Electra told her she could no longer be photographed, Lolo interpreted this as an indication that Electra felt herself to be older and less attractive to the kind of photographer Roper had been. In spite of her apparent malleability, perhaps she had grown less naïve. If she met someone like Roper in La Bermudez Grocery or at Shimmel's counter now, she would throw coffee at him and tell him to leave her alone. Lolo reassured her, she was under no unwritten contract to Roper. He had moved away.

Electra explained that when she squinted the lines painted on the basketball court looked like Klee's or Kandinsky's, she couldn't remember which. She couldn't even remember who they were, physicists or electricians, she guessed. Dr. Atlas had not really prepared her for life on Earth. The books she remembered from her spaceship seemed to describe another planet, not this one, not this city. She wanted to return to space, to Orion, to the security of a fixed story. (It's always a sign in fairy tales that when a character veers off a chosen course there will be trouble, but I could think of no point of closure for *Electra*. Readers often start stories knowing how they will end, but they read them nonetheless. The writer might try to put off the ending, putting as many adventures between reader and the end of the story as can possibly be managed and will not tax the reader's memory. The Fantômes *Electra* could have gone on forever and Electra would have been relatively safe, adventure after adventure, but the Fantômes serial was over.)

Electra's hair was matted, while Lolo's had been dyed red so many times it was thin and hung in limp reddish spikes. Both women had small pointed noses and perfect teeth. Lolo's lapels were shiny, her shoes cracked around the toes where they were too tight. She looked ordinary seen from a few yards away, but on closer examination, her clothing was on the edge of crumbling into as bedraggled a state as Electra's. The sharp noses and flawless teeth gave them an air of no-nonsense trapped in flighty tatters. To those who drove by the meridian, their clothing signified disorientation, but their manner resembled that of two women who met at a college reunion; two who had had an uncertain relationship, the ambiguities of which they were both still well aware. They approached each other with reserve. The one who had been domineering might not now be in control, her aggressiveness done in by disappointment and store managers. The dormouse might have grown less timid. They'd been speaking for only a few minutes. Neither one of them yet knew much about the other.

At first Lolo reminded Electra of the woman in black who had thrust a wallet into her hands, but Lolo didn't make the claims that the charitable woman in black had made. She was curious about Electra, tried to save her once, but wasn't sure she wanted to get involved. The woman in black had gone the way of many minor characters: traitorous shipmates, converted felons, and confirmed saboteurs, they are lost over a cliff or fall into the archives, ignored and forgotten.

If Electra still copied her surroundings, it was possible Lolo's appearance was a copy of herself which she didn't yet recognize as such. Or perhaps, as they spoke to each other, Electra would begin to imitate Lolo. It might take Lolo a while to realize what was going on, but once she did, Electra was afraid she'd gather up her want ads and go home. Had her defensiveness grown so involuntary that she was doomed to solitary confinement within a big city, scaring everyone away? Or was Lolo too narcissistic to notice? Electra just went on talking, combing her memory for uniquely autobiographical shreds: Kandinsky, Klee, a test tube buried under a mountain. Lolo didn't look as if she believed a word of it.

It started to rain. Lolo took Electra's arm out of one of the sleeves and put her own into it. Although Electra looked better than she had at Roper's loft, Lolo took a partly eaten Mars bar out of her bag and offered it to her. They looked like Siamese twins or, from a distance, like a large insect.

The coffee shop wasn't crowded, so I sat in a booth by myself and drew pictures on the paper place mat with a ballpoint pen. A man in a white suit sat in a booth opposite me and looked out the window. His head was turned so I couldn't see his face. The suit fit him well, but it was wrinkled. He ordered scrambled eggs, and in the moment he spoke to the waiter, I saw his face. The man in the white suit wasn't Martin but looked so like him, the same pointed eyes and funny hair, like a cartoon character escaped from Fantômes. He might have been Martin's half brother, the one who, despite an absent father, grew up to be everything Martin was not. The one who kept his nose to the grindstone, the one who lived in a building with a doorman, the one who remembered everything he read, the one who gave ten-dollar bills to anyone who asked him for a handout but wouldn't give Martin the time of day. The man in the suit not only looked like Martin but he had what looked like a back issue of *Electra* rolled up in one of his pockets. He slouched in a chair like Martin, and the expression on his face was one of distraction and boredom, just as Martin's had been.

It would have been easy for me to start a conversation with him. I could have overcome my reluctance to talk to strangers. He was almost more of a lost acquaintance than a stranger. I could just ask him why he was reading an out-of-date episode from a serial long out of print, and never to be revived, but I didn't. If Martin himself had walked in, I would have gulped my coffee and left as soon as possible. Why, I thought, bother with an imitation who may or may not be a relative? Instead of working long hours as a doctor or lawyer, as Martin had imagined, the man in the wrinkled suit could well have been an out-of-work letterer or actor. Perhaps as a child, he, too, had done local commercials here in New York. Perhaps he, too, had spent hours sitting in the laps of artificial grandfathers, both pretending to have a good time while they secretly hated every minute. The half brother may have had an apartment full of lamps he found in his mother's garage (if she had one) and left scraps of paper containing ideas for unwritten filmscripts lying around his desk. He, too, might live in the middle of trails of clutter from desperate projects which had no conceivable way of ending.

Late at night I had once taken a cab ride home with Martin. The driver spoke with an Israeli accent and talked incessantly. He was difficult to understand, but seemed to be telling us about how much he had recently paid for the car and how he took care of it himself. He spoke quickly, nervously, and Martin made exaggerated faces of agreement in the mirror. Martin would later say that the driver had probably invaded Lebanon and he had wanted to stiff him because he talked too much. Well, maybe he had, I said, but driving a cab is an awful job. I had begun to notice that Martin treated cabdrivers and waitresses badly, but I'd said nothing to him about it at the time. This habit was something I had noticed with annoyance, cringed, felt embarrassed or ashamed about, but hadn't asked him to stop. I didn't have time to wait around the restaurant to see what kind of tip the possible half brother left.

His scrambled eggs arrived. He noticed me staring at him, and so I turned away. It was a relief to have an excuse not to appear riveted, because I was partly riveted and found my concentration embarrassing. He looked enough like Martin to be disturbing, but a lot of people look like a lot of people they have never met. The waiter handed me a check and I got up to leave. After I put on my jacket, I moved the place mat to the end of the table, anchoring it with a green water glass. I hoped he'd see my drawings of Electra before the paper was thrown away.

Just when Ladder's business picked up and I had more coloring deadlines than I could meet, I got a call from Mr. Regozin. Fantômes was beginning a new serial with characters based on a popular science-fiction movie. I hadn't seen it. Mr. Regozin said it was a summer movie and probably I'd been away. I hadn't been, but I listened quietly as he told me how much Fantômes had paid for the rights to the characters to create the comic. I don't know why he told me the amount. It was not the sort of information colorists need to have or are expected to know. He sounded very excited. The serial was certain to be successful. The episodes would be similar to the movie, the characters were already designed, and each subsequent plot followed along the lines already laid out in the summer movie. It was considered not only a lucrative project but an easy one. He insisted I must not repeat his ideas about the new serial to Laurel or anyone else. He insisted twice. I assured him that I wouldn't, but as I was assuring him, I imagined how I would tell Laurel to what low depths the art of comics had sunk.

Though the story would probably be dull and coloring Egyptian reproductions paid more, a few days later I went uptown to Fantômes to talk to Mr. Regozin. Guests needed a special pass to enter the offices, and this was obtained at the reception desk. They were in the form of stickers with a cartoon character printed on them. The character changed every month. Electra had been the pass character several times. The receptionist gave me a yellow sticker with a creature on it that looked like a machine and reminded me of Loonan's flattened chocolate robot wrappers. The character was one I didn't recognize and must have been established after *Electra* was terminated. I peeled off the backing, stuck it to my jacket, was buzzed through double glass doors, and walked down the hall. I wondered where the cardboard man with the magnetic face had disappeared to; bald and neglected or broken, iron filings spilled and swept away. No one had heard from Mr. Loonan since his last day.

I had never been in Mr. Regozin's office before. It was in the corner of the building and had windows on two sides. Comic awards, in the form of little silver- and gold-plated Supermen lay on a shelf, framed citations placed nearby. He moved a stack of storyboards and letters to one side of his desk and asked me what I had been doing since *Electra* had been wrapped up. Painting Egyptian mythological characters couldn't be more different from working in the comic business, he said. Not that different, I told him. Creatures with animal heads were not very popular and winged gods were a little old hat, but Isis, a sorceress who had known all there was to know in ancient Egypt and still had problems, might have made an intriguing heroine for the new serial. At night, she could be brought back to life in Jack Ladder's studio in the Bowery. On Allen Street, no one would find her costume outlandish, and she could team up with Electra, but I didn't suggest this to him.

Mr. Regozin described some of the special effects from the movie which would effortlessly translate into two-dimensional comic-book space. He showed me some storyboards for the new serial. They were still black-and-white, but he told me that because of the movie, colors were predetermined. There wouldn't be much responsibility. I would barely have to think. Mr. Regozin explained this in terms of color classicism. Superman's costume is always red and blue. Archie's hair is always orange. Tintin's is always blond. He sounded almost like Mr. Loonan, but while Loonan was at least open to suggestion, Regozin's approach to color was more totalitarian. I tried to pay attention when he went into details about the new insurance plan. As if it were a minor point, he told me that I would have to begin at a slightly lower salary than when I had left Fantômes last year. Comics were going through hard times. They had to compete with television, video games, and illiteracy. I could see Spider-man, Dazzler, and The Thing standing in line at Unemployment, being sent to wait for Mr. Belvilacqua in Section C. That was why he hadn't called Laurel or the others. He thought I could be had cheaply. He spoke as if I'd already accepted the job, even when I told him I would think about the new serial for a few days and call him when I decided. We didn't shake hands, but he walked me to the door of his office. Down the hall, a glance at my old studio, and goodbye to the receptionist at the front desk. There was a new crew in what had been the *Electra* studio. They were probably working on the serial based on the pass character still stuck to my jacket. I unpeeled it when I got to Thirty-fourth Street and threw the sticker away.

I always want the characters to live in the city, in the present; stripped of their superpowers, see how they do. In my version of the story, Clark Kent barely makes it to the telephone booth, and when he does, there's no point in taking off his suit and tie unless he wants to get arrested.

Eamonn's mother sent him a box of photographs a few days before she died. There were pictures in it of friends and relatives whose names and relationships he would now have a difficult time discovering. A pair of women at Coney Island, dated 1957, an old man sitting on a screen porch, a picture of his mother as a war bride. Although Eamonn didn't speak to me about having regrets, he would look at the pictures only when he was alone, arranging them into two piles, those of people he recognized and those who were unfamiliar to him. He looked through the box two or three times. He wanted to sell the house in Brooklyn and all its contents as soon as possible. He was indifferent about the sale and saved very little. I went back to the house with him after the funeral. Although I hardly knew Mrs. Hanratty, I associated her possessions with the voice at the other end of the telephone and felt a small, almost sentimental attachment to the remains of a woman I'd never met. There was nothing special or valuable in the house. Eamonn wanted everything to be final; no lingering bits, he said. Broken teacups were useless. He could remember that she saved them without his saving them, too. Eamonn was systematic about the disposal. He didn't want to be burdened by things. Did he feel he must be able to leave at a moment's notice? He didn't answer. I helped him sort and label, but he was so methodical I had to go outside and sit on the porch, alienated by his energy and what seemed like callousness. This box to the church, that box for the homeless, this box sent to her sister. I didn't know what disturbed me more, that he controlled his grief or that he might not have any to control. Curators would not find strips of previously unprinted negatives in the basement of this house, because he was not going to keep it. He needed the money. All Laurel had was one picture of her mother at twenty in China. Eamonn had boxes; he was rich in comparison, and it didn't matter to him. He sealed the boxes with tape and tied them with string. Won't you regret that you've gotten rid of everything? I asked him. No, he repeated, he didn't need reminders. He was haunted by Weegee's room: the pictures of guns and pinups; he wished he'd never seen it. He didn't want to leave any embarrassing evidence. Eamonn was getting rid of everything. A human vacuum cleaner couldn't have done a better job. The house was soon empty. Eamonn kept little more than he could fit in his pockets. All these tea cups and crucifixes, he told me, we have no room for them. *If I kept this house, which I don't need, it would be worse to come here and see all these things.*

The way he let me know was innocent, and at first I didn't guess what he intended. He told me we should see the landlord about having my name put on the lease. It was just a formality, he said, but the landlord's sister might make inquiries if she found me alone in the apartment. The landlord lingered on in his wheelchair, barely aware of conversations around him. He lived next door with his sister, and she left him to sit in the sun if the weather was nice. She had asked the super if we were married, and he pretended not to understand her English. In order to raise rents she had begun to evict tenants on the flimsiest of grounds. I was only too happy to sign a lease. It was awful to come home and find an eviction notice pinned to your door. Two tenants had returned from work to find these stuck in jambs or under buzzers, both in one week. Coloring museum reproductions had become fairly dependable, but Ladder's shadier deals might turn on him, and an apartment could easily become the only secure thing in my life. At first the landlord's sister said no, absolutely not. Eamonn argued with her; they argued about who had a right to what in New York. Eamonn wanted to shout at her, but with her brother sitting there drooling in his wheelchair, he just couldn't do it. She had rented to him and only to him. Arguing with her was useless in any case. I thought that was the end of it, until there was some problem with the front of the building, whether it was about the sidewalk or garbage collection I never found out. She wanted to sue the city but needed documentation. Eamonn was there with his camera. They made some kind of deal and I put my name on the lease.

Eamonn was out when the telephone rang. I wrote down the message: *Call Freddy Driscoll.* Might it not have been Nell's Auntie Fredericka tracking him down after all this time? The wedding pictures were lousy. She wanted her money back. Perhaps she was getting divorced. The separation was acrimonious and she wanted to return the pictures to their source, as if the wedding had never taken place. Each wedding had been so much like the others, he had said, but neither Nell nor her aunt would be making long-distance calls to complain about wedding pictures taken months ago. I hoped, stupidly, that the caller was another phony Driscoll. I didn't give Eamonn the message right away. Let Driscoll reach him in his own sweet time. The danger associated with Driscoll's business dissipated. Eamonn's mother had just died. I thought it bad odds, one calamity coming right on the heels of the next in the same small family. I continued to suffer from the gambler's fallacy, but what did I know about Freddy Driscoll? He lived in Staten Island. I looked him up in the telephone book, and he was listed. Anyone could call him. Perhaps he was some kind of low-level arms dealer, not the ones who have big houses in Virginia, Rome, or Tel Aviv. Staten Island seemed innocent, inculpable, but the number looked to me as if it was beckoning suicide. Would it have been more dangerous to have given him the message, was it dangerous at all? Maybe Driscoll wanted to thank him for a job well done. The next time he called, Eamonn was at home to answer the telephone.

When he left a few days later, Eamonn took his Irish passport and left the American one in New York. Driscoll continued to call. Sometimes he made threats, but I couldn't have told him where Eamonn was even if I'd wanted to, because I didn't know. I think he went to London, but probably not back to Saint Paul's Crescent. The building was scheduled to have been torn down soon after he left, I do know that much.

I don't look at the Mets parade pictures. The ones of Quality Meats and the Blanket Men are gone. The super next door asks me where Eamonn is and I tell him he's in New York, just very busy, and therefore he's not in much. If the landlord and his sister are sitting on folding chairs on the sidewalk, I answer in Spanish. She strains to listen, even though she can't understand the language she makes such an effort to overhear. I no longer trip over boxes of photographic paper in the bathroom.

I might miss the stacks of pictures and the stories that accompanied them. When I walked into the apartment I never knew what I might see. Now I always know things will be as I left them when I locked the door behind me. I didn't go with Eamonn. His escape was a private one, it was his hunt, not mine, and even if he wrote for me to join him, I'm not sure I would. I'm not like Weegee. I can't just get up and go. I have my characters to take care of, and I was afraid of this trip. Even after Driscoll gives up and forgets about Eamonn, even if he is able to start taking pictures again, even if it becomes safe to join him, I'm not sure I will.

O ▭

One day when I returned to the apartment it was not as I had left it. Someone had broken in and ransacked the place. Every drawing had been torn apart, paint and ink were spilled, pools of red and yellow lapped into each other creating streams of orange seeping into cracks in the floor. Back issues of the Fantômes' *Electra* lay scattered in the pools, and my own drawings of the serial, my Electra who came to earth and survived only in a confused and marginal state, lay saturated in colors beside the damaged bound comics. My most recent renderings of Osiris, Nephthys, and Isis lay bleeding in a sea of Nile-blue paint, Nephthys stabbed by Venetian coral. I turned on my radio. It was in exactly the same place I'd left it. I found my answering machine and bits of jewelry lying under piles of clothes and papers. Nothing seemed to have been stolen. I called Ladder and told him this week's consignment was ruined. He was very sympathetic, said he would pay me anyway and I should call the police. I didn't. I couldn't tell the police about Driscoll, how it started with the *Grace O'Malley*, a pickup spot a few miles east of Mount Desert, Maine, and the two passports.

Laurel came over to help me clean up. As we sorted through the mess and wiped up the paint, it became apparent what they had taken. Every picture of Eamonn, including his American passport, was missing. Laurel noticed it first when she found torn pictures; usually the remaining half was me. Driscoll was either after him in a serious way or was taking an odd kind of revenge.

It was almost as though I'd arrived at the apartment, a

new tenant, and had never met Eamonn Archer/Hanratty. No evidence of him remained. Even the postcards and letters were obliterated by splatters of Prussian blue and lemon yellow. So now I have no choice, I'm forced to remember, and there are no reminders.

ABOUT THE AUTHOR

Susan Daitch is the author of *L.C.*, a novel. Her short stories have appeared in *Between C & D*, *Bomb*, *Fiction International*, *Central Park*, and *Top Stories*. She has taught at Bennington College, Sarah Lawrence College, and the University of Iowa Writer's Workshop. She lives in New York City.

VINTAGE
CONTEMPORARIES